Not so Wicked

Scandal Sheet Survivors Book 2

ADELE CLEE

This is a work of fiction. All names, characters, places and incidents are products of the author's imagination. All characters are fictitious and any resemblance to real persons, living or dead, is purely coincidental.

No part of this book may be copied or reproduced in any manner without the author's permission.

Cover by Dar Albert at Wicked Smart Designs

Chapter One

One would think the devil lived in a cavernous basement, a dark, unearthly place where he stalked through the shadows and committed a host of wicked sins. Yet Mr Masters' Palladian-style house on Dover Street looked to belong to an elegant man about town, not the ruler of the underworld.

The grand windows and decorative pediments were neat and symmetrical, the stucco clean and freshly painted. It did not look like the house of London's most notorious rogue. A cruel man who lived life to excess—a lover of gaming hells and the cause of untold misery.

Mina stood on the pavement, staring at the soft glow of candlelight spilling out onto the street, trying to calm her ragged breathing.

Her life depended upon two things.

Mr Masters agreeing to speak to an unmarried lady at midnight, and him withdrawing from the duel with her dissolute brother. Should she fail either task, she had to pray the man was a terribly poor shot.

Keeping the hood of her cloak raised and gathering every

ounce of courage she possessed, Mina mounted the stone steps and knocked on the imposing black door.

At this late hour, she expected to wait while the butler made himself presentable and trudged from the basement to the hall. Then she remembered Satan's minions were accustomed to strange comings and goings in the dead of night.

Indeed, the butler yanked the door open as if he were a guard at hell's gate, then scanned her figure with some irritation and pulled her inside. "Mr Masters expected you to arrive half an hour ago," he snapped.

Mina blinked at the servant's effrontery. "He did?"

People said the devil had the power of second sight, that he could predict his opponent's gameplay before a card hit the green baize, which surely accounted for his success at the tables.

"Perhaps you failed to understand the urgency of the situation." The butler glared through cold, grey eyes. "Time is of the essence."

"Yes, that's exactly why I'm here."

She had less than seven hours to convince Mr Masters her brother would issue a written apology, which meant lying through her teeth because Thomas didn't have an honourable bone in his body.

"Then stop dallying and give me your cloak." The rude fellow tugged the ribbons and practically ripped the garment off her shoulders. Then he scanned her plain blue dress and loose hair and screwed up his nose in disdain. "Is that the best you could do?"

Mina raised her chin. "Had I known I was to meet His Majesty, I would have worn white silk and a diamond tiara." Except she had sold the latter to keep her brother's creditors at bay.

The snooty man grasped a lock of her hair, his frown

deepening. "Brown? Mr Masters prefers women with hair as fiery as their tempers. He'll not tolerate timidity."

"As I am not marrying the man, I don't see why it matters." Doubtless, he would throw her out once the introductions were made.

"But everything about you is so… dull."

Mina breathed deeply through her nose to stop tears forming. She did not need reminding of her failings. "I'd heard Mr Masters was shallow, though I hoped he would prove me wrong."

The butler contemplated his dilemma, then huffed. "The master will have my guts for garters for this, but it's too late to fix the problem now." He ushered her towards the stairs. "It's the first room on the left. Be quick before he curses us all to Hades."

Mina gripped the newel post, but that didn't stop the butler from pushing her up the stairs. "Wait! I cannot barge into Mr Masters' bedchamber. Can he not come and speak to me in his study?"

Matters were progressing far too quickly.

"Mr Masters would never allow a woman to enter his private domain. You're to meet him in the guest chamber. Now button your lip before I complain to your mistress."

Her mistress?

Clearly, he had confused her with someone else.

She might have raised an objection, but she likely had a bruise from the constant jabs in the back, and she did not want to look a gift horse in the mouth. This could be her only chance to meet the man who would invariably kill her brother.

The impatient butler knocked on the chamber door and turned the handle. "Do as you're told, and no more complaining." He pushed her inside and shut the door.

The devil's lair was dark but for the faint glow of firelight casting flickering shadows about the room. A huge poster bed with thick blue curtains dominated the space, and the potent smell of amber and cedarwood filled the air.

"You're late," came the rich, masculine drawl. "A man might look less endowed when he's spent an age bathing. Take off your clothes and wait on the bed. There's wine on the nightstand."

Mina's heartbeat thumped hard in her throat as her gaze settled on the naked man relaxing in the tub. His shoulders were broad, his hair as black as Satan's soul. He didn't look to see if she had followed his strict instructions but continued to stare at the fire's flames.

Recognition dawned, along with mild panic.

There was only one reason he wanted her naked.

"Sir, there has been a dreadful misunderstanding."

He rose in the tub like Poseidon, a muscular figure of perfection, a destroyer of mortal men. Water slipped over every hard plane. Rivulets ran down over his tight buttocks.

"Evidently." He turned his head a fraction to study her form. Disappointment flashed in his dangerous eyes. "I demand obedience in all things, yet you're standing there quivering like a frightened doe. Take off that hideous dress and drink some wine."

She tried to straighten her spine, though it seemed to be made of jelly. "I—I am not the woman you ordered."

"No, it appears your mistress has poor eyesight or cannot read. I prefer auburn hair and a slender figure. You possess neither attribute, madam."

She swallowed past a lifetime of inadequacy. "Thank heavens. Although when a man must pay for female company, one would think he'd be less fussy."

He hissed a breath and stepped out of the tub, mindless of

the puddle pooling at his feet or the fact he was naked. "Now I know you're an imposter. I'm told Madame LaRue's ladies have a touch more elegance."

As they were trading insults, she should be thinking about her reply, not the sight of his flaccid manhood. While she had seen intimate drawings in a physician's book, being the object of the *ton*'s ridicule, she had never thought to see one in the flesh.

"Forgive me if I do not take offence. A man who uses a bawdy house is hardly considered a good judge of character."

"The complex nature of my current problem leads me to take drastic measures." He prowled boldly towards her, his thick shaft hanging like a weapon between his muscular thighs.

"You mean the duel at dawn?"

Dark brown eyes twitched in surprise. "While I am considered an expert shot, these might be my last hours on this earthly plane. If I want to live, I cannot blur my mind with liquor. Why not bed a woman instead?"

She understood his motive, not his need to pay for the pleasure.

"Do you not have a mistress?" she said, observing his full lips and the harsh angles of his face. Surely, his wealth and athletic physique would compensate for his patrician nose and stern expression.

"I thought they taught ladies not to ask impertinent questions." His gaze slipped to her nose, which was equally too long for her face, before lingering on her mouth. "So, if you're not Madame LaRue's most skilled Cyprian, who the devil are you?"

Nerves fluttered in her throat. Because of his dishabille, she had no choice but to look him in the eye. "The sister of the man you're to meet at dawn. I'm here to plead for clemency."

His face hardened, his eyes flaming with barely contained fury. "What the blazes! You're Miss Wilhelmina Stanford? You're related to that loose-mouthed ingrate?" He gritted his teeth. "And Bates let you in? What the hell was he thinking?"

He stormed to the armoire, unleashing a string of vile curses, and pulled clothes from the shelf. She watched him thrust his powerful legs into a pair of blue breeches and pull the waistband up over his damp buttocks.

"I should throw you out," he growled, dragging on his shirt, the fine lawn clinging to every wet muscle.

When Thomas was in a foul temper, arguing only made matters worse, and so she spoke to Mr Masters with an air of gentle serenity. "I should be the one stomping about in a rage. If you shoot my brother, I shall have to sleep in doorways and walk the streets selling oranges and lemons."

"How is that my fault?" He poked his chest, then pointed at the closed door. "Should you not have this conversation with the degenerate you call kin?"

"I would if I could find him." Thomas had stormed out of the house hours ago and had not returned.

Mr Masters laughed. "Check the nearest gaming hell."

"Do you know how many disreputable haunts there are in London?" Of course he did. He was a master card player. "It would take a week to visit every one. Being a woman, I wouldn't get past the front door." She stepped closer and clasped her hands in prayer, for she was not averse to begging. "Sir, I implore you to accept my brother's apology and let that be the end of the matter."

Mr Masters jerked his head. "The lout acknowledges he is at fault and agrees to pay his vowels? I must say, I'm surprised. I thought he had a death wish."

"Thomas knows he was wrong."

He paused and sharpened his gaze. "You're lying. It's written all over your face. I hear disloyalty runs in the family, Miss Stanford. I read about your escapades in the *Scandal Sheet*. Were you not jilted at the altar for being unfaithful to your betrothed?"

Shame burned her cheeks.

"Do not believe everything you read, sir." Since the story had appeared in that ridiculous rag, ladies whispered insults in the street. Men made indecent proposals. And though she went to balls, hoping people would forget the gossip, she was forced to hide in the corner as penance, feel the pain of shame deep in her gut. "Mr Wenham broke off the engagement a week before the wedding and proceeded to lie for his own end."

What a fool she had been to believe his protestations.

But a lady who lived with the threat of ruin sought security, and Mr Wenham had swept her away with his kindness. Until questions over her dowry had shone a light of doubt on his character.

I would need a substantial sum to marry a woman as dull as you!

The comment had pierced her heart like a barbed arrow.

"My brother failed to provide proof of my dowry."

"Probably because he had spent it," Mr Masters mocked.

"Still, Mr Wenham needed money and had to find a good excuse to break our arrangement." Hence, he paid someone to lie and ruin her reputation. Surely, Mr Masters could see the importance of keeping Thomas alive. "The stories in the *Scandal Sheet* are nothing but a fabric of Mr Wenham's vengeance."

Mr Masters studied her intently, then shocked her by

7

grasping her chin. "Are you trying to tell me you're a virgin, madam?"

She nodded. "A foolish one, sir. Based on the gossip and my plain looks, I will likely remain that way for quite some time." Unless Thomas died and she had to sell her wares in Covent Garden.

The man released her, though she could still feel the imprint of his warm fingers on her skin. "I believe you, Miss Stanford. Not that it makes a difference in your bid to save your brother."

A hard lump formed in her throat. "You won't withdraw your challenge?"

Had she embarrassed herself for nothing?

"I cannot."

"Please reconsider, sir. Thomas is a liar, a cheat and a reckless fool, but without him, I am lost."

For a man reputed to have little tolerance, Mr Masters surprised her by giving a resigned sigh. "Enough men owe me money. They'll tear up their vowels if I fail to make Stanford pay for the insult. However, I shall ensure the *ton* learns of Wenham's lies, ensure the gossip ceases. It may help in your quest to find a husband."

He cast a doubtful eye over her person.

"It's not that I'm ungrateful, sir, but how will that help me if I am destitute? You may kill my brother tonight, and no man will marry me without a sizeable dowry."

Mr Masters gave an arrogant smirk. "I have no intention of killing your brother. I shall aim high or, at worst, shoot him in the arm. Someone needs to teach the fool a lesson."

She feared Thomas might lose both arms and still find a way to roll the dice and hold his cards. Cutting out his tongue was the only way to stop the slanderous remarks.

"The wound may become infected, and he might die."

"That is not my problem." Mr Masters braced his hands on his lean hips. "Madam, do you know who I am?"

Satan! Mina thought, but suppressed the urge to shout it aloud. "You're the most skilled gamer in all of London. A man reputed to be as intelligent as he is dangerous. It is said you tied Lord Kinver to a tree, ripped his shirt off his back, and gave him ten lashes."

His expression darkened. "Then you know I cannot tolerate a weasel like Sir Thomas Stanford saying I cheat at cards."

Of course she knew.

Most gentlemen would punish Thomas for the insult.

Her shoulders sagged as she realised nothing she could say would change the outcome. "Then I thank you for listening to my heartfelt plea." He had been more than fair, all things considered. "I shall leave you to enjoy the next seven hours, though I am certain you will have many more nights ahead of you. Think of me the next time you pass a woman in rags weeping in a doorway."

She turned and had barely taken a step when Mr Masters wrapped his fingers around her wrist to stall her departure.

"You surprise me." He pulled her around to face him.

"Why? Because I give up so easily?"

"Because you found the courage to come here tonight, yet lack the drive to achieve your goal." With a glint of fascination, he looked to where his fingers rested against her porcelain skin, but did not release her.

"You made your position perfectly clear."

"Yes, though there is a way for you to appease me and save your brother. Don't disappoint me now, Miss Stanford, not when you've made such a lasting impression."

A way to appease him and save Thomas? Did he expect her to play a harlot in exchange for her brother's life?

9

Despite heat radiating from his fingers and spreading to other parts of her body, she raised her chin in defiance. "Surely you don't want to bed a virgin. It will hardly make for a memorable experience, and if I'm to lose my virtue, I may as well risk a life on the streets."

The man's gaze slipped to the swell of her large breasts.

"I lack the attributes you require in a bed partner," she reminded him, though he looked quite taken with that part of her anatomy. "And I am certain Madame LaRue's ladybird will arrive to service you shortly."

A slow smile formed on his lips. "I meant you might come with me to the secret location and stage a scene. Despite what you may have heard about me, I am a gentleman, Miss Stanford. If a lady throws herself at my feet in front of witnesses and begs for mercy, I shall be obliged to act."

She tried to hide her embarrassment. Of course he didn't want to bed her. No one did. Hence why she spent her time hugging the potted ferns at balls and soirées.

"And as you say," he continued in the smooth voice that played havoc with her insides, "if your brother devises a plot to kill me, I would rather not spend my last hours balls deep inside a woman who's wincing in pain."

Shocked by his crude comment, she said, "I might accuse you of hypocrisy, sir. A gentleman would never speak to a lady in such a way."

"A lady would not come to a man's house alone at midnight. And after your experience with Mr Wenham, I thought you might prefer the direct approach."

Having lived with a liar for her entire life, she found it hard to believe any man spoke the truth.

"If we're being frank, sir, you should know a lady with larger hips tends not to feel so much pain." Her friend Lillian

was a fountain of knowledge when it came to romantic liaisons.

Amusement danced in his dark eyes. "Are you attempting to sway my decision, Miss Stanford? Anyone listening would think you want me to bed you."

Oh, the man was incorrigible.

"I plan to give my virtue to my husband, and since you have no interest in marrying me"—nor did anyone else for that matter—"accept that I merely meant to correct your misconception."

He moistened his lips. "Yet now you leave me intrigued."

"I suppose that's a feat in itself."

"Indeed." His dark eyes flashed with some unfathomable emotion. "Stay. Take supper with me. Attend my dawn appointment and attempt to sway my decision. It's the only way to save your brother."

Stay in a rogue's bedchamber for seven hours?

She considered his offer, confused why he cared. The man she'd heard tell of was ruthless and determined in his ambition. Doubtless, he would seek to use her for his own gain.

"I cannot stay. I came in Mr St Clair's carriage and said I would be but a few hours. Mrs St Clair knows to come here if I fail to return promptly." And she would not cause Helen more distress.

Mr Masters gave a nonchalant shrug. "Send a note."

"And say what?"

"That I've agreed to a solution, and you don't need the carriage. Reassure them all is well. I shall write to St Clair and say the same."

Was this all not a little odd?

And why was he still gripping her arm?

Mina pulled out of his grasp. "Why are you so keen to help me?"

He snorted. "I'm not helping you, Miss Stanford. I am encouraging you to help yourself. Leave if you must. But if Stanford shoots at me, I shall have no choice but to retaliate."

She stood there, a little stupefied.

Knowing Thomas, he would take aim and fire.

And since her brother had a personal vendetta against Mr Masters and had slandered him publicly on numerous occasions, why was the gentleman being so reasonable?

"Do you have a sister, sir?" It would explain why he had not thrown her out onto the street. Was he a protective brother? Or had he made the girl's life a misery and sought to make amends now? "Is that the cause of your benevolence?"

He froze as if words alone had rendered him immobile.

A veil of sadness fell over him, softening his features, and he turned away abruptly and marched to the washstand.

"My sister is dead, Miss Stanford." He peered into the looking glass as he scooped water from the bowl and splashed his face. "And I have no desire to discuss the matter."

He stared at his reflection as if a ghost stared back.

The atmosphere grew so tense she could barely breathe.

A warning voice whispered through her mind.

Leave now. Run!

Yet she needed him.

Grisly thoughts of his sister's death entered her head. Had she suffered a horrible accident? Had she perished from a terrible disease? Judging by his rigid stance, it was something unspeakable.

"I'll stay," she blurted, overcome by a wave of pity.

Still, saving herself was a priority.

He straightened and dried his hands on a towel. Then he faced her, and her heart stopped. Dark shadows danced across his rugged features. His mouth was set in a smug line.

She should have known the devil would appear eventually.

"If you want to stay, you'll have to oblige me." Arrogance dripped from every word as he stalked towards her. "I need something for my trouble. If I'm to die tonight, I'll not waste these precious hours."

She stiffened. "What would you have me do?"

Like a wolf considering his next meal, the beast circled her, his gaze moving over her dull hair and curvaceous hips, attributes he disliked in women. "Nothing that will spoil your plans to marry. But I mean to do something new, something novel."

"S-something to me?"

"Fear not. What I have planned will last mere seconds."

She caught the potent scent of his cologne. Cedarwood embodied his strength and determination. Amber added a sensual quality that marked the man as dangerous to the opposite sex.

"For someone who professes to be direct, Mr Masters, you seem to have a problem saying what you mean."

The devilish glint in his eyes made her wonder if she had unwittingly pledged her soul to Satan. "I mean to kiss you, Miss Stanford. If you'll allow it. Having never kissed a virgin, I'm keen to taste a little bit of heaven."

Chapter Two

Had Devon placed a wager on Miss Stanford's response, he would have doubled his money and toasted his victory. The lady wanted to be kissed.

He was damn sure of it.

His confidence came from her actions, not his own conceit. He could read people as easily as he could read a book, though at times, Miss Stanford's character had him flitting back and forth between the pages, trying to make sense of the glaring contradictions.

A virgin with a ruined reputation.

A timid chit with the courage of a tigress.

She was scared and bold, fearless and terrified.

And that fed a jaded man's appetite for something new.

"You appear shocked, madam. Am I to presume you've never been kissed?"

Her throat worked tirelessly as she tried to form a response. "On the contrary, Mr Wenham kissed me twice on the lips," she said so honestly he felt a stirring in his loins. "Though I'm certain I lack your experience in the matter, sir."

"Perhaps you might show me so I may judge his method."

She pressed a shaky hand to her chest. "As my appearance is less than appealing to you, I doubt you will find it pleasant."

He gave a half-shrug. "You might persuade me of my error."

"And risk you recoiling in disgust?"

"We could make a wager on the outcome."

"No. You always win."

Yes, because he assessed people, not cards.

"Then let us barter instead." He'd find a way to succeed regardless of the game, and he had something she wanted desperately. "Show me how Mr Wenham kissed you, and I shall tear up your brother's promissory note."

"Which one?" she mocked, clearly doubting his word.

"The one for three thousand pounds I won at Boodle's." He had warned Stanford not to play, but the fool had made a scene.

Eyes as brown as autumn chestnuts flashed in surprise. "You would forgo such a large sum for a simple kiss?"

The note was worthless. Stanford couldn't pay, and there was a chance he'd shoot Devon tonight. "On the scale of what we consider uncomfortable, it seems like a fair trade."

She fell silent and nibbled her lip while deciding whether to trust him. Hence why he captured her hand and, despite her protestations, led her downstairs to his study.

Bates hurried to light the lamps and pour refreshments. He was clearly confused that Devon had let a woman enter his private domain, and somewhat relieved his master wasn't storming about in a vile temper.

Devon reached into the desk drawer and removed a leather portfolio. "Here are all the debts owed to me." He handed Miss Stanford the file for her perusal. "You will find your brother's notes amongst them."

Devon perched on the desk and sipped brandy while she stood beneath the lamplight and flicked through the vowels.

"All of these people owe you money?" Her tone carried a hint of reproach, leaving him keen to take up arms and defend his position.

"I don't force men to the card tables." Arrogant lords lined up to be the first to ruin Devon Masters. They invariably left a few thousand pounds lighter. "They have a choice."

She glanced at the walnut furnishings and gilt-framed paintings. "You're extremely wealthy. Still, there must be debts totalling fifty thousand pounds here."

"Seventy-three, but who's counting?" He laughed, though he knew the sound lacked genuine emotion. He could bankrupt the *ton* and it wouldn't clear the debt they owed his sister.

With a huff of frustration, she found Stanford's vowels. "Mother Mary! Altogether, Thomas owes you twenty thousand pounds." She paled and had to grip the desk for balance. "You do know he cannot pay?"

"And you know I cannot tear them up and use them as kindling." He demanded something valuable in return. "I have offered a trade. You choose what happens now."

She withdrew a slip of paper and waved it at him. "What must I do for you to destroy the one worth ten thousand?"

Ah, his winnings from the game at Fortune's Den. The night Stanford made a base comment about Devon's sister, forcing him to bleed the man dry.

He considered her request. "You can kiss me for three thousand pounds or permit me to kiss you for ten."

She blinked like he'd lost his mind. "Why?"

"Because I like owning things, Miss Stanford."

"And you mean to own me for all of a minute?"

16

He'd make sure it lasted a damn sight longer. "Will it be a minute? You might spend a lifetime recalling the moment I left you hot and wet and panting. Wouldn't that be money well spent?"

Curiosity, not repulsion, shone in her eyes. "Burn it first, and I give my word I will keep our bargain."

It was evident she had a distinct distrust of men. And so he snatched the paper from her, dipped his pen in the inkwell and scrawled *paid* in bold letters along with his signature.

"You need proof of payment, madam." He handed her the slip.

Their fingers brushed as she took the note. For the second time this evening, he felt a surge of energy race through his veins.

Damnation!

Perhaps he was apprehensive about what dawn would bring. Perhaps he enjoyed pleasing a woman most would pity.

The lady blew on the ink, then folded the paper and pushed it down into the bodice of her drab blue dress. There it remained, hugging her impressive breasts, a haven from her brother's greedy fingers.

She placed the portfolio on the desk and marched around to face him. "As I am not one to renege on a bargain, you may kiss me, Mr Masters."

She screwed her eyes tight, leant forward, and puckered her lips.

Besides the obvious, Miss Stanford had a few things to recommend her. Her skin was smooth and porcelain pale. Her mouth was wide, her lips plump. Her nose was too long, her eyes too large, though they reminded him of an image of Cleopatra. Keen. Intelligent. Beguiling.

The lady opened one eye. "Have you had a change of heart?"

"No. But I should warn you to expect something different from the kiss you shared with Wenham." He hoped for something different, too. He hoped innocence tasted divine.

"Oh!"

"Might I wrap my arm around your waist, madam?"

"Why?"

"To prevent an accident." He'd wager her knees would buckle the moment he slipped his tongue into her mouth. "I'll also sign the vowel for three thousand as a gesture of goodwill. But you will need to trust my word on the matter."

She glanced at the portfolio on the desk and swallowed. "For the remaining notes, you may hold me however you please."

He smiled, impressed with her gameplay, though the sudden racing of his heart proved unnerving. This was merely a distraction. A means to gain payment for a debt. To satisfy a curiosity. To control a daughter of the *ton*.

"Agreed." He held out his hand. "Shall we seal our bargain?"

Despite him sensing her inner conflict, she slid her palm over his and clasped his hand tightly. "I pray you keep your word, sir."

"You'll soon know if you were right to trust me."

"Have you ever kissed a woman you find unattractive?"

"I did not say I find you unattractive."

In a short space of time, he had grown to like her. He admired her tenacity and need to save her sibling, and had quickly realised she had inherited the brains and the gumption.

"You have much to recommend you," he added.

"I doubt it's enough to please you." She inhaled sharply when he cupped her nape and sank his fingers into her hair.

18

"When a man pays twenty thousand pounds to kiss a lady, he is sure to be disappointed."

"On the contrary, it may be worth the gamble."

The time for conversation was over.

As Devon drew her closer, he inhaled her sweet scent. She smelled fresh and clean, her perfume conveying the natural essence of roses. Pure. Heavenly.

She set her hand to his chest, lifting it lightly as if his skin was so hot it burned through the fine lawn. "Please hurry before I expire from anticipation."

Tension thrummed in the air.

"Relax," he whispered before their warm mouths met.

She kept her lips firm, unyielding. It was like kissing a pebble found on the beach—cold and unmoving. He wanted to feel the wild rush of the ocean, wanted to be thrown off balance, and have the current take his feet from underneath him.

He was about to use his tongue to breach the barrier, but she broke contact. "Would you mind if I tested a theory, sir? As a notorious man, I cannot see why you would object. And I'm not certain I shall get the chance again."

"A theory?"

"A kiss is said to be enhanced by movement."

"A kiss is better if you open your mouth, love."

She blinked rapidly. "Miss Ware said if a couple move their bodies in a swaying rhythm, it lends to a far more sensual experience. She is writing a book on the subject to better inform women."

Devon chuckled to himself. It would make a highly amusing read. "And what else has Miss Ware told you?"

"That shyness is like water dousing passion's flames."

He could not agree more.

"Then let us begin again. A little bolder this time." A

flush of heat spread to his groin. The anticipation was killing him, too. "You will let me enter your mouth, and I shall show you the dance you crave."

Her eager nod hardened his cock.

He held her tight against his body and moved in a slow rhythm—an age-old prelude to something erotic. A dance that left him throbbing, desperate to push inside her warmth.

Her lips formed a pretty "O" when he cupped her buttocks and ground against her in a way only a lover or husband should.

"Is this the dance you hoped for?"

Miss Stanford gripped his shoulders as if she were dizzy on wine and her legs might buckle. "P-perhaps you should kiss me now, Mr Masters. Before I combust."

Wenham might have followed a pious man's guide to kissing, but the devil's lust held Devon by the ballocks.

Their mouths crashed together on the promise of something wild and wicked. A hot and frantic melding the like he had never experienced before. He was still trying to grapple with the fact, but hunger had taken command of his body, forcing him to drive his tongue into this innocent's delectable mouth. To satisfy this undeniable craving.

The lady needed only minor tutoring.

Instinctively, she thrust her hips against him, slid her tongue over his and dared to drive deep.

Mother of all saints!

She tasted so good. So good, he wanted to strip off her dress, spread her out on the desk and feast like a king.

A loud knock on the door made her dart backwards. She touched her fingers to her swollen lips, her hand to her heaving bosom. She couldn't catch her breath, though her ragged pants said she wanted him.

Witnessing the change in her, feeling her passion awake and build to a crescendo, was worth losing a king's ransom.

"Enter," he called, a little shaken himself.

Bates came charging into the room, his bottom lip quivering, his dull eyes wide with alarm. "Forgive me, sir. It seems there's been a terrible misunderstanding. This isn't the erm … the lady you were expecting."

Obviously, the butler hadn't noticed Devon's throbbing erection, else he would know there had been no mistake.

"Madame LaRue's lady has just arrived." Bates pointed at the breathless Miss Stanford. "This woman is an imposter, sir."

"Fate must have granted me a boon, Bates. Miss Stanford thought to call and settle her brother's debts."

Bates blinked in surprise. "You mean there's to be no duel?"

"We will attend the dawn appointment and put an end to this nonsense." Upon hearing the lady's gasp, he added, "I shall allow Stanford to leave the field when his sister pleads for clemency." He motioned to the door. "As for our guest, settle her fee and send her back to Covent Garden."

"But the Cyprian is everything you requested, sir."

Devon glanced at Miss Stanford's ugly dress and mussed hair. "Everything has suddenly become dull, Bates. I have company tonight." Before Bates jumped to the wrong conclusion, he said, "I am to teach Miss Stanford to play piquet and hazard."

The lady may learn a trick or two and take to the tables. If she could not rely on her brother to secure a good match, she might raise money to pay her own dowry.

"Arrange for supper to be served in the dining room, and Miss Stanford will take a glass of the 1820 Veuve Clicquot.

She might appreciate a drink named after the first woman to run a Champagne House."

Bates seemed baffled by this change of heart, but like any good servant, he bowed. "I shall ring when supper is served, sir. Will there be anything else?"

"Yes, return in a few minutes. Miss Stanford wishes to give her coachman a note." And he needed to write a letter reassuring Nicholas St Clair he hadn't ravished his midnight visitor. Well, not entirely.

"Very good, sir." The butler withdrew, and after a slight commotion in the hall, sent the Cyprian away.

Miss Stanford finally found her voice. "You would prefer throwing dice and playing cards with a novice than having your physical needs met?"

"What better way for a seasoned gambler to spend his last hours than making bets?"

Tomorrow, he might indulge his desires. He was confident he would survive an altercation with Stanford. Tonight, he wished for an unconventional way to spend the evening.

"Are you sure you want me to stay, Mr Masters?"

Doubtless, she would run for the hills were she not desperate to save her brother. "Having spent twenty thousand pounds, I'm determined to get my money's worth, Miss Stanford."

"You may have my company, sir." Her cheeks turned a pretty shade of pink. "But there will be no more kisses."

"Did you not enjoy the experience?" He dared her to lie.

"You're skilled at many things, Mr Masters. Kissing is one of them. Indeed, you might teach Mr Wenham a thing or two."

For her honesty, the lady rose a notch in his estimations.

And he meant to teach Wenham a different lesson altogether.

"Come, let us write notes to appease St Clair, and then we will get to the serious game of cards and wagers."

Her eyes sprang wide. "Wagers? I have nothing to stake."

Devon smiled. "I'm sure you will think of a suitable forfeit."

"I thought Thomas said the duel was to take place near Chalk Farm." Miss Stanford kept her nose pressed to the carriage window as she peered out across the dark landscape. Fear marred her tone. Nerves had her knee bobbing up and down. "Where are we?"

"Bromley Common. Simpkin will stop near the old oak tree where you can alight. Hide there until the others arrive." Devon had come half an hour early and had instructed his second, Bradbury, to make his own way to the common. "You know what to do when you see your brother."

Amid Miss Stanford singing and playing charades as a forfeit for losing at cards, they had formed a plan. After downing two flutes of champagne, she had almost forgotten about the dawn appointment. Climbing into the carriage had rendered her sober.

The lady wiped mist from the window, then faced him. "Now we're here, perhaps you might explain why you're helping me. You're supposed to be sinful and wicked, not an angel of hope in the darkness."

"I am sinful and wicked. I take pleasure in ruining men." He had lowered his guard briefly, but she should be under no illusion. "You're here with your virtue intact for one reason only."

"Which is?"

"My sister once needed assistance." He paused as his throat grew tight and his heart ached. "Had someone helped her, she might be wearing pretty dresses and dancing at balls. Consider this a means of honouring her memory."

He'd hoped the comment might silence her temporarily, but she sat forward. "I know you've not been entirely benevolent, but you've helped me more than I'd hoped. Your sister would be proud of you."

A sudden wave of emotion almost choked him.

The sooner he got rid of Miss Stanford, the better.

"Your efforts may prove fruitless. If your brother insults me in front of witnesses, I'll have no choice but to shoot him."

Miss Stanford's shoulders sagged. "I understand."

They fell silent as the carriage bumped along the dirt track. The secluded area of Bromley Common used for duels lay between an orchard, thick hedgerows and the broad trunks of numerous English oak trees. The nearest house was Bromley Hall, some two miles north, so it was unlikely they would be disturbed.

Simpkin brought the carriage to a rolling stop near the ancient oak tree. Sunrise was but twenty minutes away, the burnt sienna skyline giving a modicum of light, but Devon disliked the thought of leaving a lady out in the cold.

"Change of plan," he said, confused why he gave a damn. "I shall wait in the field while you hide in the carriage. Lower the blinds and wait until I cough three times in quick succession. Then sneak out and charge onto the field of battle before the pistols are drawn."

She brooked no argument. "Very well. If you think that's best."

Devon pushed aside all reservations. "Be prepared to improvise."

"I've done that numerous times already this morning."

"Remember to say you hired a hackney." He leant forward and opened the door, but the minx grabbed his arm to stall him. "What is it, Miss Stanford?"

"Have a care, sir. My brother is unpredictable at present."

For a few seconds, he merely stared at her. Why she should have an ounce of concern for his welfare was beyond all rhyme and reason. But she was right. An unscrupulous man might use an unscrupulous gunsmith to make a faulty weapon.

"I might say the same to you, Miss Stanford. We may not have cause to speak again, but I shall deal with Wenham as promised. I wish you well in your quest to find a husband."

"Thank you, sir."

Gratitude had a marked effect on his person. The lady's brown eyes appeared warm and sensual, not dull and overly large. His gaze fell to her mouth as he imagined plundering those plump lips again. Heaven had indeed tasted divine.

God's teeth!

He tugged his arm free from her grasp. "Lower the blinds, madam." He vaulted to the ground and shut the door. "Simpkin, make sure no one sees Miss Stanford. She's to sneak out of the vehicle while the seconds inspect the pistols."

"Aye, sir. I'll keep an eye on things 'ere."

Devon took a calming breath and strode into the field to wait for Thomas Stanford. The sharp nip in the autumn air might numb a man's fingers, so he took his flask from his pocket and swallowed a small swig of brandy.

Long minutes passed before he heard the rattle of carriage wheels on the dirt track. Bradbury and Anderson arrived. Devon had attended Cambridge with both men, and while he had a distinct distrust of most people, he had a little faith in his friends.

"Masters!" Bradbury shouted as he came striding across the field, the wind whipping his vibrant red hair. "You're early. Keen to put an end to that whining tosspot?"

"Something like that."

"How was your night with Madame LaRue's filly?"

"Interesting." He could not say he had spent the evening kissing his enemy's sister and teaching her to play cards.

Bradbury grinned. "Did I not say her skills surpassed all others?"

"You did." Devon glanced at Anderson, lingering beneath the light of the carriage lamp. If he found Miss Stanford hiding, the lady's reputation would be in tatters. And Devon had no intention of marrying anyone, let alone the sister of his nemesis. "Is Anderson afraid to get his boots dirty?"

"He's keeping watch for Stanford while he finishes his cheroot."

Bradbury continued talking, but Anderson was Devon's only focus.

"You seem distracted," Bradbury said with mild concern when Devon ignored his ramblings. "You'll need to keep your wits with a man like Stanford. He won't think twice about breaking the gentleman's code."

"I trust you visited his second and discussed the terms."

"Yes, I spent an hour with Crumley at the Albany."

"Did you see Stanford?" Had his sister not thought to visit the house of his second? It seemed like the obvious place to start.

"No. I waited, but he failed to show. He'd told Crumley he had a seat at an exclusive game of hazard at Boodle's and would come to the Albany once play was concluded."

No doubt Stanford hoped a win would cover his debts. Gambling was a fool's game unless one had spent weeks researching one's opponents, months studying the men at play. Years perfecting one's skill.

"And you've not heard from Crumley since?"

"No, he said he would meet us here at dawn." Bradbury glanced to where the sun was slowly breaching the horizon, then he withdrew his pocket watch and inspected the time. "Perhaps he's still looking for the coward."

Anderson raised his hand and called to them. "Be on your guard. There's a carriage approaching."

Blood pumped rapidly through Devon's veins. If everything went to plan, Miss Stanford would plead for mercy and explain she had sent the funds to settle the debts. Stanford would offer an apology. And they could all go home and get some bloody sleep.

A twisting in his gut said he was a fool to believe in happy endings. Someone would be shot dead at sunrise. He hoped to God it wasn't him.

The carriage rumbled to a stop, and Anderson went to speak to the occupants. A few seconds passed before their friend beckoned them over.

As impatient as ever, Bradbury strode ahead, while Devon lagged behind so he could send a covert message to Miss Stanford. Praying she was peeking beneath the blinds, he raised a hand, a signal to remain hidden at all costs.

"We've searched high and low," Crumley said, pushing his spectacles firmly onto his nose. He gestured to the stout man seated opposite. "Davies has visited every gaming establishment we know, but there's no sign of Stanford."

Devon suspected the fool had fled his creditors and left his sister stranded. "Did he attend the game at Boodle's?"

"Yes, he lost three thousand and left six hours ago."

Some men were beyond redemption.

"What did his servants say?" Bradbury asked.

"Something odd. We visited Stanford's abode an hour ago. The butler said Stanford was out, and his sister left the house at ten o'clock last night and hasn't returned."

Hellfire! Surely she hadn't given the butler her direction.

"Then they have both fled the country," Devon said, feigning optimism while trying to throw them off the trail. "Stanford is drowning in debt, so it makes perfect sense."

"But the lady was seen in Grosvenor Street at the home of Viscount Denton." Crumley sounded certain something was amiss. "A witness said she was distressed and left in St Clair's carriage minutes later."

"She was probably looking for her brother. I doubt Stanford has any intention of attending the dawn appointment." Indeed, Devon needed to get the lady home before she leapt out of his carriage and demanded answers. "But we'll make a few calls, see if we can find the coward."

He told Crumley to visit Boodle's, to speak to the porter and send word to Dover Street if Stanford appeared. He told Bradbury he would travel with him and search the brothels and taverns.

While the men were busy discussing where else they might look, Devon returned to his carriage on the pretence of collecting his greatcoat.

"What's happening?" Miss Stanford whispered, shooting to the edge of the seat and gripping his arm. "I cannot see Thomas. Has Mr Crumley brought a written apology?"

"No one has seen him since last night." He covered her hand with his own, ignoring the sudden lurch in his chest. "You must leave. You must leave now before you're discovered and your reputation suffers irreparable damage."

"But I must speak to Mr Crumley. He may—"

"Madam, I am trying to help you," he said through gritted teeth. "I'll visit St Clair and have his wife come to see you this morning. He will act as a mediator between us in the hope we can sort out this infernal mess."

He didn't wait for a reply.

He grabbed his coat, slammed the door shut and told Simpkin to make haste. The coachman flicked the reins, and the carriage jerked forward and gathered momentum. Devon didn't breathe easily again until his vehicle had disappeared down the lane, and Miss Stanford was on her way back to London.

Chapter Three

Two days later
Lord Denton's mansion house, Grosvenor Street.

"Perhaps Sir Thomas is embarrassed about missing the duel and is too ashamed to come home," Miss Lillian Ware said, patting Mina's knee as they sat on Lord Denton's sofa, awaiting his return.

Despair weighed heavily in Mina's chest. "It's been two days, and no one has seen hide nor hair of him." Upon hearing news of Thomas' disappearance, one creditor after another had come banging on the door. The tailor would have barged his way in and stolen the china had Nicholas St Clair not been there to frighten him off. "Maybe he's fled to France."

From her chair near the hearth, Helen St Clair sighed. "Let's hope my husband brings good news when he returns. He plans to visit the ticket offices while my brother checks the main coaching inns."

Mina felt sick to the pit of her stomach.

It wasn't that she cared about Thomas. How could she when he made her life so miserable? She worried more about her own future because the house was mortgaged and money was scarce.

"What of Mr Masters?" Lillian asked coyly.

Mina's heart skipped a beat. "I've not seen him since I left Bromley Common." She had dreamt about him, a dark, forbidden dream that left her tangled in the bedsheets, but she daren't confess to being a participant in the erotic visions.

"He met Nicholas last night," Helen said, as if she knew Mina's shocking secret. "They went to a gaming hell to question the patrons but learnt nothing new."

Heat rose to Mina's cheeks.

Was Mr Masters avoiding her?

Based on her lack of experience, the kiss must have been dreadfully disappointing. Yes, he had moaned into her mouth, but maybe it was the sound of frustration, not pleasure. And a man reputed to be dangerous did not want people learning of his benevolent streak.

Lillian pushed a stray lock of auburn hair behind her ear and grinned. "What did you do at Mr Masters' house? You've not really said."

All the things a lady shouldn't!

"I—I told you. We ate supper and played cards." And shared a kiss that had curled her toes and stolen her breath.

Helen gave a discreet cough. "He told Nicholas he was bathing, and his butler ushered you into his bedchamber, thinking you were someone else."

An image of the man's rugged physique flashed into her mind. "Yes, it was just a silly misunderstanding." She daren't say she had been mistaken for a harlot or that she had ogled his manhood for minutes.

Helen arched a brow. "You recall what the mystic said?"

How could she forget?

During a visit to the mystic's tent at the Bartholomew Fair, they were all given a glimpse of their future. The absurd premonitions had left them crying with laughter. But Helen's prediction had recently come true, and she had married a man who'd fallen in cow dung.

"Yes, I'm supposed to see my future husband's buttocks before seeing his face." She had glimpsed Mr Masters' profile before he'd charged out of the water like a god of the sea, all firm buttocks and solid thighs, so surely it didn't count. "While I am desperate enough to marry a street hawker at present, I assure you, Mr Masters will not marry me."

Lillian chuckled. "The fortune-teller told me I would marry a man who bares his knees in public. Obviously, she meant a man in a kilt."

"And you have been avoiding the Duke of Dounreay ever since."

Lillian's gaze dipped to the floor. She had something on her mind and had recently taken to disappearing at every ball and soiree. "I mean to be an archaeologist, never a duchess."

Mina might have said more on the subject, but the slam of the front door had her jumping to her feet. "Goodness. They're back."

She heard the mumble of voices in the hall before Lord Denton and Mr St Clair entered the room. Neither man looked pleased. Indeed, one would think the sky was about to come crashing to earth.

"Well?" Helen said when they remained silent.

Lord Denton cleared his throat. "You should sit down, Miss Stanford. Prepare yourself. I am afraid it is not good news."

Lord have mercy!

Even though Mina had expected as much, she gasped and fell into the seat. "Don't tell me. He has fled to the continent and left me to deal with his debts."

Nausea roiled in her stomach.

Fear left her trembling.

The future was undoubtedly bleak.

Lord Denton grimaced. "Forgive me. There is no delicate way to say this. They pulled him from the river this morning." He gestured to the hall. "Sir Oswald, the magistrate from the Great Marlborough Street police office, is here with a constable to ask some questions."

"From the river!" Her blood ran cold. "Is he alive?"

After a few grave seconds, Mr St Clair said, "N-no. He'd been stabbed in the chest. The current dragged him as far as the steps near Hawkes Wharf. He also suffered a head injury but may have been hit by a boat."

Dazed, Mina sat rigid in the seat.

Her life passed before her eyes—a three-second summary of the last twenty-four years. While she had grown to despise Thomas, he did not deserve to die in such a cruel and grisly manner.

"I have agreed to identify the body," Mr St Clair added when she failed to reply. "And we shall help put his financial affairs in order. Help in any way we can."

Lillian wrapped a comforting arm around Mina's shoulder. "I shall stay with you in Carnaby Street until everything is settled. You don't need to suffer this alone, Mina."

She patted her friend's hand and accepted a glass of sherry from Helen, downing the contents in one swift gulp. "I've always known he would meet a tragic end. When Miss Howard declined his offer of marriage, he became nothing more than an empty shell."

Unrequited love had ruined Thomas.

Unrequited love had robbed him of all sense and logic.

Hence, she had agreed to marry Mr Wenham—for security and companionship, not for an emotional connection that might destroy her one day.

"I can send Sir Oswald away," Lord Denton said. "He can call later when you've had time to process the news."

Feeling numb, she wasn't sure what to do for the best. Her mind was a whirl of confusion. For all his mistreatment, she owed Thomas nothing. Yet should she not help to bring the culprit to justice?

"No, I'll see him now. I may be a blubbering wreck later."

"We can stay with you," Lillian reassured her.

Indeed, they all remained present while Sir Oswald expressed his deepest condolences. Being a short man with an expanding waistline, he gasped his way through a speech he must have made a hundred times.

"With Great Marlborough Street being your local police office, I have been instructed to take your case, Miss Stanford."

Lord Denton gestured for the magistrate to sit.

Sir Oswald breathed a relieved sigh when he collapsed into the chair. "Do you know of anyone who may have a grievance against your brother? I'm told he owed many people money."

"Yes, he gambled away his inheritance and continued the same reckless behaviour when the coffers ran dry. If you ask at any gentlemen's club, I'm sure they will provide you with a list of members who own my brother's vowels."

"Sir Thomas played hazard at Boodle's the night he went missing," Mr St Clair said. "He left at one o'clock in the morning, adding another three thousand pounds to his debts."

Sir Oswald waved for his constable, who stood quietly in the background, to write the information in his notebook.

"I'm told one man in particular was owed a substantial sum," the magistrate panted. "Mr Masters has threatened Sir Thomas publicly on numerous occasions. He dragged your brother along the floor at the Chatterton Ball and threatened to kill him in the crowded ballroom."

Mina's pulse thumped a hard beat in her throat. Had Mr Masters killed her brother? Was that why he had quickly sent her away in the carriage?

Every instinct said no.

"Thomas provoked Mr Masters at every opportunity. I have no idea why, but all I can say is the gentleman had the patience of a saint."

Sir Oswald raised a bushy brow. "I heard a rumour the men were to engage in a duel."

"You must be mistaken, sir. It is illegal to duel in England."

"Your brother never mentioned Mr Masters calling him out?"

"My brother spouted nonsense most of the time. I had learnt to ignore his constant blabbering."

Sir Oswald nodded. "Forgive me, but you seem rather calm considering you've received such dreadful news. I mention it only to gain an insight into Sir Thomas' character, you understand."

Her cheeks grew warm. "I am in shock, sir, and am somewhat numb. I have spent two years warding off his creditors and always feared he would meet a terrible end."

He seemed appeased. "Well, I shall leave you to rest, madam. Mr St Clair has agreed to accompany me to the mortuary. If you think of anything that might be pertinent to the case, send word to Great Marlborough Street."

"I will, sir."

The magistrate hauled himself out of the chair. Mr St

Clair and Lord Denton followed him into the hall where, moments later, the men could be heard whispering.

"Sir Oswald is incompetent," Lillian said in Mina's ear. "When they found Mr Ashbury dead in my brother's garden, he wanted to arrest a suspect without evidence."

The magistrate had seemed quick to blame Mr Masters.

"Then I shall visit the office and keep abreast of developments. Many people welcome the new police force. Hopefully, Peel is monitoring the more serious cases."

Mina's heart sank to her stomach when she considered the task of finding a murderer and dealing with her brother's estate. How she wished she could sleep until next Michaelmas and wake when it was all over.

Lord Denton returned, looking as worried as when first breaking the terrible news. He glanced back into the hall, clearly keen to ensure no one would overhear him.

"I fear you have another problem, Miss Stanford. One that may play havoc with your conscience."

Her mind ran amok. "What problem?"

"Someone sent an anonymous letter to the police office last night, which is why Sir Oswald asked about Masters and the duel. I'm afraid they took Masters in for questioning and are considering charging him with your brother's murder."

"Charging him!" Mina sagged back in the seat. Had everything the gentleman said been a lie? Had he left Bromley Common, found Thomas, and killed him in cold blood? "Then they must have substantial evidence." And to think she had kissed the man who'd ruined her life.

"The coroner believes your brother had been in the water for two days. Masters has no alibi for the night Sir Thomas went missing, and they refuse to take the word of his staff."

Two days!

Her heart sank.

Had Thomas died while she'd been playing cards and drinking champagne with Mr Masters? While she had been winning back his vowels?

"And as no one wishes to admit to attending a duel," the viscount continued, "his friends cannot account for his whereabouts either."

Ah, she understood his point clearly.

"But I can," she said. Admitting to being in a gentleman's bedchamber at any time of day would see her utterly ruined, with no hope of recourse. "Is that what you imply, my lord?"

The viscount looked most apologetic. "Providing Masters with an alibi would prove disastrous for you, Miss Stanford. Along with the problems you already face, you'd be forced to leave town."

Leave her home, her friends?

The thought left her bereft.

"Not if she married a viscount," Lillian said with a grin. "You need a wife, my lord, and might save poor Mina from the poorhouse."

Lord Denton looked like he'd rather find himself naked in the middle of the Irish Sea. "Despite the desperate nature of Miss Stanford's case, we are totally incompatible," the lord said, which really meant he found her unappealing. "And I have no immediate plans to marry. A match would be disastrous for both parties."

"Perhaps my brother might draw up a list of suitable men," Helen quickly said to save further embarrassment. "Assuming Mina wishes to make a statement, of course."

Mina sat silently debating the issue.

Mr Masters may have manipulated events to suit his purpose, but he had signed the promissory notes as paid, had

37

given her twenty thousand pounds for little more than her company.

He had formed a plan to prevent her from suffering when he might have thrown her to the wolves.

I am encouraging you to help yourself.

The likelihood of her finding a husband was slim at best. And with the *ton* already calling her a harlot, perhaps she should be Mr Masters' alibi and become notorious instead.

"And the coroner is certain of the timings?" she asked, while considering the impossible. "There is no doubt my brother died in the early hours of Wednesday morning?"

Lord Denton shrugged. "The coroner has presided over thirty suicides this year from Waterloo Bridge alone. Accidents account for double that number." He did not mention murder. "It's his best estimate, but I doubt he can be more exact than that."

It hit her then.

The shock of knowing she would never see Thomas again. The choking feeling that he was gone for good. The ache in her heart as she wished she could turn back time and things could be different.

Tears filled her eyes.

Tears for herself and her foolish brother.

But crying achieved nothing, and she had cried a river this last year.

Dabbing her eyes with her handkerchief, she stood. "Then I shall visit the Great Marlborough Street office and make a statement. Mr Masters may be dangerous and wicked, but he does not deserve to hang for a crime he did not commit."

Helen inhaled sharply. "But you'll be a social pariah. You'll be top of the list of undesirables. Are you certain you want to do this?"

Mina nodded, though she would undoubtedly come to regret the decision until the end of her days.

One thing was certain.

Her life was about to change irrevocably—and not for the better.

Chapter Four

The windowless room was small and cluttered and smelled of wet boots and old books. Many hours had passed since a constable gave Devon a pisspot and a copy of yesterday's broadsheet, shoved him inside and warned it was only a temporary cell.

Damn Thomas *bloody* Stanford!

The man meant to ruin Devon's life, even from the grave.

He glanced up as the clip of booted footsteps came to an abrupt halt outside the locked door. Men began whispering, discussing his fate.

Things could be worse.

He might have been shot by Stanford or thrown into a dank cell and had a thumping from the arrogant men of the new police force.

Things could be better.

The judges and magistrates in his debt would rather see him hang than have to sell their daughters to pay their notes. And some devious blackguard had sent a letter mentioning the duel and Devon's desire to see Stanford dead.

Many men would sleep easier if London's best gambler went to the gallows. Lord Kinver would hold a week-long celebration and dance on Devon's grave.

A key turned in the lock and the door swung open.

Devon cast his contemptuous gaze at the newcomer.

Sir Oswald waddled into the room, breathless and red-cheeked. "Mr McGee puts the time of death sometime in the early hours of Wednesday. And a witness places Sir Thomas on Waterloo Bridge at three o'clock that morning."

The news sent Devon's pulse skittering, but he kept his arms folded, his legs crossed at the ankles. "How convenient. I was at home during those hours, yet you refuse to accept my butler's word."

"Were you home alone?"

Something in the man's tone made Devon sit up. What did he know? "How many times must I repeat myself? I had supper and went to bed."

"And yet your butler suggests otherwise."

"I certainly doubt it."

"He said you had female company."

Bloody hell!

Bates knew better than to contradict his master's orders, which meant the magistrate was lying. But why? Did he know Devon had hired one of Madame LaRue's Cyprians?

"Regardless, I stand by my earlier statement. I spent the night alone. Though, ask yourself why I would want to kill a man who owed me twenty thousand pounds."

Sir Oswald pondered the matter before leaving the room.

He returned moments later, carrying a crisp sheet of paper. "Miss Stanford said she came to see you late Tuesday night to settle her brother's debts." He handed Devon the lady's signed statement—his alibi. "She states she arrived in

41

Dover Street at midnight in Nicholas St Clair's carriage and left at seven o'clock Wednesday morning."

Devon swallowed past his shock.

Had the woman lost her mind?

He had created an elaborate plan to save her and her dissolute brother so she might have a modicum of peace, not tarnish her name and damage her reputation.

According to the statement, she'd claimed to use money she had secretly saved to clear two promissory notes but had negotiated for the remaining two. It mentioned supper and piquet and singing, not the kiss that had left him wanting.

Still, the world would assume he'd bedded her in payment.

Her name would appear in tomorrow's *Scandal Sheet*.

And he would be the rogue who'd taken advantage.

Hellfire!

"Women often invent stories about me," Devon blurted, despite knowing it was too late and the seed had been sown. "If you've any decency, you'll tear it up and spare the lady the shame."

"She came to the office an hour ago with Viscount Denton. The peer would not condone perjury. Rest assured. You're under no obligation to save her reputation. She must escape her brother's creditors and is leaving for Winchester after the funeral."

Devon should have been relieved.

Yet he hated being in anyone's debt.

He felt sick at the thought of what she'd sacrificed to save him.

"It grieves me to say this, but you're free to go, Masters." Sir Oswald gestured to the door. "Don't leave town. The case is ongoing, and you may be required to answer further questions."

Sir Oswald waited, but Devon couldn't move.

His heart was heavy, his legs like lead.

He'd rather deal with a murder trial than this... this act of benevolence. This utterly selfless act that made him admire the lady more than he might curse her stupidity.

"Masters, did you hear me?"

Devon dragged his hand down his face as a harrowing image of Miss Stanford weeping into her handkerchief flashed into his mind. "Did she cry?" He had heard Arabella sobbing many times. The sound was like sharp claws dragging his skin.

"I beg your pardon?"

"Did the lady cry when she made the statement?"

The questions seemed to confuse Sir Oswald. "Her brother was found murdered. Of course she blubbered. She wore black and, for the most part, kept her face covered with a veil. I don't see why you're concerned. Lord Denton will see her right."

Devon jerked his head. Yes, the viscount's seat was in Winchester.

"Lord Denton means to marry her?" For a reason unbeknown, the thought brought bile to his throat. He refused to let another man accept a responsibility that was his by rights.

"Marry her! Good lord, no!" Sir Oswald laughed. It was the sound of someone ignorant to hardship, of a hypocrite who professed to have impeccable morals. "A viscount marry a lady with such a scandalous reputation? Heaven forbid. I believe she means to live in a cottage on Denton's estate."

Spend her life tending roses, making jam and entertaining the vicar? The lonely life of a spinster forced to ward off every ageing man's advances?

"I see. Did a witness tell you she came to Dover Street?"

Had the magistrate harassed Miss Stanford until she had no choice but to confess?

"No. When she heard we'd brought you in for questioning, the lady came to the office of her own volition. She said she couldn't see an innocent man hang."

Devon stood, for the path ahead was clear.

He had a long list of people to barter with and bribe, beginning with Sir Oswald. "Give me the anonymous letter sent to the office, and I shall return your promissory note." Devon had been fortunate to receive it in payment for another man's losses.

Sir Oswald glanced behind to ensure they were alone. "I cannot give away evidence," he whispered, though the man would likely sell his soul to clear his debts.

"It's not evidence," Devon said, brushing the creases from his coat. "Miss Stanford's testimony proves I'm innocent."

"Unless she's a fraud."

Devon's blood simmered. "The lady has suffered enough in the name of justice." Why in blazes had she ruined herself over him? He would find out in due course. "Unless you mean to provoke me, you will keep your foolish comments to yourself."

The magistrate offered a mocking grin. "Who'd have thought it? Devon Masters neck-deep in debt to a lady? It must prove grating, knowing it can never be repaid."

It proved more than grating.

It was like a rusty blade twisting in his gut.

"Be assured, I always pay my dues."

He marched past the useless oaf, past the group of blue-coated constables gathered in the corridor, one thought prominent in his mind. If it killed him, he would ensure Miss Stanford received fair compensation.

After a trip home to change clothes, one to Coutts to claim a ring Devon had stored there two years earlier, he reached Carnaby Street to learn Miss Stanford was at Lord Denton's abode.

Anger surfaced.

He would rather die than let Denton deal with his problem. And someone had to shake Miss Stanford to her senses and explain only a fool ran to the home of an unmarried man. Then he recalled she was friends with the viscount's sister, and his ire dissipated.

What the devil was wrong with him?

He had not felt this unsettled in years.

Denton's butler answered the door with cool aplomb and politely told him the viscount was not receiving visitors. "If you would care to leave a card, sir, I shall ensure his lordship knows you called."

Devon whipped a card from his case and thrust it into the butler's hand. "Tell his lordship I'm here to make Miss Stanford an offer. I shall wait to receive his reply."

The glum servant looked like he'd been told the recipe for filbert biscuits, not that London's most notorious bachelor planned to shock the world and take a bride. He closed the door and returned a minute later. "Follow me, sir."

Devon was shown into the viscount's study and found Denton seated behind his imposing desk, his face like thunder.

"So, Sir Oswald released you. I was hoping he would find a reason to detain you indefinitely."

"Why? I'm innocent of any crime."

"Innocent, not blameless." Denton firmed his jaw. "What the hell do you want, Masters? What blasted game are you playing?"

"Did your butler not tell you? I'm here to see Miss Stanford. In the absence of relatives, I was told you are helping to put her affairs in order and have offered her a rent-free cottage on your Winchester estate."

"Why is that of any interest to you?" Denton shot out of the chair and braced his hands on the desk. "Is it not enough that she had to make that shameful statement? You should have sent her home that night, not forced her to partake in some ridiculous charade."

He studied the lord. Was the man in love with Miss Stanford? Did that account for this sudden outburst? Or was he merely playing the role of a protective brother?

Devon breathed deeply to curb his temper. "She came begging for her brother's life. I offered a solution to the problem. How was I to know someone would murder Stanford and attempt to blame me for the crime?"

Denton pushed his hand through his mop of golden hair. "Maybe you hired someone to kill him and put an end to your troubles."

"Make no mistake, I could kill a man and no one would ever find the body. If I'd wanted Stanford dead, I would have got rid of him months ago."

The viscount's nod was as curt as his tone. "I suppose you've come to thank the lady for seeing justice served, for saving your rotten neck."

Devon reached into his pocket and placed the velvet ring box on the desk. "Yes, and to offer marriage and present this token of my gratitude."

"Marriage? You've helped to ruin her damn life. What makes you think I would permit her to marry a scoundrel?"

"It has nothing to do with you. An intelligent woman should be allowed to make her own decisions." Devon snatched back the box, and though he lowered his voice, it was nonetheless menacing. "Fetch her or I shall tear through this house and find her myself."

Denton grumbled under his breath. "She's across the hall in the drawing room. If she has any sense, she'll have Woodley throw you out. I'll be more than happy to give him a helping hand."

Devon inclined his head. "You should know, I would fight to the death to get what I want." And then he left the lord seething and marched from the study.

His appearance in the drawing room caused a stir. Miss Stanford, seated with two friends, jumped to her feet and clasped her heart.

"Mr Masters! What are you doing here?"

He studied the woman he would marry to settle a debt. Pink blotches covered her cheeks. Her eyes were bloodshot, her lashes damp with tears. She wore the most hideous black dress he had ever seen. It made her hips look twice as wide and sagged around her breasts.

"I seek a private audience, madam."

She glanced at her friends. "For what purpose?"

"I shall tell you once we are alone." He would not have these prim ladies raising their objections before he had made Miss Stanford see sense.

"Mina, perhaps you should hear what Mr Masters has to say." The viscount's golden-haired sister came to her feet. "We shall be outside if you need us."

What did they think he would do?

Force himself on an innocent?

Ravish her on the viscount's plush settee?

He waited until the ladies left the room and closed the door before offering a respectful bow. "Let us begin again. Good afternoon, Miss Stanford."

She dropped into a curtsy. "Good afternoon, sir."

"You must be surprised by my visit."

"A little. May I ask why you're here?"

To do something he'd thought impossible yesterday.

"I come to thank you and berate you with equal measure. You saved me from an unfortunate situation and have my utmost gratitude. Admitting to being alone with me was downright foolish. What the hell were you thinking?"

She blinked, her dark lashes fluttering wildly.

"Had you taken leave of your senses, madam?"

"My conscience demanded I tell the truth. Trust me. I have no desire to be the subject of ballroom gossip, but a lady is nothing without integrity."

Cursed saints!

This woman knew how to throw him off kilter.

"Honesty is a rare quality, Miss Stanford."

"When one has lived with constant lies and deceit, one strives to do better. The truth may deliver a sharp blow, Mr Masters, but falsehoods leave an indelible scar."

He found himself smiling like a loon. "Then know, I mean to speak plainly throughout our married life."

She flinched. "I beg your pardon?"

"I might bend my knee in a romantic gesture and praise your looks and musical talents, but I know nothing about you. I might say we will make a perfect match, but I suspect we're opposites in every regard."

She shook her head and snapped, "What are you saying, sir?"

He drew the velvet box from his pocket and opened the

lid to reveal the extraordinary ruby and diamond cluster ring. The thirty rose-cut gems glistened like stars in the night sky. "I offer this in earnest, as a symbol of faith and gratitude, which will bode well for our impending partnership."

Evidently shocked, she focused on the ring. "It is beautiful."

"I wish I could say it belonged to my mother." But sadly, the woman wasn't dead and wouldn't give him the scraps off her plate, let alone something priceless.

Censure flashed in her eyes. "Did you win it at the tables?"

"No, I bought it from Woodcroft Jewellers on Bond Street. The Earl of Haversham wished to purchase it for his mistress. I offered Woodcroft double if he sold it to me. The earl refused to raise his offer, and so here we are."

She stood. "You bought it for another woman?"

"No. It has remained in Coutts' vault ever since." Keen to secure her hand, he said, "I always get what I want, Miss Stanford. I always pay my dues. You sacrificed everything to save me, and I refuse to be in anyone's debt."

"And so you offer marriage to a woman most men consider plain, because your conscience deems it necessary?"

"Indeed."

"I suppose I should admire your honesty."

"It is perhaps the one and only trait we share."

Neither spoke for a few seconds. The lady stared as if posing for a portrait and had been told to hold her breath for an hour.

"Thank you for your kind offer, sir, but I must decline."

Decline!

Had she not heard him say he always got what he wanted?

He bowed his head respectfully but insisted on pressing

49

his case. "You were willing to marry Wenham. Why not marry me?"

She gave a light laugh. "Mr Wenham is a pathetic fop. You're the most feared man in London. A woman knows when she is out of her depth."

"Does that not work to your advantage? No one will ever hurt you again. No one will dare give you the cut direct. And I shall ensure every copy of that damn *Scandal Sheet* is tossed on the bonfire."

A flicker of excitement danced in her dark eyes.

"If I may, let me tell you what I expect from our marriage," he said, for when one made a deal with the devil, one should be forewarned. "Then you may take the day to think about your answer rather than act in haste."

"Very well. I am most intrigued."

She would likely be startled.

"It won't surprise you to learn I demand loyalty. And after the kiss we shared, you understand the physical aspect of a relationship is important. In short, madam, I will not live like a monk."

Her eyes widened and her pupils dilated. "You mean to bed me?"

"At least four times a week."

"Every week?" She gulped as her gaze dipped to his mouth. "What if I don't like intimate relations?"

"Trust me. You will."

She had liked kissing him, and passion burned quietly inside her, just waiting for someone to stoke the flames.

"What if you dislike having relations with me?"

He laughed to himself, for her naivety amused him. "I won't. Men think differently about such matters."

"But I have no dowry, nothing but the trousseau I gathered for my wedding to Mr Wenham."

The mention of the fop's name roused his ire. "I don't want or need money. As my wife, you will inherit everything in the event of my death." Not quite everything, but he would explain that issue later, once he knew he could trust her implicitly. "With regard to your trousseau, give it to a women's refuge. I'll not see you in clothes meant for another man's eyes."

Dumbfounded, Miss Stanford put a shaky hand to her throat.

"You will not entertain another gentleman," he continued, perhaps too bluntly. He might be mad, but he would not be a cuckold. "Not in thought nor deed."

It was her turn to laugh. "No one wants me."

"They will once they learn we are wed." Men sought to ruin him by any means necessary, and a woman who married a scandalous devil always seemed more appealing. "You will keep nothing from me. I want to know who approaches you, who offers an enticement to have an affair."

He might have asked if her affections were engaged elsewhere, but based on the way she had kissed him, he knew the answer.

"And that is all you require?" she said, astounded. "Loyalty, honesty and to make love frequently?"

Make love! He did not correct her misconception. He meant to fuck her hard but would always see to her pleasure.

"And no dramatic displays when I go out of an evening."

She snorted. "I imagine I shall be grateful for the rest."

A rush of genuine pleasure filled his chest and he laughed aloud. "Madam, I would not be doing my job properly if you did not want me in your bed most nights."

"Will I have my own chamber?"

"You can have whatever your heart desires."

Rather than be overwhelmed with joy at the prospect of

being wealthy and admired, her smile faded. "Why shackle yourself to me when you've no need of a wife?"

Perhaps because she had breezed into his house at midnight and filled the lonely hours until dawn. He had been aware of an inner emptiness ever since.

"I feel responsible for you. You do not deserve to suffer for helping me." The memory of their kiss filled his mind. It should have been awkward and clumsy, yet their mouths had melded together like perfect pieces of a puzzle. "I have learnt to trust my instincts, and something tells me this is the right course of action."

She studied him intently.

Long seconds passed.

"I must make a few stipulations of my own," she said boldly.

"Tell me, and I shall consider them."

She swallowed. "I want to dine with you of an evening. I want to play cards with you for amusement, not money. I ask that you do nothing to embarrass me, to make people think I am less of a person, that I am a fool. I know of married ladies who are so dreadfully lonely. I want us to be friends."

Most women would have asked for a gilded carriage, for diamonds and pearls, for a house of their own amid the sprawling countryside. Miss Stanford wanted his time, his company, things he'd never given, things that would cost him more than the contents of Coutts bank.

He stood silently, contemplating the trade.

He had to eat and had no intention of taking a mistress. He enjoyed playing cards, and she was easy company.

"I shall dine with you daily, though cannot promise it will be every evening. Whether it be breakfast, dinner or supper, I will sit with you and enjoy a meal. Agreed?"

"Agreed," she said, understanding this would be a partnership, not a grand love affair. "I have one more stipulation, sir, and am not prepared to negotiate."

Doubtless, she wanted children. It was to be expected, he supposed. "I'll not dismiss Bates," he joked.

"I wouldn't ask it of you. Loyal staff are hard to find." She stiffened, as if preparing to defend an attack. "I mean to investigate my brother's murder. I'll not rest until I know who killed him. If I am to be your wife, I must know if the villain meant to frame you."

Investigate a murder!

"You want to play enquiry agent?"

Hell, he had to admire her courage. Did she even know where to start or understand the dangers involved? How could he protect a woman determined to risk her life for her dead brother?

But she had a point.

Had the culprit wanted to kill Stanford or had he meant to frame Devon for the crime? Still, he could not let her race about town, risking her neck. Yet that was not the most pressing problem.

What unnerved him most was why he wanted to marry her when she persisted in making things difficult. If she refused his suit, did that not mean his conscience was clear?

"Sir Oswald is as useless as cologne to a pig," he said, determined to make her his bride. "We will work together in the hope of solving the crime." Devon might be a free man at present, but who knew what the villain had planned?

The lady struggled to contain her excitement. "Then I will marry you, Mr Masters, though I want the conditions in writing. Will the banns be read, or do you mean to procure a licence?"

His chest grew warm. He liked winning above all else and considered himself the victor of this first game.

"I mean for us to marry posthaste, madam." There was some benefit to having many men in his debt. "I shall trade a promissory note for a special licence."

She gasped. "You own the Archbishop's vowel?"

"No, his secretary Rigby owes me a modest fortune. Rest assured, I can arrange for us to be married by the day's end."

Chapter Five

The vicar arrived from Aldgate at ten o'clock that evening and entered the makeshift chapel that was Mr Masters' drawing room.

The Reverend Parker blessed the Lord before quickly slipping a pile of signed banknotes into the small wooden box meant for his Bible. Only then did he ask to see the special licence. Or so the maid said when she came to relay the gossip.

Considering his bride's every need, Mr Masters had arranged for a modiste, a perfumer and someone's ladies' maid to attend Mina in an upstairs bedchamber.

In two hours of chaos, she was swamped in silk, stabbed and pricked with pins while being sewn into a second-hand gown by five different hands. She almost choked as Monsieur Gagneux dabbed her skin with exotic perfumes.

Then she was bundled downstairs, where Mr Masters stood talking to her friends, Helen, Lillian and Nicholas St Clair. A handsome man lingered in the background, his stern expression marking him as equally dangerous.

They all stared as she entered the room.

Doubtless because she should be dressed in black, not the deep lavender silk that clung to every curve and exposed too much flesh.

Mr Masters' keen eyes traced a slow path over her body, and he smiled. "Remind me to pay the modiste a bonus." He captured her hand, drew her closer and lowered his voice. "Despite limited time and resources, she's done a remarkable job."

"I don't know why it matters." Nerves set her on edge. This man would want to bed her tonight. The thought left her terrified and excited in equal measure. "We both know why we're here."

His gaze moved to the pretty pearl comb in her hair. "I wished to see you in something other than those ugly gowns you've worn of late."

"Am I meant to smile and flutter my lashes, happy my appearance pleases my husband?"

He must have heard the faint mockery in her tone. "I thought you would feel more comfortable if you were dressed like a bride. But I'm not keeping you prisoner here, Miss Stanford. Leave if you've had a change of heart."

Panic had her pulse fluttering wildly.

Would he always be so direct, always hold her to account?

She would do well to remember he was accommodating on all levels. No other man had volunteered to save her reputation.

"Forgive me. Matters are moving quite quickly."

"Once my mind is made up, I do not dally."

"No, then let us proceed." Many women wanted to marry the enigmatic Mr Masters. Many women longed to feel the heat from those skilled lips. To have those large hands caressing their thighs.

He bowed gracefully and led her to the lectern, where the vicar stood, trying to stifle a yawn. The Reverend Parker flicked to the relevant page in the King James Bible and read in the mumbling tone of one with little conviction.

Mina feared the Lord could not hear him, that this marriage would be forever blighted. This was not a house of God but the dim, candlelit room of a man in league with the devil. How else might one account for Mr Masters' success at the card tables?

The mumbling continued until she repeated her vows like a thousand women who had gone before her, desperate girls whose options were limited. Yet when Mr Masters claimed her as his wife, every syllable rang with steely determination.

In the blink of an eye, they were married.

The man who enjoyed owning things owned her.

Mr Masters slipped his arm around her waist and pressed his lips to her temple. "I sense your fear," he whispered against her ear. "Be assured, I will protect you always. You will not regret your decision."

She turned her head, their gazes locking. She felt it then, the sudden rush of hope, the intense need to feel his hands roaming over her body. They were so close their breath mingled in the air between them, the arousing scent of his cologne filling her nostrils with every quick inhalation.

Seconds passed.

The stranger cleared his throat and offered his felicitations, dragging Mina out of the dream where she had thought about kissing Mr Masters.

"Daventry," her husband addressed their guest. "Allow me to present my wife, Mrs Wilhelmina Masters."

"I'm honoured to meet the lady who has tamed Devon Masters." Mr Daventry glanced at her, his amusement turning to pity. "Allow me to express my sincere condolences on your brother's death, madam."

On closer inspection, he did look familiar. "Thank you, sir. Though it must seem strange to you. It is not often one deals with a death and a wedding on the same day."

"Fate has a way of propelling us in a certain direction, regardless of the circumstance." He turned to Mr Masters and handed him a note. "The information you requested. All gossip regarding Sir Thomas, and a rough timeline of his movements for the last week. My agents bribed the servants and called in debts at numerous clubs."

Mr Masters placed the note in his pocket. "I appreciate the effort."

"It's late. I shall leave you to enjoy your evening." An inscrutable look passed between the men. "Don't hesitate to call at the Order's office in Hart Street should you need assistance."

The Order? Yes, she remembered him now. Lillian's sister-in-law had once worked as an enquiry agent for Mr Daventry.

The gentleman bowed and left promptly.

Mina's friends were not far behind him, though from their grave expressions one would think they were leaving her in a dark alley in Whitechapel. She got the sense Mr Masters had already informed them the event would be a brief affair. A man who wished to bed her at least four times a week must be keen to get the preliminaries over with.

But as soon as he closed the door behind the vicar, it was evident he had other plans. "Your maid has unpacked, but I have a safe hidden upstairs for items of value. Fetch your jewels, and I shall store them safely while you find a cloak or pelisse. We're going out."

Out! Heavens! Her husband barely took a moment to breathe before moving on to the next task.

"I don't have any jewels."

His gaze fell to her bare throat. "None? Stanford once offered your mother's diamond necklace as payment, but I refused to accept an heirloom."

"Yes, I sold the necklace last week to pay the butcher, farrier and chandler. It was the last item left to me by my mother."

He firmed his jaw. "That scoundrel made you sell everything?"

"Yes. When I said I had no money, I meant it."

He cursed Thomas beneath his breath. "Then hurry and fetch something warm to wear. We will call at a place in Bond Street before venturing across town."

"Is it not a little late to go gallivanting?" Despite his bold claim earlier today, he was not desperate to strip off her clothes and ravish her senseless.

She had failed as a wife before she had even begun.

Her insecurities must have been etched on her forehead because he gripped her chin between gentle fingers and uttered, "You need a little time to become accustomed to me. I'll not have you tonight, Wilhelmina. But we—"

"Mina. I would prefer you call me Mina."

"Mina," he repeated softly. "I'm sure you would rather we moved at a slow pace. And we have an investigation to conduct, a killer to catch before Sir Oswald finds another reason to charge me with murder."

Despite stating what he required in a marriage, evidently he needed to get used to the idea of bedding her, too.

She forced a smile and stepped out of his grasp. "Of course. I shall fetch a cloak and change shoes, and we can be on our way."

If he sensed her confusion, he did not say. Still, she felt his gaze on her back as she mounted the stairs, felt it keenly during the quiet carriage ride to Bond Street as she watched raindrops pattering the windowpane and contemplated her bleak future.

When they reached their destination, she remained inside the vehicle while he stood outside Woodcroft's, banging the door knocker against the brass plate.

"It's late," she whispered through the open carriage door. It was almost midnight. "The proprietor is either out or asleep in bed. And you're getting wet. We can return tomorrow."

Her stubborn husband thumped the door with his fist.

A face appeared at the window upstairs, and a man wearing a white nightcap lifted the sash and rubbed his tired eyes. "Who goes there?"

Mr Masters got as far as introducing himself before the fellow almost fell out of the window in excitement. Within minutes, the proprietor was dressed and ushering them into his shop.

"Can I fetch refreshments, sir?"

"No. We have another appointment, but my wife wishes to purchase the most expensive necklace and bracelet you have." Mr Masters stood like the epitome of masculinity— strong, forthright, determined. Yet he foolishly believed money could solve every problem. "Indeed, we will look at anything you consider the best example of its kind."

This insight into his character would prove invaluable during the difficult months ahead. What was the impetus that drove him? What made him crave such power over people?

Mina coughed discreetly to gain his attention.

He faced her and closed the gap between them. "What is it? Is there somewhere else you would rather look?"

"No, but you are acting under a misconception."

He frowned as if no one ever questioned his judgement. "How so?"

"You presume my distress over selling my mother's jewels stems from their monetary value. You're quite wrong."

His blank stare confirmed her suspicion.

"Sir, do you—"

"Devon," he corrected, "or Masters, if you prefer."

Yes, he'd stated his full name while pledging his troth.

"The diamond necklace was a gift from my father on their wedding day. It was a symbol of hope, a token of his esteem, an object of breathtaking beauty. It could have been made of seashells and would have meant the same."

"You mean it is irreplaceable?"

"Yes. I pray a gentleman bought it with loving thoughts in mind." The man admired honesty, and so she made a heartfelt plea. "Ours is not a love match, but if you must purchase something for me on my wedding day, ensure it holds some meaning."

He glanced briefly at the walnut counter, at the gold bracelets laid out on burgundy velvet, at Mr Woodcroft's desperate smile. "I understand. Return to the carriage and wait for me there."

Intrigued, she obeyed his command.

Ten minutes passed before he emerged from Woodcroft's, a small velvet box in hand, and climbed into the elegant conveyance.

Mr Masters waited until the vehicle jolted forward and picked up speed before handing her the gift. "I pray you are not disappointed. It's the first time I have purchased a gift while considering a woman's character."

"Doubtless you're used to women who value quality and expense over silly things like sentiment." The devil on her shoulder prodded her to ask the obvious question. "Have there been many?"

"Gifts or women?" he said bluntly.

"Power radiates from you like a beacon." It left a nervous energy in the air that played havoc with her senses. "I'm sure you don't have to trawl the ballrooms looking for female company."

"I've not kept a mistress for three years."

A light laugh escaped her. Not because he was quite frugal with explanations. "What of your criteria for marrying? If you don't use brothels or keep a mistress, why stress the importance of …" She waved at his groin rather than say the words.

"Because I'll not be unfaithful to my wife, nor will I live with a stranger. Don't expect a grand affair. I doubt I'll fall in love. But if we're to survive this marriage, we must create the intimacy couples share."

Mina might have reeled from the verbal slap, but she admired the man's honesty and was not a believer in fairy tales.

"I should be grateful for small mercies."

He merely stared. "Open the box, Mina."

She nearly dropped the box when the carriage bounced through a rut in the road, but she settled back in the seat, lifted the lid and studied the gold bird-shaped brooch inside.

Tiny diamonds covered the head and tail. The bright wings were made of rubies and orange stones, perhaps topaz or citrine.

"It's beautiful. Like the ring you placed on my finger, it catches the eye and holds one's attention." As that did not apply to her, she was at a loss to know why he'd picked the brooch.

"It's a phoenix." He watched her through intense, dark eyes. "In mythology, the bird rose from the ashes a stronger version of itself. After all you have suffered, I felt it was apt."

Heat warmed her chest. She had spent hours crying, yet had found the strength to marry Mr Masters. And while he meant to control every aspect of their life, she was determined to have a say, too.

"I have spent too long cowering beneath the weight of the *ton*'s judgement, sir. In the coming weeks, I mean to be a more forthright version of myself."

"I shall look forward to seeing your rebirth. Like the phoenix, there is something exciting about a woman who strives for greatness."

Mina traced her finger over the vibrant gems. "I shall remember that every time I wear it." She removed it from the box.

"Allow me." Her husband crossed the carriage. He sat beside her, his firm thigh pressing against hers, and set about pinning the brooch to her cloak. His fingers brushed against the material. "You've not asked how much it cost."

"It is of no consequence."

He touched her chin. "You really are quite unique."

Feeling the urge to give him a gift but having not a single penny to her name, she pulled the pearl comb from her hair and twisted a bead until the thin wire snapped.

"This is for you." She captured Mr Masters' large hand and placed the bead in his palm. "Pearls are often compared to the moon—a powerful force in the universe. They convey a sense of wealth and wisdom and the quality I admire most about you. Patience."

He inhaled deeply before wrapping his fingers around the pearl. "I shall treasure it always."

She suspected he was merely humouring her, playing the game, and so she slipped the comb back into her hair and straightened. "Now we've exchanged gifts, perhaps we should consider Mr Daventry's note. You hid it in your pocket. I trust it is still there."

Looking curious about the sudden change of subject, he reached into his coat pocket, handed her two folded letters, and then returned to his seat.

Beneath half-lowered lids, she watched him roll the pearl around in his palm before tucking it into his waistcoat pocket.

Mina tried to concentrate on the first letter, the unsigned note sent to the police office. "A woman wrote this."

"I thought so, too."

"That's rather odd, don't you think?"

"Had your statement not saved me from the noose, you would have been my first suspect."

She considered the exaggerated flourishes. "I tend to write the way I do most things, with quiet obedience. This was written by a woman who wants people to stare as she descends the ballroom stairs."

Mr Masters chuckled. "Wait until your next soiree. All eyes will be upon you, madam. You'll be the most sought-after woman in the room."

Her pulse raced at the thought. She was used to hiding behind potted ferns. "You forget I am in mourning for the next three months. I couldn't possibly attend a function."

"A new bride is not expected to be in mourning."

Blast. Had he researched the rules just to prove a point?

"My brother is dead." Her voice cracked on the last word. Oh, the reckless fool thought he was invincible. "I must show a modicum of respect." She took advantage of the opportunity to learn more about her husband. "May I ask how long you mourned your sister?"

Darkness moved like storm clouds across his eyes. "I have never stopped grieving."

"You must have loved her deeply." Whereas Mina's heart was cold after her brother's selfish antics. Would it ever bloom with love again?

"When one's parents are imbeciles, the sibling bond is strong."

Her parents had been the epitome of perfection, kind and loving, always forgiving. "When your parents are blind to your faults, one struggles to cope with one's failings."

Her mother's constant praise and insistence that Mina would be the belle of the ball had left her unprepared to deal with cruel jibes and taunts.

Silence descended, and so she turned her attention back to the letter.

Someone wanted the magistrate to know that Mr Masters had a motive for murder. But who? The true killer? Or a lady out for revenge?

"Do you know of a woman who wants to hurt you?"

His mocking grin said yes. "I receive at least one letter a week from a wife begging I tear up her husband's vowel." He sighed as if the dilemma weighed heavily on his shoulders. "While I cannot be seen as weak, I may pay her child's school fees or the butcher's bill. Anonymously, of course."

Mina stared at her husband as he sat in the shadows. Who was this man the *ton* considered dangerous? He destroyed his peers with his skilled card play, yet privately found ways to be benevolent.

"Why do you gamble?" she dared ask him.

The devil leant forward and whispered, "I may tell you that when I know you better. And I mean to know you better,

Mina." His gaze slid over her body, leaving the promise of something wicked. "On the subject of the letter sent to the police office, I told no one other than Bradbury and Anderson about the duel. Therefore, the obvious conclusion is the sender knew your brother."

"Or you cannot trust your friends."

"Yes, though that is an unlikely possibility."

She focused on the second letter and peeled back the folds. "Perhaps if we study Mr Daventry's note, we may find a clue as to who the culprit might be." And she was curious to know where her brother had been this last week.

Thomas had visited thirteen gaming houses in the space of seven days, and those were the ones Mr Daventry's agents could confirm. Most surprising was a trip to Great Queen Street off Drury Lane. It wasn't the home of a mistress but of an artist hired to paint her brother's portrait.

She handed Mr Masters the letter. "My brother made no mention of having his likeness painted. It would cost in excess of three hundred pounds. Where did he hope to get the funds?"

"I doubt he considered money a problem."

"No. Somehow, he always found the funds to gamble."

Mr Masters gestured to the letter. "According to gossip, he was obsessed with Miss Howard. Would that be Captain Howard's sister?"

"Yes." Embarrassment warmed her cheeks. "Thomas offered marriage, but the lady has sense and refused him." She went on to explain how Thomas had stalked Miss Howard night and day. "The captain has a motive for murder and is not averse to killing the enemy."

"We will add him to the list of suspects."

The carriage rumbled to a stop, and a quick glance out of the window confirmed they were outside her home in

Carnaby Street. The house was in darkness. Matters had proceeded so quickly today she had not had an opportunity to explain the situation to Grimsby, the butler.

"What are we doing here?"

Mr Masters sat forward and opened the carriage door. "Searching for clues and questioning the servants."

"Could we not have called in the morning?"

"And give the murderer a chance to enter the house and steal crucial evidence?" He vaulted to the pavement with athletic grace and offered his hand. "Come, let us go inside. We have much to discuss."

She accepted his hand, suppressing the sudden rush of awareness that reminded her of the night they'd kissed. Was it wrong to admire his physical attributes? To want to drug her mind and experience the pleasure of his skilled touch?

He released her once they had mounted the steps. The door was locked, and she reached into the boot scraper buried in the wall and removed the hidden key.

"I'd rather not wake Grimsby and the others." She slipped the key into the lock and opened the door gently in the hope it didn't creak. "And I didn't tell them I was getting married today."

"Why ever not?"

"They are not exactly enamoured of you, sir."

When money was short, the staff often cursed Mr Masters to Hades. Grimsby would likely drive a poker through Devon's heart if he appeared in the darkness. Heaven knows what they would do when they learnt she was the devil's bride.

"Stay behind me," she whispered.

The house was bitterly cold and deathly quiet.

Upon hearing the pad of footsteps on the boards, Grimsby would appear at some point, and so she sent Mr Masters to her brother's study while she went to inform the butler she was home.

The basement was as quiet as the rest of the house. Grimsby had to be awake. His snores were usually loud enough to rattle the shutters. And yet she found his door open, his bed made, his drawers empty.

Cook had left, too, along with the maid and the footman. Fearing they wouldn't be paid, they had fled into the night. Who could blame them?

Mina joined her husband in the study, surprised to find he had already lit the lamp and was sorting through the vast pile of papers scattered over the desk and floor.

"Wouldn't it have been better to attend to them one at a time?"

He shrugged. "It was like this when I entered."

She brought a shaky hand to her throat. "But I tidied everything away last night. There was nothing on the desk but the lamp and the inkwell."

"Then fetch the butler as someone has been rummaging in the desk drawers." He reached for the mahogany waste paper bin, scooped up the documents and dumped them inside. "Would this be all of Sir Thomas' private papers? Did he have a safe somewhere?"

"A safe?" Mina snorted. A safe held treasures and jewels. "Money burnt a hole in Thomas' coin purse. He sold everything of value. And I cannot fetch Grimsby. The servants have taken their belongings and deserted their posts." She would have expected the butler to leave a note, but then he hadn't been paid for six months.

Mr Masters frowned. "Did they give notice?"

"No, though it's only a matter of time before the bank forecloses on the loan and takes the house in payment."

"*Who goes there?*" came the sudden screech from across the hall.

Alarmed, Mr Masters placed the bin on the floor and straightened his broad shoulders. "Someone's in the house."

"*State your name and your business.*"

Her sudden panic died, and she laughed. "Oh, it's only Miss Marmalade. If the servants have left, I shall have to bring her with us."

"Miss Marmalade?"

"My brother's parrot."

"What the devil! I'll not take the bird. A man feared amongst his peers cannot own a parrot."

Mina raised her chin. "Then I shall remain here until we can find a suitable person to take care of her."

"My wife is not sleeping across town on our wedding night."

Mina wasn't sure why it mattered. She wasn't sleeping in his bed either, by all accounts. "Then your wife will need to bring Miss Marmalade to Dover Street." Mina laughed to lighten the mood. "Come and meet her."

"And have her mock my every word."

"Thomas taught her lots of interesting facts in the hope of pleasing Miss Howard. The lady has a fondness for our feathered friends."

He muttered something beneath his breath. "Then fetch the damn thing and we'll be on our way." He glanced at the pile of papers. "No doubt the thief has stolen a vital piece of evidence. But we'll take what's here and examine it in detail at home."

Home!

The word roused a tightness in her chest. This house had been her home for the last twenty years. There had been happy times, and times she had wanted to cram her belongings into a carpet bag and board the first ship leaving Dover.

Now, she *was* escaping to Dover, to a street that housed the most notorious man in London. And yet, as her husband carried the cage containing Miss Marmalade and placed it carefully in the carriage, one thought entered her head.

Mr Masters was not so wicked after all.

Chapter Six

Ensconced in his bedchamber and dressed in nothing but a pair of loose black trousers, Devon lounged in the fireside chair. The flames roared in the grate, the heat warming his skin, yet he was unsettled.

He should read through Sir Thomas' papers, try to find a motive for murder, but he preferred to sit quietly with his thoughts.

Logic always found a way through the chaos.

One just had to be patient.

In the room next door, Mina was undressing for bed. By now, she would have found his gift, an exquisite cream silk and lace nightgown he'd purchased this afternoon. Had she slipped into the garment ready to play the dutiful bride, or merely cast it aside?

The suspense was killing him.

On the journey home from Carnaby Street, he had made his position clear. If Mina wanted his company, she must seek him out, and so he couldn't knock on her door and make idle conversation. He would not force himself on his wife.

Devon snatched the goblet of brandy from the side table

and tossed back the contents. He hissed against the burn, though it did little to temper his restless spirit.

He had meant what he'd said.

His new wife needed time to become accustomed to him.

But that didn't stop lust rippling through his veins. It didn't banish the memory of that night in the study where she had escaped her restraints and fucked his mouth with her tongue. Hell, he was near desperate to experience it again, to feel genuine human contact.

He slid his hand into his trousers and stroked his aching cock. "Mina," he breathed, conjuring an image of her glorious breasts.

But the sudden knock on his chamber door jerked him from his erotic musings. He paused, unsure whether he was dreaming, and upon hearing another light rap called, "Enter."

Mina opened the door slowly and stepped into his room.

He stood, hoping she wouldn't notice his erection in the muted light. "I thought you'd be asleep. I trust everything is to your satisfaction?"

"Yes, but I'm finding it hard to settle." She pulled the plaid blanket tightly around her shoulders—a shroud to hide the delights beneath. "Forgive me. Am I disturbing you?"

"Not at all." He merely sought release from the lust clawing his veins, but he was eager to learn what she wanted. "Would you care for a drink?" He gestured to the other chair flanking the hearth. "You must be cold. Close the door and come sit by the fire. Here, give me the blanket."

She obeyed his instruction, though seemed reluctant to relinquish her makeshift cloak. "I feared you might be annoyed with Miss Marmalade."

Annoyed? The damn parrot had Lucifer's impertinence.

"Do you mean when she commented on the size of my beak or when she chirped 'Masters is a muttonhead'?"

The lady struggled to hide her amusement. "I'm sure we can train her to be polite. For the time being, I have asked Bates to keep her downstairs in the servants' quarters."

Poor Bates. "I'm sure he was thrilled at the prospect of hearing Miss Marmalade's witty repartee."

She laughed, her shoulders relaxing a little. "Perhaps Lillian might take care of her for a while. In the meantime, I shall try to ensure she is not a pest."

To distract his thoughts from the ill-bred bird, he considered his wife's bare feet and the cream silk evident beneath the blanket. "You're wearing the nightgown I purchased for you. It's meant to be worn loose. May I see if it fits?"

He was keen to discover what lay beneath the swathe of plaid.

"It's a gown one would wear for a lover, not a man I married to ease his conscience." A crimson blush touched her cheeks. "But I appreciate the gesture."

"We will be lovers at some point soon." Hell, if he let his body rule his head, she would be on the floor in seconds. He prowled towards her. "And this is our wedding night. Give me the blanket, Mina, and then you can tell me why you're really here." It wasn't to talk about the annoying bird.

She relinquished her hold. "I suppose it is only fair."

He understood her meaning as soon as he pulled the blanket from her shoulders and it came to rest on the boards in a pool of Scottish tartan. The silk was so sheer he could see the outline of her nipples, the flare of her hips, the dark hair at the apex of her thighs.

Devon swallowed hard.

She had seen him naked. Now he had the pleasure of knowing her more intimately. And the sight was so damnably arousing.

"I should have made another stipulation when listing my

requirements for marriage," he said, his fingers tingling at the thought of slipping the diaphanous material off her shoulder and kissing her soft skin. "I should have insisted on buying all your nightgowns."

A nervous smile touched her lips. "I haven't a penny to my name. Everything new comes from your purse."

The hungry imp on his shoulder demanded he peruse her form further. "You look like a queen of Egypt. If only you believed in the power of your own sexuality, then you might command a room."

"For what purpose?"

The question had him stumped.

"The truth is, I cannot prance about like a peahen," she added. "Make up your mind, husband. First, you demand honesty. Now, you want me to pretend to be something I am not."

He cupped her bare arm gently. "I want you to know I find you attractive and should have spoken in earnest rather than skirting around the issue."

"You didn't find me so appealing at first glance."

No, but like the sun edging slowly above the horizon, the more she revealed her character, the more she brightened his day.

"You were not what I'd asked for, that was all."

"This won't work if you try to change me, Devon."

It was the first time she had used his given name.

Hearing the sound on her lips stirred something warm inside.

"I don't want to change you, Mina. You're the first woman I have met with an ounce of substance." The first woman he believed he might come to trust. And he needed to make certain provisions before some bankrupt bugger shot him dead.

She glanced at his large tester bed. "I want to sleep here with you tonight as expected. I'll not have the servants think there is something wrong with me. And we've not shared a meal together today. I've arranged for Bates to bring a light repast. All we need do is ring."

"Yet I suspect you seek intimate relations, not food." While his heart darted for cover, another part of his anatomy raised its head, eager for her answer.

She scanned the entire length of him, her gaze returning to linger on his bare chest. "I am not sure I'm ready to entertain all of you. But we could share another kiss. Make a move towards becoming accustomed to one another."

He welcomed the move.

"I trust Miss Ware told you what to expect when you wake beside a naked man." One used to having the bed to himself.

She flapped her fingers in his direction. "Yes, I know how it all works. Although, a man's morning erection may be due to the sudden stimulation of the blood supply, not arousal."

"And yet most men would not look a gift horse in the mouth."

"Perhaps this is a conversation to have at first light."

He chose not to inform her he would be stiff numerous times throughout the night. "Then, before we ring for Bates and discuss our plan to catch a murderer, let us test another of Miss Ware's theories."

Her eyes widened. "Which one?"

"That kissing is a more sensual experience when both parties are almost naked." He slid his arm around her waist and brushed his mouth over the shell of her ear, yet he was the one panting. "And you are practically naked, love."

She was responsive to his touch, her head lolling to the

side as he sucked her earlobe. "Devon, why does everything you do leave me with such a profound ache?"

"Because I swore to always please you in bed, and I pride myself on being a man of my word." While they hadn't married for love, he was certain they would have many passionate encounters between the sheets. "Soon, I shall show you how to ease the tension."

The air crackled with it—an electric blend of lust and need and utter desperation. His blood pumped fast through his veins. He had never been so hard from anticipation alone. Perhaps knowing he had to wait to take what he wanted accounted for his heightened senses.

Indeed, when their gazes met, he saw his own hunger reflected in her brown eyes. A second later, they were devouring each other's mouths, plunging their tongues deep to satisfy the craving.

Such was this newfound addiction, he wanted to rip the fine silk from her body, feast on her flesh and make her come hard.

He was always in control of the game, yet hadn't anticipated having such a skilled opponent. He hadn't studied her methods. He couldn't read her hand. Didn't know when she might play her best card.

The sobering thought had him tearing his mouth from hers. "It's late. I'll not rush you tonight."

"Yes," she breathed. "We should ring for Bates."

He could have seduced her and claimed her virtue.

He could have taken the prize.

Instinct said patience would bring a greater victory.

"I told Simpkin we'd walk from the corner of Great Queen Street," Devon said, aware his wife was a little subdued since he'd stopped kissing her rather abruptly last night. They had slept in the same bed, but she had teetered on the edge, as still as a tomb effigy. "If Mr Goldman sees us alight, he may shut the shop."

"Whatever you think is best," she said in the same absent tone she used when they had discussed the investigation over breakfast this morning.

He might have explained his actions, stressed the importance of not rushing into something that might cause problems between them. Besides, her brother had died, and she had dressed in a black pelisse and pillbox hat and watched him from behind the lace veil. Perhaps that was the reason for her quietude.

Maybe she disliked feeling out of control as much as he did.

Whenever their mouths met, they lost their heads.

His abdominal muscles clenched at the thought.

The same happened again as he handed her down to the pavement. Hell, he needed to drive deep into her body and banish this damnable craving. Then they might return to some semblance of normality.

Mina accepted his arm. Her hand slid over his bicep in a sort of covert exploration. "It's strange we have found no receipts for the portrait. Nor has Mr Goldman appeared at the house demanding payment."

"I doubt Daventry has made a mistake."

"But who told him?"

"Probably Crumley or your butler." Daventry's agents could be very persuasive but rarely revealed their methods.

They approached Goldman's Portrait Studio, a four-storey building in good repair. Paintings of horses and hounds filled the bow window, miniatures in oval gilt frames were displayed in a glass case. The artist was skilled, the portraits lifelike.

"Good morning," said a middle-aged gentleman whose paunch was so pronounced he may have been growing it since childhood. "Do you have an appointment or have you come to browse the collection?"

He introduced himself as Mr Dowling and gestured to the paintings filling every available wall space.

Mina raised her veil and offered the man a warm smile. "We were hoping to speak to Mr Goldman. He is the portrait painter who captured Sir Thomas Stanford's likeness, is he not?"

Recognition flashed in Mr Dowling's eyes, yet he said, "Mr Goldman rarely paints portraits these days, and I can recall no clients of that name."

Devon knew when an opponent was lying. Mr Dowling clutched the oak counter while his gaze darted left and right, like a rabbit escaping a fox.

"You must be mistaken," Mina said with a card sharp's confidence. "Might you check your records? It is a matter of the utmost urgency."

Devon stepped forward and hit him with a stare guaranteed to leave him trembling in his boots. "We wouldn't ask if it wasn't important."

The assistant's bottom lip quivered. He nodded, then disappeared through a door behind the counter. The plod of footsteps on the boards said he had ventured upstairs.

"I'm confident your brother has visited this establishment."

"Yes, Mr Dowling had a hard time meeting my gaze."

"How do you wish to proceed?"

Perhaps unused to men asking her opinion, she blinked in

surprise. "We need answers and must employ Mr Daventry's methods if we mean to find the killer."

Devon noted the sudden tilt of her chin. Thomas Stanford had joked his sister was timid and easy to manipulate, but desperation had left her fearful and fainthearted. Devon saw a spirited woman whose determination would frighten most men.

"Then I shall follow your lead," he said.

Mr Dowling returned with a heavy ledger which he said contained the names of previous clients, all listed in alphabetical order. "You're welcome to inspect the tome." Dust particles wafted into the air as he placed the book on the counter and turned it to face them.

Mina removed her black gloves and flicked through the foxed pages until she found the relevant section. "Freeman. Ferguson. You're right. There is no one named Stanford in the records."

"That is what I said, madam." The assistant snapped the book shut so quickly he almost trapped her fingers between the pages. "You might try Thomas Phillips at the Royal Academy. He paints many distinguished gentlemen."

Mina snatched her gloves off the counter. "Perhaps I have not made our position clear, Mr Dowling. We are dealing with the matter of murder. We have proof Sir Thomas spent many hours in this studio. Your refusal to acknowledge the fact means I must fetch the magistrate and have him inspect the premises."

Mr Dowling paled. "I—"

"I suggest you speak up, sir," she continued, so brazenly pride flickered in Devon's chest. "My husband wishes to rip this place apart in a bid to find answers. I would hate for anyone to get hurt in the process. The worst accidents happen amid chaos."

Mr Dowling raised his hands in surrender. "I cannot give you the answers you seek and would tell the magistrate the same." In a panic, he glanced at the door behind him. "I assure you, the man you mention has never had his portrait painted by Mr Goldman. Now, I must ask you to leave, else I shall call a constable."

"What an excellent idea," Mina said. "We will wait while you fetch him. Perhaps then we might discover the truth."

Aware the assistant's resolve was crumbling, Devon added, "We are not leaving until we've spoken to Goldman."

A tense silence ensued, broken only by someone muttering in the hall. The door behind the counter creaked open a fraction, and a man whispered an instruction and closed it again.

Mr Dowling gestured to the door and stepped aside. "Mr Goldman will see you in his private studio. First floor. There's a cavalier painted on the door."

Mina tugged on her gloves and led the way upstairs.

All four doors were painted with portraits of different people. A man in a red military uniform. A scholarly figure. The naked goddess Venus. A cavalier.

Devon knocked, and Goldman called for them to enter.

They found him seated in a red velvet throne chair on a small dais. He wore a gold silk banyan over a white shirt and black trousers. His feet were bare, and though Devon suspected the man was approaching forty, there wasn't a single streak of grey in his dark brown hair.

"I would offer you a seat," Goldman said, gesturing to the lay figure perched on a wooden stool and dressed in the black and gold coat of a naval captain, "but as you can see, there are no more chairs."

There was nothing else in the room but easels and paints, the floor scattered with drawings and crumpled paper.

The pompous popinjay roused Devon's temper. "A gentleman would offer the lady a seat, not prattle on like an indulgent coxcomb. Be assured, Mr Goldman, I could ruin you in a heartbeat, so I suggest you take our visit seriously."

The man's arrogant grin faltered. "I might if you'd bothered to introduce yourselves and state your business."

Devon straightened. "I am Devon Masters, and my wife is sister to the late Thomas Stanford. Unless you've spent the last few days with your nose pressed to the canvas, you will know the man is dead."

"Murdered," Mina added. "We are helping the magistrate with his inquiries. Evidence confirms my brother spent time here and visited your premises only last week."

"Murdered?" The news wiped the smirk off Goldman's face.

"I doubt you were painting Stanford's portrait," Devon scoffed. "The man hadn't a penny to his name, and you strike me as someone who charges over the odds." Though one could not dispute he was talented.

Mina stepped forward. "If we are wrong, show us the portrait. Failure to offer an explanation will result in a visit from Sir Oswald of the Great Marlborough Street office. The new Metropolitan Police Force deals with crimes swiftly."

Goldman sighed and scrubbed his hand down his face. "You leave me in a predicament. If I tell you, do I have your word you will not mention the matter to anyone else?"

"That all depends," Devon said, suppressing a grin.

"We must report evidence of a crime, sir."

"Oh, there has been no crime committed here." Goldman stood and brushed imagined dust off his silk banyan before stepping off the dais. "But should the ton learn of my *private* art classes, all parties would find themselves scandalised, and I shall be forced to flee to France."

While Mina appeared confused, Devon understood. He would bet these private classes took place behind Venus' door. Doubtless, Goldman charged an extortionate rate for his services.

"Stanford couldn't afford your classes."

Goldman strode ahead, his banyan billowing behind him. "No, but the wealthy ladies of the *ton* will pay anything for the experience." As predicted, he led them to the door decorated with the naked goddess. "I would advise your wife waits downstairs."

Mina huffed. "I have a name, Mr Goldman."

"Mrs Masters' courage knows no bounds," Devon said, suspecting they were about to gaze upon erotic images.

Goldman grinned. "Don't say I didn't warn you."

The room was dark and smelled of linseed and resin and, to the seasoned nostrils, the sweet scent of burnt opium. More went on in this room than teaching a lady how to master the perfect stroke.

Goldman tugged the heavy red curtains aside, sending a burst of daylight into the large space.

For long, drawn-out seconds, they gazed at the theatrical setting. A gilt chaise stood on a carpet of red silk. Different hats and masks and wigs bulged from a basket in the corner. There were marble busts, standing candelabra and a chest of old daggers and swords.

Was that where Goldman got the murder weapon?

"I provide the life model." Goldman moved to stand near the easel and beckoned Mina forward. "Still, I encourage my students to paint a background that reflects something of their state of mind."

Mina crossed the room, eager to know what was on the large canvas propped against the easel. Her eyes widened, and her chin sagged.

"Good heavens!" She shook her head, as if struggling to comprehend the vision before her. It proved so repugnant she turned away. "Mr Masters, you should look at this, though I warn you, I have never seen the like."

Devon closed the gap between them and came to stand behind her.

Mother of all saints!

He met Goldman's arrogant smirk. "Are you telling me a lady painted this?" He stared at the depiction of a naked male figure lying on the chaise. A pig mask hid his face. A sword covered in blood stood in place of his phallus. "It's grotesque."

"Beauty is in the eye of the beholder. I assure you, it's her best work to date." Goldman pointed to the figure of a woman dressed in a black shroud, ten puppies nipping at her feet. "My student believes it represents the plight of young women, though you can see it isn't finished."

Mina snorted. "Now I know why I find it so abhorrent. There is some truth to the symbolism. But what has any of this to do with my dead brother?"

"Why, Sir Thomas is the life model. I paid him handsomely, though he begged me for the opportunity. You see, the models always remain hidden behind a mask of the artist's choosing. The student has no notion who the subject might be."

If Mina had looked shocked before, she looked positively astounded now. "I don't know what evil trick this is, sir, but why would a baronet don a mask and prance around naked?"

"Sir Thomas had his reasons."

"I don't believe you."

"I have a signed contract. You can inspect the signature."

Mina pursed her lips.

Devon placed a reassuring hand on her back for fear she

might cast up her accounts. "Am I right in assuming the student is Miss Howard?"

It made sense. Sir Thomas was obsessed with the woman and the thought of spending hours in her company must have been the motivating factor.

"I cannot reveal such sensitive information. I've shown you this because you have as much to lose as I do. Heaven forbid, someone should learn of my student's hobby or Sir Thomas' deviant tendencies."

The devious bastard!

"How many students have painted Sir Thomas?" Devon asked, eager to discover as much as possible while Goldman was willing.

"He would only sit for one student." Again, he motioned to the canvas. "It's not finished, so I doubt the lady murdered him. Indeed, she will be most aggrieved to learn of his death."

Mina gave a weary sigh. "Is there anything you can tell us that might help catch my brother's murderer?"

Goldman maintained eye contact. "No."

"Do you have relations with your students?" Devon asked, much to the man's surprise. "This place stinks like an opium den. Artists proclaim to do their best work when under the influence."

A lady who felt trapped by the confines of her sex might like to experiment with a man she admired. Had Stanford witnessed something and made a scene?

The lothario winked at Mina. "I dabble occasionally. Please let me know if you would like art lessons, Mrs Masters. I'm known to give expert tutorage."

Devon was on him in seconds.

He knocked the reprobate on his arse, grabbed a handful of his gold banyan and stuffed it into the bastard's mouth.

"Speak to my wife like that again and they'll be burying you in this peacock's outfit."

Goldman's arms and legs flailed as he choked.

"If I discover you're lying, I shall be a little less forgiving." Devon straightened and tugged his cuffs. "I'm sure you don't want Captain Howard learning of his sister's antics."

He left Goldman squirming on the floor and led Mina downstairs and onto Great Queen Street. "After an insightful morning, we now have a motive for murder," he said, his temper burning as hot as Satan's pitchfork.

"Yes, Thomas might have attempted to blackmail both men. If so, Mr Goldman and Captain Howard had a reason to silence my brother."

"Indeed." They needed to speak to Miss Howard privately in the hope she might reveal damning information.

"We should hire a man to watch Mr Goldman. He strikes me as the sort who would do a moonlight flit." She gripped Devon's arm tightly as they walked towards the carriage. "Assuming, of course, he hasn't choked on his silk banyan."

"Forgive me if I frightened you." The mere thought of the rakish gent seducing his wife had roused the devil's own fury.

"On the contrary." She gave a light laugh. "I don't think I have ever found you more charming, Mr Masters."

Chapter Seven

Two days had passed since Devon had almost smothered Mr Goldman at the artist's studio. Two days since they had knocked on Captain Howard's door to be told the family were out of town and not due back until Wednesday.

It had been a little more than two days since Mina had felt her husband's mouth devouring hers, though the atmosphere was charged with a pulsing energy whenever they were alone together.

The air between them thrummed now, even in this house of God. Indeed, as they stood at St George's Fields chapel doors and thanked the mourners for attending Thomas' funeral, the Divine did not strike them down for entering into a sham of a marriage.

Still, when Devon placed a warm hand on her waist and pressed his mouth to her ear, her body reacted like that of a harlot from Gomorrah.

"The men approaching are my friends from Cambridge," he whispered. "The red-haired fellow on the left is Mr Justin Bradbury. He acted as my second at Bromley Common."

Mr Bradbury came to a halt a mere two feet away and

bowed. "Please accept my condolences on the death of your brother, Mrs Masters."

"Thank you, Mr Bradbury." She did not call the man a hypocrite. He had come merely at Devon's behest to ensure the pews weren't empty. Although, she sensed he disapproved of his friend marrying to settle a debt. "Devon tells me you've been friends for many years."

"Seventeen. We went to Harrow together, as did Anderson." Mr Bradbury gestured to the inconspicuous man beside him. "We're like family, as close as brothers."

Devon had mentioned his parents were alive and living in Boston. She made a mental note to ask him why he had remained behind and not made a new life in America. Perhaps it had something to do with his sister's death.

"Then I look forward to knowing you both better."

The men were forced to move on when Lord Denton stopped to express his sympathy. "Should you need anything, madam, you can call on me night and day." He shot Devon a Medusa-like glare and made way for his sister, who, despite facing many objections, had insisted on attending the service.

Helen scanned Mina's face as if looking for bruises or any sign of mistreatment. "I'm so worried about you," she whispered while her husband, Nicholas St Clair, spoke to Devon. "Was he kind to you?" she mouthed, a deep frown marring her brow. "On your wedding night, was he gentle?"

Mina nodded. "All is well. There is nothing to fear."

All was not well.

For some reason, they had lost their way the last two days. Yes, they had dined together and spoken for hours about unimportant things. They had played cards and laughed like they hadn't a care in the world. Devon was kind and attentive, but he had not kissed her again.

That said, she had not given him leave to.

She might have asked for advice, but this was not the time or place, and how could Helen understand Mina's dilemma when she was so in love with her husband?

Equally determined to defy convention, Lillian was next to leave with her brother Lord Roxburgh, and a brief conversation ensued.

Lillian reached for Mina's hand and squeezed it tightly. "Remember, you're a strong, beautiful woman with the power to create the life you want. Let nothing stand in your way."

Everyone needed a friend like Lillian, a constant voice for the downtrodden. Happiness was often a state of mind. Worrying and playing through scenarios in one's head achieved nothing.

As it was uncustomary for ladies to attend the service, let alone the burial, Mina had requested a private interment. Besides, she did not want men who despised her brother standing over his grave, silently cursing him to the devil.

The vicar waited for them to take their positions, for the burly men no one knew to act as pallbearers and ready the coffin.

"You did pay the gravedigger?" She turned to Devon, who stood beside her like a tower of strength, watching the vicar find the relevant page in his dog-eared Bible.

Skilled resurrectionists could dig up a body and fill the grave in twenty minutes. Many of her brother's creditors might be eager to see if Thomas had been buried with a secret purse of gold sovereigns.

"Yes, the grave is eight feet deep, not six. And he will ensure the stone tomb I purchased is in place before the week's end."

"Thank you." She'd never been more grateful to anyone.

They fell silent as the vicar read a psalm followed by the "ashes to ashes" liturgy, and the coffin was lowered into the ground. The creaking of wood reminded her of those nights when Thomas had crept through the house, broke and sotted. The coffin swayed on the ropes, back and forth like her brother's fragile state of mind.

Such were Thomas' debts, he might have been buried in a common grave had it not been for Devon's generosity. Devon had helped her prepare the body and arrange the service.

Had he thought it inappropriate to kiss her again?

Could he not get past the fact he found her unappealing?

It was up to her to find out.

Though she was scared of the answer.

"I couldn't have done this without you," she said, tossing a handful of soil on the coffin and blinking back tears. "You despised him more than any man, yet you have been nothing but respectful to his memory."

She found his benevolence as arousing as his hard muscles and sinful smile, as the trail of dark hair leading down past the waistband of his trousers.

"It is my duty to support you."

Is that all this was… an act of duty? Payment for a debt?

"You must have read the manual on how to be a good husband. You always say the right things, do the right things. You're kind and generous, always thoughtful."

"So why do you sound disappointed?" Reluctantly, he turned to speak to the vicar, thanking him for the service. Then he mentioned a sizeable donation, and the vicar's eyes brightened like he had witnessed a heavenly vision.

The vicar left them alone at the graveside, and Devon scattered a handful of soil over the coffin too. "I should have found a way to help you," he said, almost to himself. "It seems to be the story of my life."

The words echoed a sentiment she had expressed often. "Believe me, I tried many times. All to no avail."

Devon faced her, his dark, unfathomable eyes meeting hers. "What do you want from me, Mina? Did you hope to marry a rogue and live a life of adventure? Does it grieve you that I am not as wicked as people portray?"

Kindness had been her only consideration—until she'd kissed him.

Now she couldn't stop the sinful train of her thoughts.

She swallowed hard, debating how honest she should be. "You've not kissed me in days. What happened to your demands? One might think you cannot bear to lay a hand on me."

Amusement played across his rugged features. "Did I not tell you to inform when you might welcome my advances?"

"I don't want you to think I'm heartless. My brother is dead. It hurts that we weren't close." That she had grown to despise him. "It hurts that I'll never get a chance to put things right. Indeed, I have never felt so alone."

Was that why she longed for his touch?

He cupped her elbow. "You want me to pursue you? You want me to seduce you? Make you my wife in more than name?"

"I want to feel like a desirable woman, Devon." She glanced at her poor brother's grave, deep in the cold ground. "Life is precarious. I am tired of hiding in the shadows, of tiptoeing around the *ton* for fear of causing offence."

"I need a simple yes or no, love."

"Yes, I want you to seduce me."

"Very well," he said, as if it were all part of repaying his debt to her. "Your needs are duly noted."

Mina sighed to herself. Devon Masters hid behind an impenetrable fortress. He'd let her peek through the window, but she wanted to gain admission. Was there a special key?

Had he ever let anyone cross the threshold? And how did she go about achieving her goal?

How might she seduce him, too?

"Do you mean to start immediately?" she said, her attention suddenly drawn to the iron railings and the line of trees flanking the road.

The hairs on her nape prickled to life.

Someone was watching them.

"If I'm to tempt you into bed, it's best to catch you unawares." Noticing her attention waning, he frowned. "What is it?"

"I don't know. I thought I saw a figure by the railings." She laid a hand on his arm. "Don't make it obvious, but look a few feet to the left of the oak tree."

"Pretend you're whispering in my ear so I can turn my head."

She came up on her toes and wrapped her arms around his neck. He smelled of leather and expensive cologne, and she resisted the urge to press her mouth to his jaw and nip gently.

"Can you see the figure?" she uttered against his ear.

A hum escaped him. "It's a woman in widow's weeds."

"Oh, thank heavens. Doubtless, she means to visit her husband's grave and is waiting for us to depart." Still, it was most odd.

"Damn it, she's seen me and bolted." Devon grabbed Mina's hand and sprinted towards the gate. "If she's visiting the churchyard, why run?"

They navigated the old headstones, though Mina struggled to keep Devon's pace. "Wait. I cannot run in these skirts." She couldn't hike them up any higher.

He slowed. "I'll not leave you alone. It may be a trap."

They burst through the open gate onto the Uxbridge Road and spotted the woman climbing into a hackney parked two hundred yards ahead. Though her face was hidden behind a black veil, she stared in their direction before slamming the door shut.

The jarvey flicked the reins, and the vehicle jolted forward before picking up speed and disappearing amid a host of carts, carriages, and cabs.

"Interesting," Devon mused.

"She was young." She'd covered the distance quickly.

"Yes, she raised her skirts and ran."

"Do you think she came to pay her respects to my brother?"

Devon stared into the distance. "Undoubtedly."

"But why hide in the shadows?"

Devon frowned. "That's what we need to find out."

Mina sighed. In a case that was already proving complicated, and with very few leads, the last thing they needed was to add another suspect to their list.

"But I already have a gown suitable for a ball." Mina glanced at the sign above the door of the elegant shop. Mrs Clancy of Chancery Lane was renowned for her daring evening dresses. Every lady of fashion had paid the extortionate sum to have a gown made by her magical hands. "Besides, the modiste has a waiting list as long as Hadrian's Wall."

Devon cupped her elbow and propelled her forward. "If we're to attend Captain Howard's ball tomorrow night, you need a new gown."

"We don't have an invitation."

"We don't need one." He gave a devilish grin. "But you

need to look like the wife of a notorious devil else it may damage my reputation."

He was joking, yet she supposed he had a point. It was time she accepted her new life, and she had been wearing the same dowdy old dresses for years.

"Maybe I do need to look the part if I'm to steal into a ball uninvited and question the guests." Would Miss Howard confess to her scandalous meetings at the artist's studio? Would the captain admit to murdering Thomas? It was unlikely. "But the party is tomorrow, and I doubt a modiste like Mrs Clancy has dresses already made."

"Trust me. It's all in hand." Devon opened the door, the overhead bell tinkling. "I sent her your measurements on Saturday once I learnt of Captain Howard's ball."

"My measurements?" Keen to tease him, she whispered, "So it was a wooden ruler prodding my buttocks in bed last night. You wished to be certain you hadn't made a mistake."

She had lain awake for hours, waiting for him to slide his arm about her waist, to draw her closer, an unbearable anticipation hardening her nipples and tightening her core. Yet still he had not taken her virtue, nor had he kissed her passionately or eased the infernal ache as he had promised.

So what was he waiting for?

"Perhaps I've been watching you closely while you sleep." His deep drawl slipped over her like a lover's caress. Warm. Stimulating. "Studying every curve."

"I—I would have known."

"I promise you, I have the lightest touch, love."

"You promise a lot, Devon. Yet I am still waiting."

The thrum of energy passing between them was as powerful as ever. Her husband had a magnetic presence, a confidence that left her a little in awe. And when their mouths met, he made her feel like she was the most desirable woman in the world.

He dared to run his finger over her lips. "If there's any hope for us, I need you to want me, Mina."

She shivered as he whispered her name. "I do."

"You must want me with a hunger that defies the odds."

As the hours had stretched into days, she had felt starved for his attention. The time spent together at home created an intimacy that physical affection would enhance. "I find I am counting the minutes until you kiss me again."

His gaze dipped to her mouth.

He looked at her mouth a lot of late.

"Then I must rectify the problem posthaste," he breathed before a discreet cough behind broke the spell.

Captivated by her husband's seductive banter, Mina had almost forgotten she was in the modiste's shop. She swung around to find the celebrated designer standing behind a gilt and glass counter. Based on her exquisite pieces, one might expect to find a young woman, not a matron of sixty.

"Ah, Masters. It's you."

"Good morning, Mrs Clancy."

"Close the door quickly and come in out of the cold." Mrs Clancy spoke in the lofty tones of a society grande dame. She wore her white hair in the once fashionable *fontage* style, had a black beauty patch near the corner of her eye and three strings of pearls wrapped around her bulging neck.

"Allow me to present my wife, Mina Masters."

Mrs Clancy rounded the counter and beckoned them closer before raising a quizzing glass to her right eye. "Unbutton your pelisse, gal, and let me look at you."

Mina glanced at the door, then to the screened area at the rear of the shop, near the glass case filled with gloves and fans. "What, here?"

The modiste flapped her hand impatiently. "One must have an appointment to enter this establishment. One does not walk in off the street. Still, lock the door, Masters, so your wife might relax. Is she always so fidgety? I have never seen shoulders so tense."

Devon obliged the matron by turning the key in the lock. "It's been a while since she's had a new gown, and as I explained, her brother met a tragic end recently."

"Yes, hence this ghastly black ensemble." Mrs Clancy tugged at the stiff bombazine and tutted. "Crepe would sit better on her hips."

"I do have a voice," Mina snapped.

"Then use it, gal."

"Very well. Let me begin by saying my husband does not choose what I wear." She shot Devon a determined look. "Nor will I be browbeaten into wearing something too revealing."

She had heard Mrs Clancy's gowns always caused a stir.

Mrs Clancy stared down her narrow nose. "Each gown is unique, designed to reflect something of one's character. As such, you determine the colour and the cut, though based on Masters' description of you, I've chosen midnight blue."

Mina stared at Devon, and the devil smiled. "What exactly did my husband say?" she asked but then thought better of it. Perhaps it was best not to know.

Mrs Clancy captured Mina's chin in her cold fingers to better assess the angle of her cheekbones. "Oh, that you're bold and courageous, but sometimes let nerves overwhelm you. That you have a natural elegance which is often hidden beneath ugly dresses."

She could not argue with that.

"Yes, you're right, Masters." The modiste ran her hand over Mina's waist. "She has the curves of Venus herself."

Venus?

The mention of the goddess roused thoughts of the lecherous painter in the gold banyan. "Is that meant as a compliment, madam?"

"Yes. In the right clothes, we will have every man drooling."

"She need please no one but her husband," Devon said sternly.

"I need please no one but myself," Mina corrected.

Mrs Clancy clapped her hands. "Indeed. Now, come behind the dressing screen and let's get you out of this monstrosity so Penelope can measure you properly. The six of us will have to work overnight to have you ready in time. Thank heavens I've hired an extra seamstress."

While Devon relaxed in a leather wing chair and opened the broadsheet he found on the side table, Mrs Clancy ushered Mina behind the six-foot screen and had her out of her dress and petticoat within a minute.

"Merciful Lord. How old is this corset?"

Heat flooded Mina's cheeks. "I've had it a few years."

"The boning is all wrong for the silhouette popular these days." Mrs Clancy set about unthreading the ties. "Masters will want his wife to reflect something of his status."

A week ago, Mina might have joked about wearing devil horns, but Devon was nowhere near as wicked as people believed. "May I ask how you know my husband?" Had the modiste made a dress for a mistress or three?

Was playing the gentleman part of Devon's game?

Mrs Clancy leant closer and lowered her voice. "My grandson would have landed in debtors' prison had Masters not taught him a harsh lesson. Now he's a lieutenant on the *St Vincent*."

"I see," was all she managed to say because her chest grew warm whenever she thought of Devon's kind gestures.

"I've no appointments until February," Mrs Clancy said, tugging off Mina's corset to leave her standing in her chemise. "Yet I'd cancel the King to appease Mr Masters."

"Because he did your grandson a great service?"

"One I'll struggle to repay in this lifetime." She gave a light chuckle. "Regardless of gossip, his heart is not entirely black. But woe betide anyone who crosses him, gal."

"Yes, he can be quite determined." Though she might not want to admit it, she found his dark side as attractive as his tight buttocks.

Mrs Clancy gestured to the thick wool blanket on the chair. "Keep warm while I send Penelope down to take your measurements. Masters had the foresight to send us one of your old gowns, so we've already cut and pinned the silk and sewn the sleeves and skirt."

"Thank you for going to so much trouble." It would take six women working for the next thirty-six hours to have the gown finished in time. "It's been a while since I've known the kindness of strangers."

Mrs Clancy patted Mina's arm. "Well, you've been lucky enough to marry the kindest man I know, so I doubt you'll have cause to feel deprived again."

And yet she did feel deprived… deprived of his hot kisses and sensual touch, deprived of his amorous attentions. It was like the worst hunger she had known, and she had gone days without a decent meal because Thomas hadn't paid the grocer.

The modiste left Mina alone and exchanged hushed words with Devon before a door clicked shut.

A shiver rippled through her, though it had nothing to do

with the chill in the air. She was almost naked, and her husband was on the other side of the dressing screen.

"You don't have to wait," she called, needing to hear his voice. "Come back in an hour, or I can have them wave down a hackney to bring me home."

The rustle of the newspaper preceded the scrape of chair legs on the boards. "I'll not have my wife riding in a hackney."

"Why?" Thomas had left her to make her own way about town. "It must be tedious sitting there. We're sure to be another hour or two."

He did not reply, and she almost jumped out of her skin when he appeared behind the screen, looking so handsome it stole her breath.

Depthless, coal-black eyes raked over her. He inhaled sharply when his gaze reached her bare toes. "I'm waiting for you. And I'll not hear another word on the matter."

"If you're sure."

"I'm sure." He prowled towards her, shrugging off his dark blue coat and draping it over the screen. "I thought about what you said earlier, about wanting to feel desired."

His rich, compelling tone was like an overture to a romantic opera. A story of a fool lured to sin by a fallen angel. A quest for erotic pleasure that led to a profound life-long love. Just silliness, really.

"And what did you deduce?" Nerves left her shaking.

He came to stand a mere foot away, his long, elegant fingers settling on her collarbone and stroking back and forth in an arousing rhythm. "That if I touched here, in the modiste's shop, it would convey something of my desperate need to bed you."

In the shop!

Despite stuttering, she managed to say, "W-what about

Mrs Clancy?"

"The door is locked, and I told her not to send Penelope down for fifteen minutes. We're quite alone, love."

Heat pooled between her thighs at the mere thought of his hands on her body. "What will you do to make me feel like a woman?"

"I doubt you've ever come by a man's hand."

She had never *come* at all. Lillian had explained the process after reading a book hidden in her brother's library, though Mina could not think of a man she liked enough to rouse her to feel anything amorous.

Until now.

Devon Masters made her tremble with need.

Being skilled at reading facial expressions, his frown said he'd arrived at the obvious conclusion. "You've never experienced release?"

She shook her head. "I have never felt the inclination."

"Then you're in for a treat, love." He gathered the hem of her chemise and slipped his hand underneath to cup her bare buttocks. "As time is of the essence, let us save this conversation until later." He lowered his head and held her gaze. "You do want me to touch you?"

"Yes." More than anything.

Her breath came quicker, his male scent filling her nostrils—such a powerful aphrodisiac she wanted to taste every inch of him. Her lips parted in anticipation, begging for him to claim them.

Although the clock was against them, he took her mouth in a slow, drugging kiss that left her knees weak and her heart near thumping out of her chest.

And then he slid his tongue over hers, plunging deep into her mouth, the sensation tugging at a forbidden place low in her belly.

Now she knew what it meant to be drunk with desire. Her limbs had a mind of their own. She couldn't stop touching him, running her hands over his broad shoulders, slipping her fingers into his hair, rubbing her leg against his muscular thigh.

"Devon!" she breathed, bereft when he broke contact.

"Fear not." He spun her around and drew her back against his chest. "I shall make you feel so good, Mina." He sucked on her earlobe and gave it a gentle nip before tracing the shell with the tip of his tongue.

A moan slipped from her lips.

And another when he cupped her breast with his left hand and stroked her sex with his right.

"You're so responsive to my touch," he whispered against her hair as he played her like a maestro—a master of sinful pleasures. "Perhaps I've made you wait too long."

"I'm glad you like this game," she panted. Despite being a novice, she was determined to make him suffer the agonising wait, too. "Somehow, I shall find a way to tease you to dis-distraction … oh, God!" She could barely get the last word out as she came closer to reaching the pinnacle of something wonderful.

He pressed the thick ridge of his manhood against her buttocks, her core pulsing hard in response. "I'm already desperate to be inside you, love. Take comfort in the fact I shall ache for you all day."

She might have offered a witty retort, but the second he pushed two fingers into her sex, she came apart, shuddering and whispering his name.

"As the sensations ripple through you, know you will experience it again soon." His arm circled her waist. "I have you. You're safe. I'll not let go."

And she believed him.

Chapter Eight

"I feel like an imposter." Mina brushed her hands down the midnight-blue silk before gently tapping the ringlets her maid had spent an age perfecting. "I'm unused to people looking at me with even the merest hint of admiration."

Music and candlelight spilled out onto the crowded street. Those queuing to enter Captain Howard's house in Soho Square had stared as Devon handed his wife down from the carriage. Shocked gasps mingled with curious whispers. Some ladies pointed.

"You look divine." Devon hadn't stopped ogling her since she had appeared wearing Mrs Clancy's magnificent creation. "I shall find myself threatening every man who drools over your bare shoulders."

Her mouth curled into a weak smile. "I'm not sure why you insisted we come here. There are other ways to achieve our goal."

He had a list of reasons.

He wanted to present his wife to the *ton* and dare them to say an unkind word. Kinver would likely attend, and Devon meant to threaten the lord to establish if he was behind the anonymous letter. And he hoped Wenham was in the card room because he planned to shame the fop.

"We need to question Miss Howard."

"I doubt we'll get past the receiving line."

Devon grinned. "You're going to ensure we do."

Mina jolted in response. "Me?"

"You're in charge of the investigation." He could make a scene, storm past the line, and no one would dare throw him out. But Mina needed to be as confident around these people as she was with him.

"I'm only an amateur. What will I say?"

He cupped her elbow and moved to join the queue.

"You're skilled at holding your husband's attention." He had made her come again last night but had denied himself the pleasure. It had nearly killed him, but he was keen to take small steps to secure his wife's affections. "You'll have no issue commanding these ingrates. Play on the captain's weakness."

They stood behind Lord and Lady Mayweather, who congratulated them on their nuptials, and spoke about the chilly autumn weather and Mina's exceptional gown. All those waiting acknowledged them with a smile or a nod. Devon got a thrill from knowing he owned these men's promissory notes, so they had no choice but to be civil—unlike the tragic night his sister was assaulted at Lord Kinver's ball.

People had watched Arabella stumble through the garden, her torn gown hanging off her shoulder, mud covering the hem. No one had offered assistance. She had managed to find the gate to the mews, where an unmarked vehicle ploughed into her, leaving her a crumpled mess of broken bones.

Arabella was the reason he started gambling.

She was the reason he sought to ruin every pompous lord.

Mina clutched his arm, drawing him from the morbid

memories. "Captain Howard just caught my eye and frowned. He hated Thomas with a vengeance and will probably curse us to the devil."

Devon considered the captain, dressed in full military regalia. The gold shoulder chains on his red coat twinkled in the candlelight. Like most men burdened with great responsibility, he appeared miserable.

"He's standing with his sister. I doubt he'll be rude."

Indeed, when they reached their host, the man lowered his voice and, through gritted teeth, said, "I don't recall issuing you an invitation, Masters." He looked at Mina as if she were something foul on his shoe. "Should you not be in mourning, madam, instead of parading your wares for all and sundry?"

"Brides are not bound by the same rules," she said so sharply, Devon didn't need to punch the captain for disrespecting his wife.

"Still, you should be at home mourning your brother," the mouse-like Miss Howard found the courage to say. "You're not welcome here."

Mina cast Devon a sidelong glance, not knowing what to do.

Devon arched a brow, a prompt to take action.

She gathered her wits and straightened her spine. "Miss Howard, how forgetful of you. Do you not recall inviting me when we met in Craddock and Haines bookshop?"

The captain glared at his sister.

"You remember," Mina continued before Miss Howard could refute the claim. "We spoke about Mr Goldman and his paintings. Indeed, I visited his studio yesterday, as you suggested, and was lucky enough to admire one of his student's works."

Miss Howard paled. "What! Oh, oh yes, of course."

"You invited her?" came her brother's whispered growl.

"Yes." A little panicked, Miss Howard said, "There's a dreadful queue, Clarence. Let them pass. People are catching a chill on the doorstep. Come now. What harm can it do?"

Annoyed, the captain lowered his head. "I want no trouble tonight, Masters. And you'll avoid the card room. I'll not have men ruined in the name of entertainment." Then he waved them away as one might filthy street urchins begging for a penny.

"It's fair to assume Miss Howard has something to hide," Mina said as Devon led her into the lavish ballroom.

"Undoubtedly."

As the grandson of a viscount, Captain Howard was not short of funds. But people were not gazing at the crystal chandeliers or the impeccable footmen serving flutes of champagne.

All eyes were on them, not the host of military men in red coats. Whispers of their arrival spread like an infectious disease, leaving the guests' eyes bulging, their muscles rigid, their chins touching the polished parquet.

"Devon, can we not find somewhere quiet to hide?" She slipped her hand into the crook of his arm, her nerves evident.

"Hold your head high." He felt like calling in every man's debt and replacing their gawps with looks of horror. But despite wanting to punish the *ton*, he would not ruin men without just cause. "We shall give them a show they'll never forget."

She faced him and whispered, "But after that terrible comment in the *Scandal Sheet*, they know you only married me because I saved you from the noose."

"Gossip is a game." A game far worse than any played by greedy lords in the card room, a game that broke hearts and destroyed innocent lives. "Let's discredit the rag and give them something else to ponder."

"What do you mean to do?"

He smiled. "Dance with you."

The first strains of a waltz rippled through the room, and she glanced at the couples heading out onto the floor. "It's been so long since I've danced I shall probably trip over my own feet."

"I suspect you're as good at dancing as you are kissing." And she was so good at the latter he could not shake the memory of their last encounter from his mind.

Her anxious lips curled into a coy grin. "That has more to do with my partner than any skill on my part."

"Then anything we do together should be exceptional."

His own comment stirred him in a way he wasn't expecting. He'd thought to delay her deflowering until she was used to the feel of his fingers. Yet his patience was strung as tight as a bow, ready to snap.

Devon led her through the crowd, aware all the women in the room had noticed Mrs Clancy's signature sash tied around Mina's waist. Some men attempted to engage him in conversation, but he explained he lived to please his wife and meant to spend the evening dancing, not playing piquet.

"Lord Ambrose did his best to persuade you to join the game," she said, inhaling sharply when Devon held her so close it bordered on scandalous.

"Lord Ambrose can afford to lose but enjoys watching his peers suffer." A man had to focus if he wanted to win. Presently, Devon could only think about two things: his wife and discovering who murdered her brother. "Besides, I am not here to gamble and punish the *ton* for their crimes."

Mina's brows knitted together. "Punish the *ton*? You make it sound like you're pursuing a personal vendetta."

"I am."

The words left his lips before he had engaged his brain.

He was too relaxed in her company, and the secret he kept buried was slowly digging its way to the surface.

"You should know vengeance is like a poison tainting my blood," he said when she merely stared at him. "I mean to make the *ton* pay for their rigid rules and lofty opinions."

"But why?"

She had a right to know. His actions affected her, too. "Do you see the man with coal-black hair standing near the marble column? He's watching us dance like he's an angel of death come to claim our souls."

While Devon twirled her about the floor, she glanced at the devil in the crowd. "Yes, you speak of Lord Kinver. He's throwing daggers of disdain at your back."

Hence why Devon wore impenetrable armour. He didn't give a toss about Kinver and the man's pathetic protestations.

"His sister, Mrs Ellwood, has joined him," Mina continued, craning her neck to look. "She's attempting to distract him, but he refuses to turn away from the dance floor. Now he's pointing. People are looking."

Bloody hell! Did Kinver want another beating?

"Are you not keen to know why I gave him ten lashes?" Devon should have shot the rake for disrespecting Arabella.

"Since we are newly wed, I did not want to press the matter."

Devon chose to stick to the basic facts. "My sister Arabella hoped to marry the buffoon. During a ball he hosted, Kinver assaulted her in the garden." He had to stop there before he shamed his wife by dragging Kinver onto the dance floor and kicking the seven bells out of him.

"Assaulted her?" Mina's chin dropped. "Based on the crime, ten lashes seems tame. I'm surprised you didn't kill him."

Oh, he had wanted to drive a blade into the beast's black heart, but he would have swung from the gallows, and he needed the silent bystanders to suffer as much as Arabella had.

"She fled the garden half naked, her hair in disarray, and not one member of the nobility offered assistance." Painful knots twisted in his stomach. "I thought she was in the retiring room with Mrs Ellwood and was only notified when they found her body crushed by carriage wheels in the mews."

The horrific scene flashed before his eyes.

The shock. The panic. The excruciating pain.

He wanted to vomit.

Mina stopped dancing, forcing him to come to an abrupt halt amid the twirling couples. Water filled her eyes, and she pressed her gloved hand to his cheek.

"It all makes sense to me now," she said softly.

"What, my angry disposition?"

"No, why a good man would want to wreck lives."

He scoffed. "I'm not a good man, Mina. I'm cruel and wicked and would murder everyone here if I could go back to that night and make different choices."

Deep down, he blamed himself.

He should have kept watch night and day.

Mina made to reply, but Bradbury appeared at Devon's shoulder. "You're standing amid the dancers like bedlamites. For God's sake, make out that you're ill. This sham of a marriage already has everyone talking. Now, you're proving you married just to save your neck."

The need to defend Mina burned like the devil's fire in his chest. "I don't give a damn what people think. And who said this marriage is a sham?"

Bradbury sighed. "I am merely relaying the gossip.

107

Forgive me for looking out for your welfare," he snapped before stomping away.

Mina glanced at the crowd and groaned. "Come. Doubtless, we will feature in tomorrow's *Scandal Sheet*. Moreover, we have work to do. I must seek an opportunity to question Miss Howard."

Devon gathered himself. He shot the onlookers an arrogant smirk before kissing his wife's gloved hand and leading her from the floor.

He noticed Kinver heading in their direction, his sister tugging at his coat sleeve to stop him, and so steered Mina to the supper room in the hope they would get lost amid the crush.

Quickly downing a glass of champagne, Devon took another from the footman's tray and tossed back the contents. "We should search Howard's study while we're here."

"The captain is skilled in strategy." She swallowed a mere sip of her drink. Perhaps because the last time she'd consumed champagne to excess was the night someone murdered her brother. "It's unlikely we will find anything incriminating."

"There could be a letter from Goldman."

"You saw Captain Howard's face when we mentioned the artist. He didn't even flinch. He cannot know of his sister's scandalous *hobby*."

"No. He would have held a rapier to my throat, keen to discover what we'd learned." Captain Howard was skilled enough to stab a man on Waterloo Bridge and hurl him into the Thames.

To their good fortune, Miss Howard entered the supper room with a female companion. The lady locked gazes with them, turned beetroot red and made an excuse about using the retiring room before darting away.

"Excellent," Mina whispered. "I shall follow her and see what she knows about Mr Goldman. You go in search of Mr Bradbury. He was only trying to help earlier, and you were rather sharp with him."

Without another word, she thrust her champagne flute into his hand and hurried away to accost Miss Howard.

Devon remained rooted to the spot, a sense of foreboding sending a shiver to his toes. The last time he let someone he cared about visit the retiring room, it ended in tragedy.

The fact he felt sick to his stomach confirmed two things.

He feared the same might happen again.

And he held some affection for his wife.

The ladies' retiring room reflected the needs of a practical military man, not women requiring rest and a place to attend to the neatness of their gowns. There was but one huge looking glass, and the queue to have the maid tidy stray curls and fix hair combs was ten deep.

Hard wooden chairs stood in place of plush couches. One glance at Miss Howard and the ladies were quick to complain.

"A ball this size requires three maids in attendance."

"You cannot expect us to wait in line like paupers queuing for bread."

"No one serves tea anymore."

Taking advantage of the verbal assault, Mina cupped Miss Howard's arm. "Ah, there you are, Miss Howard. You promised to show me the Egyptian roses. I'm told they bloom until the first frost."

Like a chick waiting for a worm, Miss Howard opened her tiny mouth, only a strained squeak escaping.

"I'm told we can access the garden from this room." Mina had heard a tale about Thomas chasing after the poor girl at her brother's midsummer ball and she had used the retiring room to make a hasty escape.

Miss Howard nodded and pointed to the heavy brocade curtains.

Before the ladies could pounce and make demands, Mina pulled the timid creature through the gap in the curtains and out of the double doors.

With numerous people strolling about the garden and warming their hands on the lit braziers, she drew Miss Howard to an alcove hidden in the shadows.

Before Mina could gather her thoughts, Miss Howard grabbed her hands and whispered in a frantic voice, "I'm so sorry to hear about Thomas. But if you think my brother had anything to do with his death, I must tell you, you're grossly mistaken."

Clearly, the lady had thought it possible.

Else she would not plead his case.

"And yet Captain Howard was not at home that night." It was a wild guess based on the lady's assertion.

Miss Howard glanced nervously left and right. "It's not something one should discuss, but he was at Mrs Fitzroy's home until the early hours."

Mrs Fitzroy was an attractive widow of thirty with more money than sense, though there had been no mention in the *Scandal Sheet* of her being the captain's paramour.

"I presume a servant relayed that information."

Miss Howard averted her gaze. "Not a servant, but someone whose word I trust implicitly. A dear friend, if you will." Her cheeks flamed.

"A male friend?"

"Y-yes."

Unwilling to spend the next ten minutes dragging the truth from the timid woman's lips, Mina decided to take a leaf out of her husband's book and hit the target directly.

"Miss Howard, I am trying to discover who murdered my brother. Now, you will tell me who this mystery friend is, and anything you know about Mr Goldman and his gallery, else I shall fetch the captain and ask him the same questions." Mina made to leave.

"No!" Miss Howard flapped her hands and was suddenly gasping for breath. "I'll tell you what I know, but you must swear not to mention a word of it to Clarence."

Satisfaction rippled through her, but she kept a stern expression when addressing Miss Howard. "Then save us both time and begin at the part where Thomas was so obsessed with you, the captain had a reason to kill him."

Miss Howard gulped. "Thomas hounded me night and day. He wrote me letters, sent me gifts and followed me everywhere, begging and pleading. When I refused his suit for the tenth time, he chased me into the ladies' retiring room at our midsummer ball."

"That's when Captain Howard said he would kill Thomas if he saw him harassing you again." There had been witnesses.

"Yes, but he didn't mean it literally."

"And then you discovered Thomas was the life model at Mr Goldman's studio." Mina could not believe her brother had stooped so low, but his obsession with Miss Howard had left him mentally unstable.

Tears filled the lady's eyes and trickled down her nose. "You must think me a terrible person, Miss Stanford."

"Mrs Masters," she corrected.

"Forgive me. It's impossible to imagine you, a disgraced wallflower, marrying a man with such a wicked reputation. One would think you had learnt your lesson."

The need to defend Devon soared to the surface. "One's reputation does not always convey the truth. One would think you're as pure as a vestal virgin, yet you paint naked men in masks for amusement."

"Hush! Someone might hear you."

"Yes, heaven forbid your brother learns of your intimate lessons with Mr Goldman. The artist explained the nature of your relationship when we questioned him yesterday."

Miss Howard sagged forward, clutching her stomach as if she had eaten rotten fish. "I'm in love with him, but we can never marry. And so I must choose another suitor before it is too late." She gripped Mina's arm and squeezed tightly. "Thomas learnt of our affair and threatened Jasper, but I swear we had nothing to do with your brother's death."

Evidently, Jasper was Mr Goldman.

So, Captain Howard, Miss Howard and Mr Goldman all had a motive for murder. But how did one catch a killer? Perhaps Mr Daventry might give his advice.

"Yet you had every reason to get rid of him." A woman had sent the note to the police office, blaming Devon. Like how she painted, did Miss Howard write with a bold flare? "And Mr Goldman has many secrets." Mina recalled the lady's earlier comment. "He is the friend who confirmed your brother's whereabouts on the night of the murder."

"Yes, because I feared Clarence had lost his mind and committed the awful deed. Now I know he had an alibi."

"But how did Mr Goldman know your brother was with Mrs Fitzroy? Unless he was there, his account is inadmissible."

Miss Howard flinched. "What? Erm, Mrs Fitzroy told him."

"And why would Mrs Fitzroy do that?"

The lady pursed her lips and refused to say anything more.

"Wait here while I fetch the captain." Mina moved to step away.

"B-because she is also Jasper's student," Miss Howard confessed. "And she is ... she is blackmailing me." A wracking sob escaped her, and she gathered her skirts and darted away, back through the retiring room doors.

Heavens above! Murder, now blackmail!

Matters were becoming complicated.

She would add Mrs Fitzroy to the list of suspects. One rotten apple could spoil the cart. Was the widow using the captain merely to frighten Miss Howard into paying? Was she manipulating Mr Goldman? That seemed unlikely.

Mina stepped slowly out of the shadows, mulling over which suspect had the most to gain from Thomas' death, when matters did become more complex.

Mr Wenham was marching across the grass, heading in her direction, and he looked most displeased. The lock of golden hair over his brow whipped about in the wind. His thin mouth quivered like an arrow seconds away from maiming its victim.

"What the hell has he done with it?" Mr Wenham grabbed her elbow and propelled her into the darkness. "You'd better bloody well tell me, or there'll be hell to pay."

She tried to tug her arm free, but his fingers were like pincers digging into her flesh. "Who? To what do you refer?"

"That damn wastrel you called a brother broke into my house and stole the deed to the land I planned to mine. The investors won't commit without seeing proof of blasted ownership."

Mina bit back a smile. Thomas was not clever enough to think of such a cunning scheme. Still, she would like to thank the man who'd scuppered Mr Wenham's plans.

"When did the theft occur?" she said, praying Devon was not involved because she did not wish to wage a permanent war with the likes of Mr Wenham.

"Two weeks ago while I dined at my club."

"I assure you, I know nothing about it. But I have my brother's papers and will go through them tomorrow. If I find your deed, I shall return it at once."

"And you expect me to believe you?" He shook her violently, and she was suddenly glad Thomas had squandered her dowry. "You'll use it to punish me for the lies I told, for not marrying you."

"She won't need to punish you," came a cold, sinister voice behind them. "I mean to avenge my wife's name, and I mean to do so now."

Chapter Nine

Anger, as hot and fiery as hell's coals, eradicated the panic Devon had felt moments ago. He had witnessed Miss Howard leave the retiring room, tears flowing as fast as her brother's champagne, and waited for what seemed like an age for Mina to appear.

That agonising minute roused memories of the night he couldn't find Arabella, and so he burst into the ladies' boudoir, shouting Mina's name, which was barely audible amid the women's screams and squeals.

A matron had pointed a shaky finger at the closed curtains, hence why he found himself outside in the dimly lit garden. There, he witnessed a scene that fired his blood—Mina being manhandled by that blasted fop Wenham.

"Get your hands off my wife," he growled when the cretin failed to respond to his initial threat. Before the man could reply, he smashed his fist into Wenham's face.

Wenham hit the ground with a thud.

"Touch her again and you'll not live to see sunrise." Devon was not one to kick a man when he was down, but he booted Wenham in the back. "You lied. You made her suffer.

I want an apology posted in *The Times* before the week's end, clearing her name, else I'll do everything in my power to see you ruined, if not dead."

He could feel Mina's penetrating stare, but she said nothing.

"I—I just want my damn deed." Wenham dabbed his fingers to his bloody nose and cursed. "That fool Stanford—"

"We'll speak about the deed when you've published an apology." He crouched down and grabbed the man by his foppish cravat. "You do not want to wage a war with me, Wenham. You'll not live to tell the tale."

With his mind a violent maelstrom of emotions, Devon captured Mina's hand and drew her deeper into the darkness.

"Thank heavens you came when you did," she panted, jogging to keep his fast pace. "I've only seen him that angry once, when Thomas refused to give details of my dowry."

Wenham wasn't the only one seething.

Consumed by a murderous rage, Devon couldn't think straight. "Despite everything I've said, clearly you're blind to the dangers." He spotted a small orangery tucked away in the corner of the garden and meant to use the private space to berate his wife.

Upon entering, feminine giggles and a man's muffled moans drifted through the gloom. He found the amorous couple on a stone bench amid potted lemon trees, rare roses and a marble statue of a winged Eros.

"It's time to leave," he snapped. "Get out."

The gentleman shot to his feet in protest, his untucked shirt hanging over velvet pantaloons. "Now listen here, I—" Recognising Devon, he stopped abruptly and almost swooned. "Yes, well. I suspect we've been out here long enough."

He ushered his startled lover to the door, glancing back

like a frightened buck as Devon stalked behind them. He watched the couple dart into the darkness before turning the iron key and locking the world out.

With his blood pumping too rapidly in his veins, he crossed the orangery to where Mina hid in the shadows. "Don't ever do that to me again."

She blinked, looked confused. "Do what?"

"Leave without telling me where you're going."

"But I did tell you." Her tone carried a hint of annoyance. "I went to question Miss Howard. She happened to provide a wealth of information. I thought you'd be pleased."

"Pleased?" Pleased to see Wenham's claws marring her skin? Pleased to feel the same rush of panic he'd experienced three years ago? "Pleased to see you in a dark corner of the garden with the man you'd hoped to marry?"

Her laugh rang with mockery. "You make it sound like I arranged an assignation. And I didn't *want* to marry Mr Wenham. Thomas' reckless actions left me in a precarious position. I had no choice but to seek an alliance before it was too late."

"Just like you had no choice but to marry me?" He was being unreasonable, but he couldn't calm his temper or shake the fear of— What? He wasn't sure, but he disliked feeling so out of control, so vulnerable, so damn needy.

She threw her hands in the air and gave an exasperated huff. "I had a choice, Devon. I could have taken a different road."

"Yes, and lived as a spinster on Lord Denton's estate."

"It was the best I could have hoped for until you made me an offer."

"An offer you refused." Pride and honour had left him using every trick to persuade her to accept. "You didn't marry

117

me, Mina. You married an idea, a vision of a life where you felt safe and protected."

She stared at him, bemused. "The one thing we have in common is honesty. I've never lied to you. I married you for security. You married me to ease your conscience. That has never been in dispute."

No, it was more than that.

An invisible energy bound them inexplicably.

He felt it thrumming in the air whenever they were together. Yes, he had married her because she had ruined herself for him. But when their mouths met, something magical happened. Their first kiss had roused a hunger he couldn't sate. And though he wanted to feed like a man starved, he struggled to know how best to proceed.

"And yet when you're coming hard around my fingers, Mina, I might think you married me for a different reason entirely."

She inhaled sharply, but based on the hazy look in her eyes, he knew she recalled every delicious tremor. "The intimacy we share has nothing to do with the reasons we married."

"No," he mused. "I want you with a desperation that defies logic."

"Then why delay the inevitable?" Her hand came to her throat, and he imagined pressing his mouth to the sensitive skin and sucking softly. "We married for necessity. Yet beyond my better judgement, I desire you with a passion I can barely contain."

He stepped closer. The need for physical contact drew him to her like the earth's magnetic pull—a force beyond a mortal's understanding.

"Tell the truth, love." He captured her chin and brushed

his lips over hers. "You married me because you hoped to share more kisses like the one in my study."

The minx nipped his bottom lip with her teeth. "Admit you married me for the same reason."

"Damn right, I did." He angled his head, inhaled her ragged breath before closing his mouth over hers as he'd longed to do for hours.

The kiss was unlike all others.

It was soft, slow and so sensual their bodies melded into one. Her essence had the power to penetrate his armour, to seep deep into his body and stoke passion's flames. He knew he'd be lost if he slipped his tongue between her lips, but he—

She drew her mouth away on a gasp. "Before we continue, I must know why you're waiting to consummate our union."

Because he had never taken a virgin.

Because he was mindful of her situation.

Because sex complicated things.

If one kiss left him floundering like a besotted fool, what would happen when he gripped her hips and pushed inside her, when she hugged his cock tight, when his climax tore through his body and he was left moaning her name?

"I—I thought it was me. That you were struggling to find the enthusiasm. But you're hard every time we kiss," his observant wife added.

Evidently, Miss Ware had been filling her head with facts.

"I'm hard when we sleep together in the same bed." He lay there, stiff and swollen with need, fighting the urge to mount her or take himself in hand.

Lust ripped through one's body like a hurricane, a wild, tempestuous power that eventually dwindled and died. Perhaps that's what he feared most. That they would soon tire of each other and remain stuck in a tedious, loveless marriage.

Still, he was in the eye of the storm and had no choice but to open his arms and get swept up in the momentum.

"If you're willing, we might make love tonight," he suggested. The term *fuck* seemed too harsh a word for what they might do. "Let us leave now. I'll not resist the chance to make you climax in a moving carriage."

Such talk might have been too lewd for a virgin, but Mina was unlike other women. She was hungry for new experiences. Hungry for him, it seemed.

Indeed, she gripped his coat lapel and tugged him closer. "A survey of married ladies concluded most have used a carriage for their amorous activities."

"A survey conducted by Miss Ware, no doubt."

"After our interlude at the modiste's shop, a carriage seems tame. Did I not marry the most dangerous man in London? A wicked devil who lives for sin?"

Intrigued, he arched a brow. "What do you have in mind, madam?" But he could read her thoughts and knew she meant to take her pleasure while Eros looked on. "I am yours to command."

She swallowed deeply. "Make love to me here."

My God! He'd been right all along.

This tigress had courage abound. He needed to pander to her wants and desires if they were to engage in such activities regularly.

Yet the need to gain the upper hand was in his blood. "If we're to make love here, on the bench, you'll have to take me, Mina. And we must be quick."

Her frown said Miss Ware's instruction had some limitations. "But I don't know the first thing about it." She shook her head. "It was foolish of me to suggest—"

120

"It wasn't foolish." It was damn arousing. He cupped her nape and stroked his thumb along her jaw. "I'm flattered you want me, and I promised to give you whatever your heart desires."

Oh, he meant to make all her dreams come true.

She splayed her hands on his chest. "The ache is unbearable. But I need you to tell me what to do, Devon."

"You'll know instinctively what to do. I mean to own your body, Mina, but tonight you get to own mine. Is that not an empowering thought?"

The current of arousal was so strong now it hardened his cock.

He captured her hand and let her feel how thick he was. How much he wanted to spread her legs and plunge home.

She inhaled sharply but did not tug her hand free. "And you're sure no one will find us? We'll be perfectly safe?"

"I locked the door, but if we're doing this, we must hurry."

Her eyes widened in excitement, and then her mouth was on his, hard and urgent, as if she had been desperate to do this for days. He fought to remain in control, but she slid her hand over his rigid length, slipped her tongue deep into his mouth.

Desire licked his body like hell's flames.

Every muscle clenched as he imagined pushing into her wetness.

Remember she's an innocent, he told himself as an idea formed.

"Turn around," he panted, tearing his mouth away briefly. "Grip the back of the bench and bend over. When you've found your release, you can take me any damn way you please."

She offered no protest and did his bidding. "Hurry."

He tossed the expensive silk skirts over her back, baring

121

her buttocks. Mother of all saints! She bent down a little lower, her sex glistening in the moonlight. It was a sight he would never forget. Still, he wished he could watch her delightful expressions as she came apart.

"Hurry," she repeated.

He unbuttoned his trousers, his cock springing free. The urge to mate burned in his veins. "Don't be afraid. I'll not take you like this. I merely mean to tease you. Let you get used to the feel of me."

With great restraint, he pressed himself to her entrance, nudged just enough that she would soon be begging him to fill the emptiness. He reached round to stroke her swollen bud.

"Devon," she breathed, pushing back against him.

"I'll be inside you soon, love." He prayed he would not shame himself by spurting his seed over her buttocks.

His wife was determined to test his resolve. She rocked her hips to the rhythm of his fingers, panted his name and cried, "I need to feel all of you."

He couldn't hold back and pushed an inch inside her. One hard thrust, and he could bury himself to the hilt. But he'd made a promise he meant to keep.

Mina came then, jerking and shuddering, her pleasurable moans echoing in the small space. The need to feel full had her pushing hard against him, taking him another inch deeper into the delights of her warm body.

He closed his eyes and clenched his teeth against the urge to pound. "Let me sit on the bench, and you can straddle me."

"Yes." Her legs shook like a newborn foal's, but she straightened, and they swapped positions.

He fell onto the bench and held his cock rigid while she gathered her skirts, the rustle of silk not as loud as their breathless pants. "Sit on me," he commanded. "Lower yourself down slowly. You're so wet. You'll take me deeper this time."

She knelt astride his thighs. "Hold me. Don't let me fall."

He pushed at her entrance, slipped his arm around her waist and guided her down. "This isn't the easiest of positions. Not here, at any rate. But you need to ride me, love."

She was so tight, hugging him like a glove.

She took one inch, then another. "Oh, Devon!"

"I need to push past your virtue, love. Tell me when."

"Do it now," she said.

"I can't promise I won't hurt you."

"You could never hurt me."

Her comment made his heart swell. "Kiss me," he growled.

Less than a second later, he was driving his tongue deep into her mouth, drinking from her sweet lips, preparing her for the worst. A moan rumbled in her throat, so he gripped her tightly and thrust upwards until buried to the hilt.

She dragged her mouth away and gasped, "Good grief!"

He stilled. "Are you all right?"

She nodded and sucked in a breath.

"You belong to me now," he teased, but the power of those words spread through him, warming the heart he thought was frozen beneath the cold weight of vengeance. "Move when you feel able."

She swallowed deeply. "Show me."

He gripped her hips and rocked slowly in and out of her until she found her own rhythm. "That's it, love. Take what you want."

She rode him, breathing as she came up on her knees, sighing sweetly as she sheathed his cock. He'd never witnessed such a glorious sight and watched in awe as a sliver of moonlight kissed her rosy lips, caressed the soft swell of her breasts.

God, she was divine.

When his climax came, it surged through him, and he withdrew with nary a second to spare. He would not spill his seed inside her until she'd confirmed a desire for children. It was a conversation they needed to have soon.

Very soon.

Although his heart was pounding, he wanted her again.

"Well, one thing is certain," she said between ragged breaths.

"What? You're my wife in the only way that matters?" He removed his handkerchief from his coat pocket and wiped the evidence of their lovemaking from her thigh.

"Yes, but I was thinking about something Lillian said. That lovemaking can leave one a little dazed and delirious."

For once, he agreed with Miss Ware.

His infatuation for his wife had reached a fever pitch.

Chapter Ten

Mrs Fitzroy was not at home.

Which was just as well because Mina couldn't think clearly. She could barely recall her name let alone form complex questions to catch a blackmailer.

"We'll call again tomorrow. Let's visit Goldman." Devon cupped her elbow, the physical contact sending a delicious shiver rippling to her toes. "We'll see what he has to say about Miss Howard's revelation."

He sounded calm, collected, as if joining bodies had not left him desperate to perform the act again, as if he was not bathing in an odd kind of euphoria.

Would they make love tonight? Naked this time?

Would he wait until tomorrow to ravish her again?

She had thought four nights a week excessive.

Now it wasn't enough.

"Mina?" he prompted.

"Y-yes?" She almost jumped a foot in the air.

"You've hardly spoken a word since breakfast. Did you hear what I said about Goldman? We need to press the man harder."

"Harder. Yes." Good Lord. Her cheeks and forehead burned, and she could barely look him in the eye.

"Are you well?"

"Yes, quite well." Just a little obsessed with her husband, just sickening for the closeness they had shared last night when she had expected to spend her life alone. An undesirable no one could love.

Devon handed her into the carriage, gave the coachman instructions and climbed inside.

Her traitorous gaze slid to the muscular thighs she had straddled last night. Everything about him was so hard, so perfectly formed.

The carriage lurched and picked up speed. All the time, he watched her intently, his gaze caressing her face the way his hands had caressed her flesh. Had she seen a flash of hunger in his eyes too? Was he thinking about her as he ran his tongue over his bottom lip? Was he just as keen to make love again?

It all became too much.

"Is it always like this?" she blurted, tired of suffering in silence. "After the initial event, is it natural for one to think of nothing but doing it again?"

"It?"

"What we did in the orangery last night."

A sinful smile curled his lips. "Surely Miss Ware told you."

"Told me what?"

"That when it's good, it can be addictive."

"She said if a woman excites a man, he will never venture far from home. But that is the limit of her expertise." Mina often wondered if Lillian's research was a means of understanding her own confused feelings about love and marriage. "And how does one define what is good?"

He smoothed his hands down his solid thighs. "It's good when you're shuddering in each other's arms and both find release, when you feel satiated beyond compare but are compelled to make love again."

That explained her position perfectly. "There we have it. I am addicted to lovemaking. Is there a cure, do you think? I sincerely hope not." If there was, she would empty it into the chamber pot and hope it got tossed out too.

He chuckled and held up his hands in mock surrender. "I'm also addicted to lovemaking, but only with you, Mina."

"You are?" Her heart thumped wildly. "I find that quite surprising."

He hadn't given the slightest clue.

"I have a habit of keeping my cards close to my chest."

Marriage wasn't a game, but she demanded to see his hand. "Are we to continue in the same vein this evening?"

She expected to hear a teasing reply, words to heat her blood, but he shifted awkwardly in the leather seat. The grin softening his features faded as fast as a misty breath.

"I won't be at home tonight."

The comment sent her heart skittering. It took her a moment to gather her wits. He'd specifically asked that she not make a fuss when he went out of an evening. Still, they were newly wed, and she'd thought he might spend the first week at home.

"Is there an important card game?" she said, forcing a smile.

"No. I have business in Aylesbury and must leave this afternoon. I shall be home at dawn." Coldness coated his tone, a coldness as unnerving as an arctic frost, and it occurred to her she didn't know this man at all. "Ask Miss Ware to stay if you'd rather not be alone."

Not wanting to appear like a simpering miss, she said,

"No. It will give me an opportunity to become accustomed to the staff. I've barely had a moment to confer with Bates."

He shrugged. "Do whatever pleases you, Mina."

She would if he stayed at home.

Thankfully there was little time to dwell on her husband's impending absence. They arrived in Great Queen Street, the carriage slowing to a halt outside Mr Goldman's studio.

Devon was quick to alight, but when he captured her hand his grip wasn't as firm, his smile not so hypnotic. The intense energy that usually left them breathless was more a faint flicker than wild flames.

She brushed all worrying thoughts aside and entered the shop.

Mr Dowling stood behind the oak counter, clutching his paunch as if it were a heavy basket of apples. He staggered a little to the left when he looked up from his ledger and recognised her.

"M-Mr Goldman is out, madam."

"Then you won't mind if we check for ourselves." She rounded the counter while Devon strode behind. "No need to play escort. We know the way."

"But you cannot enter his private room," Mr Dowling protested. But Devon threatened to whip the assistant with a birch, and the poor fellow's legs buckled beneath him. "You don't understand. Mr Goldman cannot be disturbed when he's working. It ruins the creative process."

Creative process? Doubtless, he was plotting to seduce another naive woman while charging her an exorbitant fee.

Beating Devon to the upstairs landing, she reached the cavalier's door and burst into the room without knocking. The banyan-clad Mr Goldman was making fine brushstrokes on a large canvas.

"God's teeth, Dowling. Did I not say—" In an obvious

temper, he swung around. He was naked beneath the flowing silk, and his frown quickly gave way to an arrogant smirk. "Ah, Mrs Masters. I see you were tempted by my offer of tutorage. Come inside and take off—"

"Do not mistake my wife for one of the simpering fools you seduce." Devon marched into the room. He took one look at the artist's flaccid manhood and laughed. "No wonder you have to drug them into submission. Then they may not notice you lack the necessary tool to create a masterpiece."

Goldman threw his paintbrush on the floor and whipped his banyan around his body. "What the hell do you want, Masters?"

"My brother was murdered," Mina interjected, her temper stemming from her many frustrations, including her husband's lack of information about what he planned to do in Aylesbury. "So you will answer our questions, else I shall fetch Sir Oswald."

Mr Goldman groaned and gave a nonchalant wave. "Ask your questions, but this is the last time you will call without an appointment."

"Do you know Miss Howard is in love with you?" she said.

The man's confident smile grated. "I cannot be held responsible for the lady's feelings. She's of marriageable age and knows her own mind."

"Yet Captain Howard will likely shoot you when I tell him you drugged and seduced an innocent."

Mr Goldman shrugged. "In doing so, he would ruin his sister's chances of making a good match. I'm told she has four men vying for her hand."

Was there no way to unsettle this fool?

If she didn't get information from him soon, Devon

would likely shove the banyan down Mr Goldman's throat until he choked.

"It is not a crime to take a woman's virginity," she said, trying not to think how exquisite it felt to have Devon pushing inside her. "Nor is blackmail a punishable offence, not yet at least, yet both might be considered a motive for murder. You had every reason to kill my brother, sir."

Mr Goldman narrowed his gaze. "Blackmail? Why would I blackmail a penniless fool like Sir Thomas?"

"Not Sir Thomas, Miss Howard."

The artist scoffed. "I'm not blackmailing Miss Howard. She comes here of her own volition and cannot wait to begin our lessons. She's out of her pelisse before she climbs the stairs."

Devon cursed beneath his breath, his energy growing more volatile. "Men like you should be castrated," he barked. "My sister suffered at the hands of a rogue who couldn't keep his cock in his trousers."

His blunt phrasing tore a gasp from her lips, yet his boldness left her in awe. "Mrs Fitzroy is blackmailing Miss Howard," she said, returning to the matter at hand. "But as the widow is a student here and knows of your relationship, you probably agreed to accept a percentage of the profits."

"What?" Mr Goldman jerked back so quickly his banyan flew open. "I swear, I know nothing about Mrs Fitzroy's plot. Yes, I let her paint Sir Thomas but—"

Devon charged at the fellow, grabbing the silk in his fist and raising the artist off the parquet floor. "You said Sir Thomas sat for no one but Miss Howard. He would not have embarrassed himself for any other woman but her."

Mr Goldman wriggled and squirmed. "He didn't know it was Mrs Fitzroy. I needed a model and so made him wear a hood. She spent many hours painting him."

The sudden ache in Mina's heart tightened her throat. For all her brother's faults, he did not deserve such disrespect. "You used a man suffering from an uncontrollable obsession. All the time, you were bedding the woman he loved, mocking him, abusing his trust."

Devon released the scoundrel.

He might have punched him had she not rushed forward and launched her clenched fist into his chest. "I shall make it my life's mission to expose you, to ensure everyone knows what sort of man you are. I shall see this studio closed. Have you driven out of town."

She continued thumping the scoundrel until Devon wrapped his strong arms around her and drew her away. "You'll only hurt yourself, and this ingrate isn't worth it. He will receive his comeuppance. You have my word."

She sagged back against his hard chest and let the warmth of his body soothe her. "Take me home, Devon. Before I murder this fool myself." She locked gazes with the lothario in the gold banyan.

Mr Goldman did not look like a man consumed with shame. He did not offer an apology or reassure them he would put an end to his lecherous ways.

No. Mr Goldman's smirk spoke of nothing but vengeance.

Chapter Eleven

Devon hated leaving her.

Mina had smiled and rubbed his upper arm affectionately, but like the best card sharp, she had seen deceit in his dark eyes. The truth had rebounded back and forth in his head, but he'd resisted the urge to confess. It was not his secret to tell. And he barely knew the woman he had married.

That wasn't entirely true.

For a reason that defied logic, he felt like he had known her for a lifetime. Like the night she tumbled into his bedchamber, the magnetic pull was undeniable. She was unlike any woman he had ever met. He'd known it the moment she asked to test a theory, when she offered her mouth as payment for the debt.

Any gambling man would have claimed the prize.

A kiss from a woman who didn't know her own appeal.

The carriage bounced through a rut in the road, jolting Devon from his reverie. He peered out into the darkness.

Like stars in a black sky, candlelight glowed in the windows of The Convent of St Margaret, a sanctuary for those who had travelled a long, treacherous road and sought salvation. The gothic spire surely stretched to the heavens because the Sisters of St Margaret possessed a kindness beyond that of mere mortals.

Devon brushed his coat sleeves and rubbed his tired eyes. All attempts to sleep on the six-hour journey had left him grappling with his conscience. He was unused to worrying about anyone. But since leaving London, a heavy foreboding swamped him like a sodden greatcoat.

Indeed, he would cut his visit short.

Attempt to return home before dawn.

Simpkin brought the carriage to a halt alongside the convent's boundary wall. Every Thursday, the coachman followed the same routine. He ate supper, hummed country tunes, and slept atop his box.

"I'll not stay so long tonight," Devon said as he alighted. The sick feeling in his gut did not abate. "I mean to return home posthaste."

The quirk of Simpkin's brow was the only sign he found the change shocking. And it was shocking. Being a creature of habit, Devon had kept the same routine for three years.

"Aye, sir. I'll have a nap now if it suits."

Devon nodded. "Assuming all is well, I shall stay for an hour, two at most." A prickling at his nape sent a shiver to his toes, and he peered along the dark lane. "You're quite certain no one followed us from town?"

"There ain't no need to worry, sir. There's been no one behind us since we turned off the road five miles back."

The news did not ease the tension.

Devon sighed. "Still, keep your eyes peeled."

He approached the gate and rang the bell, though he did not have to stand in the cold for long. The Reverend Mother came to greet him. Through the iron railings, he watched her glide slowly along the path. She had more grace than any matron of the *ton,* though the white wimple covered her hair and pulled her cheeks taut, making it impossible to guess her age.

"Mr Masters." Her serene smile might cleanse a man of his sins. "Welcome." She unlocked the door in her usual unhurried manner and beckoned him inside.

Devon crossed the threshold. He waited while she secured the gate, then fell in beside her as he'd done a hundred times before. They took the winding path back through the vegetable garden and spoke about the never-ending list of repairs.

"I trust there are no more problems with the tower." He glanced up at the vast shadow rising against an inky sky. "Mr Jacobs is the best stonemason north of the Thames."

"He assures me it's sturdy. Being so open to the elements here, he has agreed to inspect it yearly." The Reverend Mother spoke in a tranquil tone, regardless of the topic. "I must thank you again for your generosity. The Lord delivers angels in times of crisis."

The comment brought an image of Mina crashing into his mind. She was divine on every level. "Yes, angels come in many forms."

"Hence why we should not judge on appearance, Mr Masters."

They fell into a companionable silence as they walked through the cloisters. Words were a gift people often abused. He recalled the Reverend Mother saying so during those first few visits.

They came to a halt outside an arched oak door.

The Reverend Mother touched him briefly on the arm, her benevolence warming him like a fire on a chilly winter's night. She left him there, alone, as she always did. Except this time, his heart didn't feel so cold, so empty. He didn't feel like one man against the world.

Mina!

He knocked. And the gentle voice—that broke his heart every time he heard it—called for him to enter.

Wearing her usual dull grey dress, Arabella sat on the neatly made bed, her dark hair tied in a plait, her hands folded in her lap. "Devon." Her brown eyes twinkled with excitement.

His gaze moved quickly past the horrid scar running down her cheek. "You look well. As beautiful as ever."

His stomach clenched.

After all these years, the pain was just as intense.

Tears choked him when Arabella reached for her crutch and tried to stand. He knew not to help her. She wished to master the feat on her own.

"I took two steps without it yesterday."

He forced a smile. She should be riding in the park, strolling around the Serpentine, picnicking with friends. "Soon, you'll walk the length of the transept unaided."

She hobbled towards him and fell into his arms.

They didn't speak.

He held her tightly, stroked her hair, cried inside.

Arabella had been his only focus these last three years. But he'd let his foolish pride get the better of him. Despite being an expert shot, he might have died had Thomas Stanford attended the duel.

What would happen to Arabella then?

"Devon, what is wrong?" She pulled away to look at him, a frown marring her brow. "You're more tense than ever."

"I—I have a confession." He would tell her about Mina and pray she was happy for him. He couldn't make another visit to Aylesbury without giving his wife a reason for the trip. "But first, you must sit down." And take the weight off her weak legs. "Tell me all that's happened this last week."

She tapped him playfully on the arm. "As if I could talk about my studies when you have something scandalous to tell me."

"How do you know it's scandalous?"

She arched a brow. "Everything you do is considered scandalous. The Reverend Mother knows your donations are funded by gambling."

"The donations are funded by the interest on my investments," he corrected. "I don't need to gamble, Arabella." But he thought of his sister every time he punished the lords who had attended Kinver's party.

"The Reverend Mother knows you don't force people to play. She said God means to teach men lessons and often uses angels to carry out his tasks."

He chuckled. "I'm not an angel."

"The Sisters of St Margaret think you are." She shuffled backwards, managing to sit without the support of her crutch, then gestured to the chair opposite. "If you must make a confession, you've come to the right place."

He flicked his coattails and sat down. "You must prepare yourself for a shock. My actions will disappoint you, but you must know I did what I thought best." And he'd wanted to take a risk, to risk everything for her, for Mina. "I have no regrets."

"You've never let me down, Devon."

I let that bastard hurt you.

Is that why you won't come home?

He inhaled deeply. "I'm married. I married Miss Stanford last Friday." He told her about the duel and being a murder suspect, about Mina's sacrifice. But he had to be honest. "We may not be in love, but there is something between us, something I cannot explain."

Arabella's eyes brightened. "You enjoy her company. The air changes when she is in the room. The world seems a better place."

"Yes." It was all of those and more.

"I felt the same with Lord Kinver." Her smile died, and she looked at her legs. "I pray you have more luck in love than I, dear brother."

She rarely mentioned the man who had abused her so cruelly, and he thought to probe her mind a little in the hope she remembered something of that night, something to use against the evil rogue.

"To meet him in a secluded corner of the garden, you must have felt a deep affection for Lord Kinver. He hurt you. In more ways than one."

Her shoulders sagged. "Yes. It makes no sense to me."

"Because you can recall very little of that night?"

"Because you describe a man I do not know."

"He fooled you, fooled us all."

"Yes," she said with an air of melancholy.

"Is that why you won't come home?" They touched on the subject now and then. "I'm confident Mina would welcome a sister."

Her fingers settled on the scar marring her face. "I like it here. It's quiet. Peaceful. The sisters are kind and encouraging, and I get a bit better every day. Besides, people think I'm dead, Devon, and I'm not sure I can cope with the shame."

She had wanted it that way, wanted to hide.

The night doctors worked on mending Arabella's legs, they had met Sister Agatha by chance at the hospital, and the wheels of fate were soon in motion.

"I need to tell Mina the truth." He could not disappear

137

every Thursday and leave her in the dark. "We can trust her. I'm sure of it." Else he would not have married her. "She will not tell Lord Kinver."

Arabella gave a half-shrug. "Sometimes I wish he did know. That he would come here, and I could ask him why he chased me, why he hurt me that night."

Devon sat forward. "So he did hurt you?"

She had insinuated as much, never confirmed it as fact.

"I think so. That is what you said."

Days after the attack, she'd said Kinver had chased her into the mews. Still, he did not correct her. After hearing Lord Kinver's half-hearted confession, he had repeated her statement many times.

He dragged a hand through his hair. He could not risk Kinver finding her and silencing her for good. But by God, he wished he could make sense of what happened that night.

They spent an hour drinking tea, taking supper and talking about Arabella's studies, Mina and the murder case.

"Mr Goldman seems the most likely culprit," she said.

"And yet it wouldn't surprise me if Sir Thomas blackmailed Captain Howard, not for money, but for his sister's hand in marriage. Killing Sir Thomas would be the only solution." The captain was eager to find his sister a husband, hence the frequent balls.

"Or Miss Howard acted on impulse. Sir Thomas may have met her on Waterloo Bridge."

Miss Howard lacked the strength to kill a man.

There was another suspect. Perhaps Kinver meant to punish Devon by having him tried for murder. He should be the next person they question. Yet Devon couldn't bear to be in the bastard's company, and he refused to let the rogue intimidate Mina.

Mina!

He stood, the sickening feeling rising in his stomach.

The six-hour journey would be unbearable.

"I must go. My wife has no idea where I am. When we married, I insisted she should always be honest with me, yet I am the one at fault."

Arabella remained seated. "She will think you're a dreadful hypocrite. You will have to grovel and buy her a gift."

He kissed his sister tenderly on the head. "Yes. She deserves better. But I shall endeavour to make amends."

Thoughts of their reunion entered his mind.

He would find her asleep in bed, her silk nightgown bunched to her waist, her lithe legs on display. She'd stir as he kissed her ankle, tug his hair and moan in pleasure as he worked his way up her thigh.

"Well, I wish you a comfortable journey," Arabella said.

Devon inwardly groaned.

The next six hours would be pure torture.

Chapter Twelve

She missed him.

How was it possible after a week of marriage?

Still, she had grown accustomed to sleeping next to his warm body in bed. Longed to hear the deep timbre of his voice. Smell his tantalising cologne. Feel his tender touch.

Devon had left without explaining why he had business in Aylesbury, who he planned to meet, or why she could not accompany him on the long journey.

The house felt cold and empty without him. Mina had eaten supper alone, as she had done so many times she should be used to the silence. As she undressed for bed, she conjured an image of him leaning against the jamb, his dark eyes glinting with the promise of something illicit. Tried to tell herself all was well.

Then her maid uttered the comment that pierced her heart like a barbed arrow. That made her doubt her husband's word.

"Don't be upset, miss—" Daisy still hadn't come to terms with the fact Mina was married. "Happen he's gone to tell her he can't see her no more, that's all."

"I beg your pardon?" Her heart sank like a brick in a well.

"The lady Mr Masters meets every Thursday."

Even now, an hour later, as Mina held the lit candle against the row of volumes in the bookcase and studied the spines, her stomach tied itself up in knots.

Honesty is a rare quality, Miss Stanford.

Yes, a quality her husband lacked.

The flame flickered in the darkness as her hand shook with barely contained rage and ... and shame for being such a love-sick fool.

It wasn't love, not yet, but as one nurtured and tended a new rose, she had hoped their feelings would bloom into something strong and lasting, something beautiful and—

The library door creaked open.

And her heart nearly burst through her ribcage.

"You'll stay in here tonight," Bates said sharply. "How's a man to sleep with the constant chatter?" He looked up from the object he carried—the parrot's cage covered with a dark blanket—and jumped in fright. "Mrs Masters. Forgive me. I didn't know you were up." His tone always hinted at annoyance, like she had chained herself to his master's leg, a permanent shackle.

"I couldn't sleep and thought to read for a while."

"If you wanted a book, you should have rung for Daisy."

"I'll not disturb her at this late hour." She glanced at the cage. "What do you have there, Bates?"

Before the butler answered, Miss Marmalade chirped, "*Bates drinks the master's brandy. Bates drinks the master's brandy.*"

The servant's eyes widened in horror. "It's the parrot, ma'am. She keeps the staff awake with her constant chatter, and we are all desperate for a decent night's sleep."

Mina knew firsthand how annoying the bird could be. "As I'm on my own tonight, she can remain upstairs with me."

What would it matter? She wouldn't sleep until Devon got home, and then she planned to confront him about his trip to Aylesbury.

"I'll not have you disturbed, ma'am, not with the master away."

Mina saw an opening to ask the question that had been burning in her mind for the last hour. "How long has Mr Masters been making his Thursday night trip to Aylesbury?"

Bates paled. He looked like he would rather suffer Miss Marmalade's jibes than confess, but then decided to defend his master. "Three years, ma'am, ever since Miss Arabella died. He found it hard to cope that first year. And a man must find a haven from his troubles."

I've not kept a mistress for three years.

Why lie? The man she had come to know prided himself on telling the truth. But then she had been foolish enough to believe him.

"Give me the bird," she said, keen to return to her chamber before tears welled and the emptiness consumed her again. She crossed the room to take the cage, but Bates insisted on carrying it upstairs and placing it on the mahogany chest.

Perhaps Miss Marmalade sensed Mina's pain because the bird fluffed her green feathers, closed her tiny eyes and barely made a sound.

Mina lay awake, staring into the darkness.

The eerie chill in the air made her shiver. Had Thomas returned to haunt her, to gloat about what a mess she had made of her life?

She considered dressing and visiting Mrs Fitzroy, who would surely be home at this late hour, but she had promised Devon she would not leave the house. One of them had to be trusted to keep their word.

Long before dawn, she heard the faint creak of footsteps on the stairs. Still in a temper, she turned away from the door and feigned sleep, though the pounding of her heartbeat in her ears proved deafening.

The door clicked open, and Devon slipped into the room.

Would he attempt to wake her?

Would he climb into bed and pretend all was well?

The wait was torture.

He approached the bed and stood behind her for agonising seconds, his breathing unusually shallow. He smelled of dust, leather and musk. Not the stimulating cedarwood that fired her senses, not the sickly stench of another woman's perfume. That's when she noted the air didn't thrum with the same wild energy. A need to join bodies and make love.

He bent over her and brushed her cheek with gloved fingers.

Her blood chilled.

The man touching her intimately was not her husband. The man fondling a lock of her hair—as if he might rip it from her head and keep it as a trophy—had probably murdered Thomas.

Panic surfaced.

She pursed her lips and held her breath.

The air in her lungs fought to escape.

What should she do?

Without a weapon, her only hope was to stall him and make a hasty escape. But how? He might bludgeon her to death any minute.

"Hmm," she moaned softly, rolling onto her back and feigning sleep. She peered through half-closed lids, for she would know the identity of her would-be attacker.

The dark figure lowered his head.

That's when she realised he wore a black hood, holes cut

for eyes. He whipped a length of rope from his coat pocket and pulled it taut between gloved hands.

Fear took control then.

She gasped loud enough to let the intruder know she was awake. "W-who are you? What do you want?" She scrambled to a sitting position, but the fiend wrapped the rope around her neck before she could jump from the bed.

"To get rid of you," he growled, his voice so full of menace Thomas must have hurt him dreadfully. "Dirty sluts belong in the gutter."

She grabbed the rope chaffing her skin, yanking hard to give her space to breathe. "My husband will be back in a … a moment. He'll kill you if he catches you here."

"No, he won't," the devil sneered, his voice too deep to be natural. "Everyone knows he visits his mistress on Thursdays."

The brute may as well have punched her in the stomach.

She felt the pain just as keenly.

"W-why are you doing this?" she said weakly, knowing she had no choice but to fight for her life. She thumped his hands, kicked her legs, and tried to prize his fingers from the rope, but they were as rigid as steel. "Help!" she croaked.

"*Who goes there*?" chirped Miss Marmalade.

Panic made the monster loosen his grip.

He glanced behind and froze.

It was impossible to see anything in the darkness.

She took the opportunity to fill her lungs.

"*State your name and your business.*"

The beast cursed beneath his breath, and the rope went slack. But Miss Marmalade repeated the command, sending the attacker darting out of the door, the thud of his booted footsteps receding into the distance.

It took a few seconds for her limbs to work. She dragged

herself out of bed and tugged the bell pull so hard plaster dust fell to the floor. "Bates!" she yelled, though it hurt her throat to shout. "Bates!"

By the time the butler appeared, she couldn't stop shaking. "There was an intruder. He … he tried to strangle me. Miss Marmalade … Miss Marmalade saved me."

Oh, she would buy the bird a gold perch.

Feed her expensive preserves.

Bates seemed confused, but she pointed to her neck, to where the skin burned. "He pulled the rope so tight, I couldn't breathe."

Bates raised his candle aloft, his bushy brows arching in horror as he considered what must be red welts marring her skin. "Good heavens! Who did this, ma'am?"

She shrugged. "He wore a hood. It was too dark to see anything clearly. He thought Miss Marmalade's chirps were that of a maid."

"Oh, the master will have my hide for this."

"Had the master been at home, it wouldn't have happened."

Bates made no comment about Devon's after-dark activities. "Wait here, ma'am, and lock the door. I'll rouse the servants and check the house." Then he hurried from the room.

For ten minutes she paced the floor, wringing her hands and cursing her husband. Miss Marmalade took to repeating all the terrible things she had been taught to say about Devon.

Mr Masters was indeed a muttonhead!

Bates knocked on the door, and she hurried to greet him.

"He'd got in through the servants' door, smashed a small pane and managed to turn the key." Bates bowed his head. "Forgive me, ma'am, but none of us heard a sound. We've hardly slept since the parrot—"

145

"Regardless what you might say about Miss Marmalade, I was grateful for her company tonight." Mina dreaded to think what would have happened had the bird not scared the intruder. "Give me an hour, then summon a hackney. I shall stay with Miss Ware while Mr Masters is away."

She might remain there indefinitely. Besides, she would not wait like a sitting duck for the fiend to strike again.

The butler found the prospect of her leaving more worrying than her being strangled in her bed. "But what shall I say to Mr Masters? He'll be furious you've left the house in the dead of night."

There were many things she might say to her husband, but she needed space to clear her head, and she didn't feel safe in Dover Street. "Tell him whatever you please. And you'll be glad to know Miss Marmalade is coming with me."

Mina spent the next hour dressing and throwing garments into a valise, stopping to burst into tears and almost vomiting in the washbowl at the thought of how close she had come to dying.

She had her bag packed and was about to slip into her pelisse when she heard footsteps on the stairs.

"Bates!" she called, her stomach churning. "Bates!"

What if the beast had returned and killed the butler?

Terrified, she quickly crept to the fireplace, snatched the poker, and moved to stand behind the door, ready to bludgeon the devil to death.

The door creaked open for the second time tonight.

She raised the poker aloft and might have hit out had Miss Marmalade not squawked, "*Masters is a muttonhead.*"

"I should wring your damn neck," Devon muttered. He happened to glance right and saw her looming in the candle-light. "What the blazes?" It took him a moment to gather his wits. "Mina! Why are you out of bed? And why are you dressed at this ungodly hour?"

Relief banished her fears, but the instinct to throw her arms around Devon's neck and hug him tightly abandoned her when she remembered where he had been tonight.

"I wasn't expecting you until dawn," she said, returning the poker to the fireplace and stomping over to the bed. "Did you conclude your *business* early?"

"I was eager to return home to my wife."

Oh, the rotter! "Am I supposed to be grateful?"

He closed the gap between them and cupped her elbow. "You've not answered my questions." Through tired eyes, he looked at the valise on the bed. "What is this about?"

She couldn't look at him and so fiddled with the brass catch on the bag. "It's about you being dishonest. You profess to be a man of your word, but you're just like everyone else. Your demands gave me hope for the future, but you lack the strength to abide by them yourself."

He frowned. "Stop speaking in riddles and be specific."

"Very well. I'm leaving."

"Leaving!" A frustrated sigh left his lips.

"Yes." She found the strength to look at him, but locking gazes was like a blade to the heart. "I've been humiliated too many times, Devon. You promised you wouldn't make me look a fool."

"Why would you look a fool?"

"Because everyone knows you've been to visit *her*!"

"Visit who?" He blinked, but she saw a flash of guilt in his eyes.

"Please don't make me spell it out. You visit her every Thursday."

Recognition dawned. "Mina, you—"

"You've hardly been discreet. I listed my conditions

before we married, and you have broken them." Tears welled, but she grabbed the bag and pulled it off the bed. "I'm tired of being ridiculed. You're the one who taught me to stand up to the *ton*, to be true to my convictions."

He tried to take the bag. "Doubtless Bates told you about—"

"Bates, Daisy, the man who broke into the house and might have killed me had Miss Marmalade not scared him off." A sob escaped, hurting her bruised throat. "I hope you and your mistress will be happy together."

She made for the door, but he grabbed her wrist to delay her departure. "I've not lied to you, Mina. I had business in Aylesbury, but I needed to seek permission before explaining things properly."

"Permission?" she spat. "From your mistress?"

He pulled her close and lowered his voice. "From my sister."

"Your sister?" Surely she had misheard.

He jerked his head suddenly and frowned. "Wait. Someone broke into the house? Someone tried to hurt you?" His gaze darted over her body and stopped abruptly at her neck. "Mother of all saints! Who did this? I'll kill him with my bare hands!"

Shock took command of her senses.

The need to feel cocooned in Devon's strong embrace, to feel safe, had her dropping the valise and falling into him. "I've never been so scared. He meant to steal my last breath."

"Who?"

"I don't know. He wore a mask."

He held her tightly as she wept, stroked her hair, spoke soothing words, though his body was tense. "I'm sorry I wasn't here for you," he whispered. "But I visit Arabella every Thursday, and she has no one but me."

She pulled away and met his gaze. "Arabella is alive?"

He nodded. "No one knows but me, us, not even Bates. It is her secret. I could say nothing until she gave her permission." He dashed tears from her cheek. "I told her I couldn't keep it from you. That we could trust you to protect her as I have."

Relief rippled through her in waves. "You can. I would never break a confidence, never betray you."

"I know. We'll sit down, and I'll explain everything." He bent his head and brushed his mouth against hers, teasing her with the taste she craved. "Everyone else must think she is dead. I shall have to invent a new story to explain my Thursday night jaunts."

"Our jaunts. I should like to come with you, Devon."

"Arabella would like that." He kissed her, a slow melding that warmed her cold bones and wound the coil of desire. He felt it, too, because he broke contact. "I want you beneath me in bed, and then I want every damn detail because I mean to murder the devil who dared to hurt you."

She was already pushing his coat off his shoulders, the need to feel him inside her like the sweetest addiction. "I want you, and then I want to know why Arabella is hiding."

They nodded in unison, as desperate for each other as they were for answers. Her greedy sex pulsed, anticipating the moment he would thrust long and hard, when she would be full with him—Devon Masters.

"You may consider making love in bed rather tame," he teased, "but I mean to make you come with my mouth and tongue, come again when I'm spreading you wide and plunging deep."

His words made her wet.

She needed to elicit the same response but lacked the experience to drive her husband wild. "I want to see you

149

naked, Devon. I want to touch you, all of you." Honesty would have to do.

"Then strip me out of these clothes."

She had his gold waistcoat off in seconds. His shirt proved more troublesome because he moaned when her hands touched his bare skin. Enjoying the power she wielded, she reached beneath and caressed the rigid planes.

He sucked in a sharp breath as her fingers grazed his nipples. "Minx!" Impatience had him dragging the garment over his head and throwing it onto the floor.

Dare to be bold!

Lillian's words whispered through her mind. With the same courage she'd leant on to enter his home that first night, she stroked the hard length of his arousal through his trousers. "You do want me, Devon."

"Always," he growled, tearing at the buttons and pushing the garment down past his hips until his manhood sprang free.

Merciful lord!

She had seen him relaxed and flaccid, not stiff and swollen. Fascinated, she touched him. "You're so warm."

"I'm on fire, love," he whispered darkly. "Hold me."

She gripped him, began moving her hand back and forth.

He closed his eyes briefly, his head falling back as a groan slipped from his lips. "That's so damn good. I've spent the journey home longing for your touch, aching to push inside you."

She'd spent the time hating him.

Now, she couldn't wait to spread her legs and lie beneath him. "Make love to me, Devon. Take me to bed now."

His mischievous grin only made him more appealing. "Feeling hungry, love? Rest assured, I'll not stop until you're full. But first, I need you naked."

She wanted him to tear the garments off her back, but

Devon took his time removing each one. He kissed her bare shoulders as he pushed her dress past her hips. When her corset hit the floor he pulled her against his chest, caressed her breasts through her chemise, rolling her nipple between his thumb and finger.

"I mean to watch you this time," he said, his voice low and husky as he pressed his erection against her buttocks. "I mean to own you, just as I promised." He slid her chemise to her hips and drew it over her head. "You belong to me, Mina."

The cold air chilled her skin, but Devon swept her into his arms and carried her the short distance to the bed. He eased her down gently, giving her a moment to appreciate his physique.

He was beautiful, all hard lines and dark features, a man made for sin. Every bit as dangerous as the rogue who'd charged naked from the bath tub and paid twenty thousand pounds for a virgin's kiss.

The old feelings of inadequacy surfaced.

But his gaze slid slowly down over her body, and he gave an appreciative hum. He moistened his lips like he was starving too, then palmed his erection. "I mean to taste every inch of you tonight."

Nerves had her heart fluttering. "It's almost morning."

"I lose track of time when I'm with you." He climbed on top of her, his hot skin touching her skin, his muscular body pushing her down into the mattress. "Open your legs, love."

She obeyed his instruction, expecting to feel the pressure of his manhood breaching her entrance. But Devon kissed her wildly, tangling his tongue with hers before edging lower to kiss her neck, to take her nipple into his mouth and suck.

The sensation had her sex pulsing. She needed him to fill

the emptiness, but he moved down between her legs to sate his hunger.

The first slide of his tongue over her aching bud had her arching off the bed. "Devon? Should you be doing that?"

Embarrassment burned her cheeks. Of course he should be doing it. Lillian had shown her a drawing detailing the very thing. Though she did not recall where it said one should lick a lady like she was an ice at Gunter's.

Still, it felt divine.

Her shame was soon forgotten, her panicked gasps replaced with sweet moans of pleasure. She gripped his hair and ground her hips against every wicked flick of his tongue. The same tongue penetrated her entrance, had her convulsing and coming hard.

She would never forget the first time he'd kissed her so intimately. Nor would she forget the devilish glint in his eyes or his satisfied smirk as he took himself in hand and pushed into her body.

"Devon," she breathed, wrapping her legs around his hips as he entered her fully, stretching her until they were a perfect fit.

Buried to the hilt, he stilled and looked down at her, his dark eyes warm and tender. "How does that feel?"

A giggle escaped her. "Truthfully?"

"Truthfully."

She swallowed past her reservations. "Like we were made for each other. Like you possess me body and soul." Like I was always meant to knock on your door on a cold autumn night.

He withdrew slowly, rolled his hips and plunged deep. She gripped his back and mimicked his rhythm. Their bodies moved as one. They breathed in unison, their lips parting with each measured thrust.

Then he quickened the pace, pumping fast and hard, the bed creaking beneath them, their breathing ragged now.

"I can't stop," he panted. "I need to come. I need you to come again." He angled his hips so each thrust proved stimulating. "God, Mina. You're so tight and wet I fear I won't withdraw in time."

They had spoken about children, but she'd said she wasn't sure. Without them, it was easy to walk away if things went wrong. And yet, despite the misunderstanding earlier, she trusted this man to stand beside her through a lifetime of hardships.

"Mina!" he cried. "God, how I need you."

She came apart then, her inner muscles clamping down around every solid inch of him. "Don't stop, Devon."

She gripped his buttocks and urged him on. She wanted him to spend inside her. She wanted everything this man had to give.

Chapter Thirteen

While a man experienced many emotions during the course of a day, since marrying Mina, Devon knew only two.

Lust held him in its powerful grip. It pulsed in his veins and left him so hard he could barely function. Erotic visions of him pounding into his wife filled his head. Being a skilled gambler, he had mastered his feelings long ago, which made the whole thing so damn puzzling.

On the occasions when he wasn't imagining pushing into his wife's warm body, he spent the time in a violent rage.

Much like now.

"Explain how my wife nearly died tonight!" he growled at Bates. Mina had finished telling him the harrowing tale half an hour ago, then fell asleep in his arms. Needing to find the culprit before his blood boiled, he had moved her carefully and come hunting for information. "Explain why someone left the key in the bloody door."

Still wearing his nightshirt, Bates stood shivering by his bed. "Sir, we've all struggled to sleep since the bird arrived. It chirps obscenities most nights. We forgot about the key. It was a lapse in concentration. A mistake."

"A mistake that might have cost my wife her life." It wasn't Bates' fault. With little effort, the blackguard could have forced the door. The intruder had the devil's impudence and had known exactly when to strike.

"Sir, I shall prowl the corridors night and day until you've caught the monster. We will all help in any way we can."

The man's genuine remorse calmed Devon's temper.

He snatched a blanket off the bed and gave it to his servant. "Forget about the household duties. I want you to visit the Servants' Registry and see if you can find Grimsby, Thomas Stanford's butler. I want to know all his master's sordid secrets." Although what could be worse than posing naked while wearing a pig mask?

Bates looked relieved he had escaped dismissal. "It won't be difficult, sir. Servants gossip more than society ladies."

"I shall give you the names of the suspects. Learn anything you can from their servants. Ensure they know I will pay handsomely for any information."

"Of course, sir." Bates cleared his throat. "Before you retire, sir, I—I must make a confession." He shuffled his feet and waited for a prompt before continuing. "Daisy heard me say you … you visit a friend in Aylesbury every Thursday. I believe she jumped to conclusions and told Mrs Masters."

He should have expected as much.

Still, Devon should have handled things differently.

"Yes, I'm aware my wife thought I'd broken my vow to her." He wished he could tell his butler the truth, but Arabella's needs always came first. Still, he had promised not to embarrass Mina. "There is no mistress, Bates. I was in Aylesbury on business last night and plan to take Mrs Masters with me on my next visit."

Bates blinked rapidly. "I see. I shall correct Daisy at once."

ADELE CLEE

"Ensure you do. I'll not have anyone thinking my wife is inadequate. Do you understand?"

"Indeed." Bates winced. "One more thing, sir. Lord Kinver called. Mrs Masters could have received him, but under the circumstances, I knew you wouldn't want him in the house."

"Kinver!" Devon's pulse thumped hard in his throat. "What the hell did he want?" Perhaps another beating. Perhaps he meant to hurt every woman Devon was duty-bound to protect.

Had he returned in the dead of night to murder Mina?

"He refused to say, sir."

"Refused!"

Devon saw red.

Hands clenched at his sides, he left the servants' quarters and mounted the stairs two at a time. He washed in cold water, dragged on his trousers and muttered curses as he grabbed a clean shirt from the armoire.

Mina stirred. She opened her eyes and saw him stomping about the bedchamber. "Devon? Are you going out?" She glanced at the closed curtains and came up on her elbows.

The sight of her mussed hair and bare breasts stirred something primitive in him. "Yes, to visit Lord Kinver."

"At dawn?"

"I mean to murder him in his sleep."

She was out of bed in seconds and padding towards him, a feast to temper his ill mood. "Why? You said Arabella's memory is unclear. That the bump to her head meant she remembers very little."

"Make no mistake. Kinver chased her that night." His fingers itched to touch her, but he was already hard. That first caress would bring him to his knees, and he would not be

156

distracted from his current task. "He hurt Arabella. Last night, he hurt you."

She frowned. "But I didn't see my attacker's face. I'm more inclined to believe it was Mr Goldman. I don't imagine many men keep a black hood at home. And he was tall and broad. Lord Kinver is slight of frame."

"If he's innocent, he won't mind providing an alibi."

"Devon, your hatred for Lord Kinver is clouding—"

"He called here last night while you were at home."

She looked surprised. "He did? Bates never said."

"Because he knows Kinver is unstable. He knows I wouldn't let him within three feet of you." Devon shrugged into his waistcoat and set about tying his cravat. "I've ignored him for too long. He's been trying to gain my attention for years and has grown more persistent of late."

He should have put a lead ball between the bastard's brows.

"I am coming with you." She hurried to the armoire, offering him a delightful view of her bare buttocks. "Before you find yourself at another dawn appointment, and I'm forced to wear black permanently."

He should object, but his temper was like a wild beast thirsty for blood. He needed her to keep a tight hold of the leash. "You'd be as rich as Croesus. And you need only mourn me for two years."

"Don't say that." She looked at the crumpled bedsheets and then at him. "No other man alive could make me feel the way you do. I would rather sleep on the street and live on stale bread than suffer the loss."

Her comments touched him deeply, though he did not want to consider what it meant, not yet, not until Kinver was six feet under and they could sleep easily again.

"Let's hope it doesn't come to that." He released a heavy

sigh. "Though Bradbury said if I don't give the men of the *ton* a chance to win back their vowels, one of them is bound to shoot me."

She paled. "I'm sure he's teasing. Yet your friends have called every night this week, and you've refused to accompany them to a gaming hell."

He wiggled a brow. "Perhaps I have more pressing business at home." He craved her company, loved making her tremble with need. It was a better way to spend his time than sending a man to the Marshalsea. "Business that will keep me at home tonight and in your bed, madam."

She laughed. "It's your bed."

"It's ours, love."

He was a master at reading expressions, though he struggled to decipher hers. Was it gratitude he saw swimming in her big brown eyes? Respect? A stirring of affection?

Something infinitely more?

Whatever it was, it scared her a little. She turned away and quickly pulled her chemise over her head to cover her curves.

As he watched her dress and assisted her with the tiny buttons, he did what he did best and analysed the atmosphere. He could sense panic even when an opponent gave a confident smile.

The undercurrent that was sexual tension often left them both breathless. But there was something else crackling in the air, something even a man of his skill could not name.

A little after dawn, they arrived at Lord Kinver's home in New Cavendish Street and demanded the butler wake the scoundrel.

Devon expected to argue on the doorstep, to be waved away so the maid could wash the steps, but after the initial shock, the man seemed eager to alert his master.

The ageing servant returned within minutes. He took their outdoor apparel, ushered them into the elegantly furnished drawing room and offered them tea.

"When did you last speak to Lord Kinver?" Mina whispered. She waited for the maid to gather the coal scuttle and leave the room, then went to warm her hands against the fire's flames.

"Three years ago, although I tell him to bugger off quite frequently. He used to harass me at balls and accost me at the theatre." Kinver made a damn nuisance of himself. "He seeks forgiveness, but he can go to hell."

She glanced back at him, confused. "Why would he want to speak to the man whose sister he attacked? The man who punished him with ten lashes?"

"To ease a guilty conscience."

"So, he admitted hurting Arabella."

"I don't make a habit of whipping innocent men."

Her gaze turned warm. "No, the man I know is always fair, but do you not think it odd that—"

Kinver burst into the room, panting, making the same pathetic noise he must have made when chasing Arabella through the garden. A noise that had frightened her half to death and left her a scarred cripple.

Devon clenched his fists at his sides.

He'd need the patience of a saint to get through this.

Mina crossed the room and curtsied to the blackguard. "Forgive us for disturbing you at this early hour, my lord, but you called at Dover Street last night, and it's important we know why."

Kinver bowed to the woman he might have throttled had it not been for the parrot's timely intervention. "Madam, you're welcome to visit at any hour. I came seeking an audience with your husband, and have been desperately trying to do so for some time."

Devon muttered a curse. "Well? Is it him?"

Mina shot him a 'be quiet' glare. "No, it is not."

"You're certain?"

"Yes."

"But the man wore a hood."

"Yes, and he was three inches taller."

"One might be confused in the dark. Look at him. His eyes are red and puffy. A clear sign he's not slept a wink." The scene played out in Devon's mind, his wife fighting for her life, thinking she would die. It stoked the embers of his temper. "Did you break into my house last night and try to murder my wife?"

Kinver stumbled back like he'd been punched. "What?"

Devon prowled towards the rogue. "It cannot be a coincidence. You call at the house, and my butler turns you away. Hours later, someone forces the door and almost strangles her."

His stomach lurched at the thought.

Mina touched her throat, though the high-collared pelisse hid the horrid red marks. "Do you have an alibi, my lord? It is the only thing that will appease my husband. Where were you at two o'clock this morning?"

"Two o'clock? With the vicar of St James' church," Kinver said, surprising them both. "He refused to answer my questions, so I dragged him around the graveyard, insisting he show me where Arabella is buried."

Hell and the devil!

Devon's heart missed a beat. "Who said she was buried in St James' churchyard?"

Why did he care about Arabella's grave?

"You took her to St Thomas' hospital," Kinver explained. "The surgeon there sent me to the mortician who found a record for a woman who had died that week. He said records are often inaccurate, but he remembered a young woman being buried at St James'."

Devon narrowed his gaze. "What has it do with you?"

What the hell was this about?

Kinver's mouth twisted in pain. "The memory of that night haunts me still. I cannot let it rest. I want to lay flowers on her grave. I want to speak to her and try to make sense of what happened."

"Then let me help you make sense of it." Hatred kept his panic at bay. "You encouraged my sister to meet you in a secluded part of the garden. Correct?"

Kinver nodded.

"Then you kissed her. Put your filthy hands on her body."

"We were in love. Things got a little heated."

Devon took a calming breath. "She said no, yet—"

"She didn't say no. She saw someone watching us, then took to her heels and ran. I chased after her but lost her in the darkness." Kinver's shoulders sagged. "I want to know where she is buried so I can pay my respects. Is it too much to ask?"

"She was running away from you when the carriage ploughed into her," Devon reiterated. "Had you behaved like a gentleman, she would not have been outside." He shook his head to dispel an unwelcome vision. Arabella had scratches and bruises on her chest after being mauled by this monster. "Do you expect me to believe she tore her dress on a branch?"

Kinver threw his hands in the air. "You're not listening to me. You never listen to me. Someone else saw us. Someone else followed her. If she were alive, she would tell you!"

Mina pursed her lips but said nothing.

At this point, Devon always lost his head. He usually threatened the lord and cursed him to Hades, but the look of confusion on Mina's face made him press Kinver harder.

"If it happened as you say, why let me whip you?"

Kinver scrubbed his hand over his face. "Because you're right. I arranged the assignation. I overstepped the bounds of propriety. Not a day goes by when I don't regret my actions. Arabella would be my wife if we'd had more control over our emotions."

Weeks ago, Devon would have scoffed at the lord. But now he knew how lust and longing could command a man's mind. He had indulged his whims. He had kissed Mina to settle a curiosity.

Did that not make him a hypocrite?

"This is a list of all the men in attendance that night." Kinver reached into his coat pocket and removed a tatty piece of paper with faded ink. "You said Arabella's dress was torn at the shoulder, her hair in disarray. Then someone accosted her after she fled into the darkness."

Devon snatched the paper. Wine and water marks stained the page and had smudged the ink, the effects of many hours spent studying every line.

Something stirred deep in his chest.

A point he had not considered.

Kinver was still in love with Arabella.

He mentally shook himself and scanned the names that were also on his own list. Names that included Wenham, Stanford and Captain Howard, and those of a dozen men whose vowels he owned.

"It's impossible to prove anyone else was involved," Devon said.

"I've spent three years listening behind doors at gentlemen's clubs, getting men drunk in the hope they might confess to an indiscretion. All to no avail."

Guilt flooded Devon's chest.

Might there be some truth to Kinver's theory?

Mina must have sensed the shift in him because she crossed the room and slipped her arm through his. "Perhaps you might spend an hour comparing notes. You may have a mutual enemy."

Every muscle in Devon's body tensed in resistance.

"Let me think on the matter." He'd spent three years blaming the lord for Arabella's scars. And Kinver had rightly accepted responsibility. "Assure me you did not murder Thomas Stanford to punish me. Tell me you did not have your sister write to the magistrate—"

"Where you're concerned, I seek forgiveness, not vengeance." He took the list from Devon, folded it with care and returned it to his pocket. "If you think of a plan, I will do anything to trap the real villain."

The cogs in Devon's mind started turning. Might he persuade Arabella to join in the scheme and return to town? But then she would not want Kinver seeing her scars and mangled legs.

"As I said, give me a few days to consider the matter."

Kinver looked like the cat who had found the cream. "I'm not sure what has prompted this change of heart, Masters, but I'm grateful for an opportunity to uncover the truth. In the meantime, I implore you, tell me where Arabella is buried."

"I'll tell you." Devon pasted an indifferent expression. "Once the devil who hurt her so cruelly has confessed." And he had Arabella's permission.

Not wishing to press too hard, Kinver agreed.

They left the lord examining his list and were about to climb into the carriage when Bradbury came marching towards them, still dressed in evening attire.

"Bradbury lives a little further along the street," Devon informed Mina. "Doubtless, a servant saw my carriage and told him I was here."

"What the devil are you doing out at this ungodly hour? Please tell me you haven't done Kinver an injury," Bradbury joked. He bowed to Mina and wished her a good morning.

"Rest assured. Kinver is alive and well. He wants to know where Arabella is buried. The devil wants to lay flowers on her grave, but I warned him to stay the hell away." It was a small lie, but one that would placate his friend. Devon considered Bradbury's bloodshot eyes. He reeked of tobacco and cheap perfume. "Just arriving home?"

Bradbury glared at Kinver's front door, then brushed a hand through his mop of red hair. "If you recall, we had seats at Lord Stratham's game at White's last night. I went with Anderson, and then we stopped at numerous taverns and erm … houses before venturing home."

He had omitted the word *bawdy*.

"Perhaps you might like to dine with us tomorrow, Mr Bradbury," Mina said, offering a pretty smile. She was astute enough to know Bradbury mourned the loss of his gambling partner, and she did not wish to be the cause of any discontent.

Bradbury glanced at him and arched a brow. "We've the game at Fortune's Den tomorrow night. Tell me you haven't forgotten."

Bloody hell. He was in no mood for serious play.

"No, I have not forgotten."

He just lacked enthusiasm at present.

"Tell me you're coming. Stakes are high, and your presence throws other men off their game." Keen to secure Devon's attendance, Bradbury added, "I shall dine with you both in Dover Street, and we can head to Aldgate together."

With a murderer at large, Devon could not leave Mina alone while he played cards across town. Still, the owner of Fortune's Den owed him a boon. He supposed Mina could bring Miss Ware and wait in Aaron Chance's drawing room.

"You should play," Mina added.

"Faulkner relinquished his place," Bradbury said with a mocking snort. "I imagine you would like to ruin his replacement."

Devon laughed. "Who is it? Carstairs?" The rakehell had asked Arabella to dance on the night of Kinver's ball and moaned to all and sundry when she refused him.

"No, Lord Wenham."

"Wenham!" The thought of sending that bastard to the Marshalsea brought a warm glow to Devon's chest. "Then dine with us at eight. Nothing will stop me taking my seat in the game."

Chapter Fourteen

"Mina!" Devon's voice breezed over her like a gentle caress. "Wake up, love." His large hand settled on her hip, warm with the promise of an intimate liaison, but he shook her. "You might want to come downstairs and listen to what Grimsby has to say."

Grimsby?

Hearing her butler's name roused her from slumber. "What time is it?" Having had little sleep last night, she had come to rest for an hour.

"Three in the afternoon."

"Three!" She opened her eyes to see his handsome figure looming over the bed. "You should have woken me before. If Grimsby is here, he only wants one thing. He has learnt of our marriage and comes begging for his wages."

He captured her hand and helped her off the bed. "I asked Bates to find him, so we might ask questions about your brother's movements before he died."

No wonder her husband beat his opponents.

Devon thought of everything.

"He will want money before he says a word." And rightly

so, Thomas had treated the staff terribly. No one wished to work hard for a pittance.

"I'll agree to inspect the accounts and settle any amount owing. All those who worked for your brother deserve their rightful pay."

She smiled, her gaze devouring the man she had married. Then it hit her like a bolt from the sky. This intense infatuation was something infinitely more profound.

If love made a woman crave intimacy, made any form of separation unbearable, if it left her excited and nervous and all-round giddy, then she was in love with Devon Masters.

A soft sigh left her lips.

"What is it?" Concerned, he brushed her cheek with the backs of his fingers, his dark eyes softening the way they always did for her.

Don't tell him!

Lord knows it will ruin everything.

"I fear we will never find Thomas' murderer." And that meant the man who'd attacked her was free to strike again. He might be plotting to kill her at this very moment.

"We still have other people to question, and I'll not rest until the man who hurt you is marching to the gallows." Devon captured her mouth in a kiss that turned her insides molten.

Tears sprung in her eyes.

Tears of happiness and painful longing.

If she could freeze time and remain in Devon's embrace forever, she would. No more hardships or struggles, just love and the feel of his strong arms protecting her always.

"Perhaps we should leave town for a few days and visit the coast." He pressed a lingering kiss to her forehead. "I'm worried about you. You've had too much to contend with of late."

Spend time alone, just the two of them?

No plots, no distractions?

It sounded heavenly. Pure bliss.

"A trip would be wonderful, but you said I need to hear Grimsby's news, and there's the game with Mr Wenham tomorrow night." She had seen the devilish glint in his eyes when he learnt Mr Wenham would be at the tables. "And we need to speak to Mrs Fitzroy to discover why she is black-mailing Miss Howard."

"But you look in need of a rest."

"I shall retire early tonight, and all will be well."

His dark, compelling gaze journeyed over her face, settling on her lips. "I could join you, take supper in bed, massage your tired limbs."

Make love to you all night, he might have said.

Her sex pulsed as she imagined him on top of her, her thighs gripping his lean hips. "Let us see what Grimsby has to say and return here posthaste."

Devon's mouth curled into a sinful grin. He captured her hand and led her downstairs into the drawing room where Grimsby stood statue still, as if he were on trial and expected the judge to don a black cap and deliver damning news.

The middle-aged butler lowered his gaze when their eyes met. "Forgive me, miss. We shouldn't have disappeared without warning. We should have left a note, given—"

"You left Miss Marmalade alone in the house."

"We knew you would be back to tend to her, miss."

"Someone murdered her brother," Devon cried, "and you thought to leave my wife alone in that house, without servants or a chaperone?"

"We were scared for our lives, sir, and hadn't been paid in months." The man wrung his hands while making excuses.

"And we thought Miss Stanford was staying with her friend Miss Ware."

Mina put a calming hand on Devon's arm. "It is Mrs Masters now, Grimsby, and there is no point arguing. My husband said you have news relating to my brother's final days."

"Yes, ma'am." Grimsby looked at Devon and flinched. "The night before the duel, I saw Sir Thomas arguing with Mr Wenham in Carnaby Street. The gentleman grabbed the master, threw him to the ground and hit him with his riding crop."

Mina's breath caught in her throat. Mr Wenham was wicked beneath his affable facade. She'd had a lucky escape.

"What were they arguing about?" she said.

"I don't know, ma'am, but Mr Wenham broke into the house last Friday. I saw him emptying the master's desk, throwing papers about the room, and muttering he would kill everyone unless he found his deed."

"Did you confront him?" Devon demanded to know. "Did you report the matter to the magistrate?"

A blush stained the servant's cheeks. "He didn't see me, sir. He left without taking anything, and I didn't want to make trouble."

"You mean you were frightened?"

"Mr Wenham has a violent streak, sir."

"But he didn't find the deed?" she wished to confirm.

"No." Grimsby looked back at Bates.

"You can speak in front of my butler," Devon said.

After some contemplation, Grimsby nodded. "Sir Thomas did steal the deed. He said it's what the fool deserved, that everyone would soon know Mr Wenham was a liar and a cheat."

A wave of guilt washed over her. "Did he mean to bribe

Mr Wenham?" Was Thomas trying to save her reputation? "He meant to return the deed if Mr Wenham admitted to lying about me?"

Grimsby shifted like he had cramp. "Er, no, ma'am. He took the deed to a man in Long Lane, West Smithfield. He said Mr Wenham was deep in the mire and was trying to gain money for a mining project on land he doesn't own. The master wished to seek vengeance for the shame caused to his reputation."

To *his* reputation!

"I—I see," she said past the knot in her throat.

Devon's calming hand on her back stemmed the tears. "And this man in Long Lane was going to help him achieve his goal?"

"By all accounts. I assume he still has the document."

In her mind's eye, she saw a vision of Thomas handing over the deed, saw the toothy grin of a fool who always believed he could win. "I will need the name of the man in Long Lane."

Grimsby shrugged. "I know he used to be a runner at Bow Street, and now he mostly spends his time looking for missing people."

Devon pressed his mouth to her ear. "He won't be hard to find. We will search him out this afternoon."

She agreed. Finding the deed would give them leverage against Mr Wenham. "Grimsby, can you tell us anything else that might help us find my brother's killer?"

Grimsby shook his head. "Only what you already know, ma'am. He owed many people money and was under pressure to settle his debts."

Yes, and that gave half the men in London a motive for murder.

"Then leave your forwarding address with Bates. Mr

Masters will make arrangements to pay any wages owing to you."

Grimsby staggered a little in shock. "Thank you, sir."

Masters was no longer a muttonhead, but a generous man who always exceeded everyone's expectations, including hers.

He was an exceptional husband, a skilled lover, a caring brother, and the best card player in London. So why was he estranged from his parents?

He still hadn't said.

Indeed, she broached the subject during the carriage ride to Long Lane. He provided the perfect opening by asking how Thomas had gained his selfish streak.

"My parents pandered to his whims in an effort to control him. Their love proved suffocating, though it is unfair to hold them to account. Each person makes their own choices in life."

His gaze moved to the pretty phoenix brooch fastened to her blue pelisse. "Yes, else you would be arrogant and demanding, not kind and compassionate and courageous."

Oh, she could listen to his compliments all day. "You're the only person who thinks so, Devon. I'm still pinching myself, wondering if this is all a dream."

"Would it not be a nightmare?"

"A nightmare?"

"Marrying a man for convenience?"

She smiled while recalling the way his wicked mouth had devoured hers last night. "If you recall, I married you for your skill in the bedchamber. My only complaint is you keep too many secrets."

His expression turned serious. "I explained why I couldn't tell you about Arabella. She would rather people think she's dead than let them see her as a cripple."

171

"The trauma of that night must haunt her deeply." And she suspected a part of Devon liked knowing his sister was safe at the convent. "But I was referring to your parents. You said you were estranged, but have not mentioned them since."

She witnessed the sudden rigidness of his posture, the twitch of a muscle in his jaw, a darkness fill his eyes.

"I don't talk about it because it fires my blood. But I have no intention of keeping secrets from you, Mina." He glanced out of the window and stared at the passing buildings as if watching a painful scene from the past. "My father is cousin to the Earl of Farnborough."

"My brother mentioned the family connection." Often when he was cursing Devon for being an arrogant coxcomb.

"He was granted a position as the earl's personal secretary, and we were to go to Boston for two years while the earl courted an American heiress."

"So, you were asked to go with them?"

"Yes. It was all arranged, but Arabella refused to leave."

"Because she loved Lord Kinver?"

It was evident Lord Kinver loved Arabella and that he blamed himself for the accident. But what if he was right and someone else drove Arabella to run for her life? What would the lord say if he discovered she was alive?

He grimaced. "Yes, but my mother insisted Arabella would find someone more suitable across the water. Which meant they expected her to marry to help my father gain acceptance into American society."

She had heard that his parents were social climbers.

"And you disagreed?"

A weary sigh escaped him. "We were to depart the day after Kinver's ball. My parents were dining with the earl. I went against their wishes and escorted Arabella to the party."

Tension hung heavily in the air.

It was a decision that must keep him awake at night.

A decision he must regret deeply.

"And now you blame yourself for what happened to her."

He dragged his hand down his face, the strain evident. "I have spent three years living with the guilt. My parents see gossip as an irremovable stain on one's character. Because of me, Arabella was ruined."

His insistence on marrying her made sense now. He couldn't bear for another woman to face ruin because of his actions.

"Then they would disapprove of our marriage," she said solemnly.

"They disapprove of everything I do. But they stopped being my parents when they chose the earl over Arabella."

"They left for Boston as planned?" Surely not. Their daughter lay broken in more ways than one, and they abandoned her?

"They disowned us both and have decided to remain in Boston indefinitely. Doubtless, they have heard rumours of Arabella's death but have never sought confirmation or tried to make amends."

Was that another reason he gambled?

Was he punishing society for his parents' failings?

Desperate to comfort him, Mina crossed the carriage and sat beside him. She took his hand in hers. "You didn't hurt Arabella. You could see she was in love, and I imagine she pleaded with you to let her see Lord Kinver one last time."

Devon looked at their clasped hands. "She didn't have to beg. She didn't have to offer me a bribe. She's the only person who's ever loved me, and I would do anything for her, Mina."

She's not the only person, not anymore.

I love you, Devon.

173

The power of it was like a rush of euphoria.

So exquisite it left her breathless.

"Then, for Arabella's sake, we must discover if there is any truth to Lord Kinver's story," she said, stopping herself from revealing what was in her heart. "Did someone else attack your sister? And if so, for what purpose? For what end?"

Devon met her gaze. "First, let me find the devil who attacked you, for I suspect he also killed Thomas. Then we will attempt to prove Lord Kinver's tale. Then I shall decide what to do about Arabella."

He kissed her.

A slow, drugging kiss that curled her toes and melted her heart.

"Now we've no more secrets, Mina."

The flicker of guilt she felt faded as the carriage rumbled to a stop on the corner of Long Lane. She peered through the window to find the street crowded with people visiting Smithfield Market. Hawkers shouted their wares. Animals filled the wooden pens, some escaping onto the busy road.

"We'll walk from here," Devon said.

They alighted, and Simpkin agreed to wait on nearby Aldgate Street.

Mr Solomon, a cloth merchant and the third shopkeeper they'd questioned in a bid to find the runner, said Mr Flynn worked from the Old Swan tavern and could be found at the round table by the fire most days.

"Stay close to me," Devon said as they entered the rowdy alehouse and pushed through a throng of drunken men.

Mina gripped his arm and tried not to inhale too deeply. The stench of pig muck from the pens littering the street outside invaded the air, as did the smell of musty clothes and days' old sweat.

They spotted a smart man with brown hair and neat side-whiskers seated at the round table. He held a magnifying glass to the crumpled map covering the surface, stopping every few seconds to sip his ale and scribble a note on paper.

Devon cleared his throat. "Mr Flynn?"

The fellow looked up from his work. He scanned Devon's physique with a constable's discerning eye, but one look at Mina, and he must have established he was not in any imminent danger.

"Who is asking?" Mr Flynn said, his voice devoid of an accent.

"Devon Masters." He withdrew a calling card from his pocket and placed it on the table. "My brother-in-law hired you to investigate a land deed owned by a man named Wenham."

With some suspicion, Mr Flynn's blue gaze settled on the card. He remained silent for a few seconds, but one could almost hear his questioning thoughts.

"I'll need more information than that," Mr Flynn said with a sardonic grin. "I'll not discuss business with just anyone."

Devon gestured to the available chairs. "May we sit?"

Mr Flynn nodded. "I'll spare five minutes, that's all."

After helping Mina into a chair, Devon sat beside her. "Perhaps it's better if my wife explains why we're here."

Mina straightened. "Thomas Stanford is my—" She stopped abruptly and took a calming breath before continuing. "He was my brother, and someone murdered him a little over a week ago. We know you have Mr Wenham's deed and have come to negotiate for its return."

"I doubt Stanford paid you for your services," Devon added.

"In exchange for the deed and any information you may

have regarding its authenticity, we will settle my brother's bill."

Mr Flynn took a sip of ale and sloshed it about in his mouth while in thought. "The fee is a hundred pounds for the return of the deed and any information relating to the land in Staffordshire. Another fifty for expenses. Return when you—"

"I have the money." Devon slapped signed notes on the table. "There's two hundred pounds—a little extra for any trouble caused. If I discover you've lied to us, I shall hunt you down and demand double."

Mr Flynn was not intimidated, but gave a respectful nod. He took the notes and inspected them with his magnifying glass before reaching into a leather portfolio and handing Devon the deed.

"Stanford was right. The land is owned by a cloth merchant who plans to build a factory and warehouses on the site. There was talk of mining for coal, but the owner refused to sell."

Devon sat forward. "Did the owner confirm Wenham offered for the land?" He scanned the lengthy legal document containing numerous seal stamps and a basic drawing of the area.

Mr Flynn nodded. "When he refused to sell, Wenham became violent, said he already had men willing to invest. I'm told he'd hired an expert to write a geological report. I'm not sure how he came by the forged deed, but I assure you it's not the original document."

Devon looked at her, his expression grave. "There's every chance Wenham murdered your brother in the hope of reclaiming the deed."

"You may be right."

And yet Mr Wenham was not as broad as the man who

had attacked her in the bedchamber. He was as evil. But surely he would have demanded she return the deed before throttling her with the rope.

"I must say, I'm glad to get rid of it." Mr Flynn gestured to the deed. "I heard about Stanford's murder and feared the two were connected."

"We may need you to make a statement," she said, suppressing another wave of emotion. "Once we've gathered more evidence, caught the culprit and gained a confession." It was no mean feat.

"If you need me, leave a note with the landlord."

More men piled into the taproom, and it became hard to converse above the din. Devon thanked Mr Flynn and put the folded deed in his pocket before escorting Mina out onto Long Lane.

"We have him," Devon said, satisfaction dripping from every word. "A lead ball to the chest is too good for Wenham. I plan to ruin him. Let everyone know of his treachery."

"Yes," she said, doubts creeping into her mind. She took hold of his arm. "But should we not attempt to gather more evidence first?"

Devon grinned, baring his teeth like a panther eager to feed. "Tomorrow night at Fortune's Den, we'll force him to confess. Shame him in front of his friends and peers."

Mina forced a smile. Every nerve in her body said Mr Wenham was not the man who attacked her. He was not the man who'd murdered her brother.

Chapter Fifteen

Fortune's Den
Aldgate Street, London

"I might owe you a boon, Masters, but I'll not have women at the tables." Mr Chance glanced at Mina and Lillian and groaned. "It will throw the men off their game."

The owner of Fortune's Den ushered them out of the opulent red hall, where the air was heavy with the smell of exotic oils, and into his elegant office, which was more like a Mayfair drawing room.

"I'll not have them demand a refund from the house," the handsome proprietor proclaimed. "Your gripe with Wenham is your own affair."

"The man tried to murder my wife," Devon snapped.

"We don't know that," she quickly added. It was one thing to accuse a man of fraud, another to call him a murderer.

Mr Bradbury gave a mocking snort. "What other evidence do you need? He had motive, and Crumley said Wenham called at Boodle's looking for Stanford the night before the duel."

She wished Devon hadn't confided in his friend, but he'd found it necessary to explain why he couldn't leave her at home alone. During dinner, Mr Bradbury had suggested kidnapping Mr Wenham and dangling him over Waterloo Bridge until he confessed.

Mr Chance cleared his throat. "While I wish to help you, Masters, I'll not have you shame Wenham in front of other patrons. It's bad for business. And I'll not risk my livelihood for anyone."

"Then I shall beat him at cards and throttle him when we leave." Devon's tone lacked conviction. His temper would get the better of him, and he knew it. Hence why he added, "Or I'll make sure we're the only people in the room when I accuse him of treachery. You have my word."

"I want to believe you, Masters, but only a month ago you swore you would never marry." Mr Chance jerked his head at Mina. "And now you have a wife."

"He had no choice but to help the chit," Mr Bradbury complained, as if Devon had found her huddled around a brazier in Whitechapel, a helpless bag of skin and bones. "Because of Stanford, she had——"

"That's enough," Devon said through gritted teeth. "Don't speak about my wife as if she's not in the room. I had a choice, and I chose Mina." Devon looked at her, his demeanour softening. "Trust me. Fate granted me a boon."

Lillian leaned closer and whispered in Mina's ear, "How interesting. Perhaps Mr Masters is not so wicked after all."

Mina managed a smile, but heat coiled low in her belly. Devon thought their meeting was fated? He saw their marriage as a blessing?

She tried not to get too excited.

The words he'd whispered to her last night entered her mind.

I love making you smile as much as I love making you come.

Might their feelings grow into something more profound?

Might lust and longing lead to love?

"We ladies could remain in your office, Mr Chance," she said, gesturing to the opulent furnishings. The sooner Devon dealt with Mr Wenham, the sooner they could focus on their marriage. "We can occupy ourselves while hiding from your patrons. No one need know we're in the building."

Mr Chance scanned Lillian's pleasing countenance with some annoyance. "Very well. Under no circumstances are you to leave this room. I'll have a maid bring tea and a light repast."

Lillian smiled and batted her lashes. "We would prefer sherry, Mr Chance. There's a dreadful chill in the air, and one must do something to heat the blood."

Mr Chance gestured to the row of crystal decanters on the console table. "You may have brandy or port, Miss Ware. Fortune's Den is a gentlemen's establishment. What use would I have for sherry?"

"Do you not keep female company, sir?" Lillian teased.

"I'm a busy man, Miss Ware. I don't have time for self-indulgent nonsense." Looking a little tense, he turned to Devon. "You will participate in no more than half the games tonight, and Sigmund will watch you like a hawk." He looked at the hulk of a man standing near the door. "If you threaten Wenham in front of other patrons, Sigmund will throw you out."

Mr Bradbury huffed and might have objected had Devon not given him a firm nudge in the ribs and said, "We agree to your conditions."

"Excellent." Mr Chance withdrew his pocket watch and checked the time. "The first game starts in half an hour. You'll take port in the card room while we wait for the players to arrive."

Devon nodded. "Agreed."

"We will entertain ourselves here," Mina repeated.

Needing a private word, her husband cupped her elbow and drew her aside. "Promise me you won't leave this room," Devon whispered softly against her ear. "I can't concentrate on the game when all I can think about is you."

She placed her palm on his chest, relishing the feel of hard muscle beneath her fingers, and closed her eyes against his hot breath. "Be careful. I don't trust Mr Wenham."

"Promise me, Mina, else I'll go out of my mind with worry."

His words breezed through her like a lover's caress. As a drunkard might ache for his next flagon of wine, she could think of nothing but needing Devon's naked body pressed against hers.

She looked at him. "You can trust me."

He smiled. "Loyalty should be rewarded."

His husky whisper left every nerve tingling. "While you're gone, I shall think of a way you might compensate me for my efforts."

He stroked her elbow with his thumb. "My mind is running amok, thinking of all the wicked things I might do to you. There's no way in hell I can concentrate on the game."

"You must," she said, aware Mr Bradbury and Mr Chance were impatient to leave. "You must beat Mr Wenham if we're to learn the truth."

Devon released her. He delved into his waistcoat pocket and removed the tiny pearl she'd placed in his palm the night they married. "I have the lucky charm you gave me."

She was surprised he'd kept it. She'd expected to find it covered in dust at the back of a drawer. "Then you have the force of nature behind you. Fate means for us to conquer our demons."

He slipped it safely back into his pocket, brushed his fingers over her cheek, and left with Mr Chance and Mr Bradbury.

Even this brief separation proved difficult.

Consumed by her addiction, the deep yearning had her mind inventing a story of their reunion, their journey home, and how they would spend the dark hours until dawn.

"Well, who would have thought it possible?" Lillian's laugh drew Mina from her reverie. "Your marriage of convenience is now a love match. Mr Masters is besotted with you."

Mina turned to her friend, the rush of excitement making her a tad unsteady on her feet. "He is not besotted. You spend so much time researching your book it has clouded your judgement."

Lillian shook her head. "I have spent the last few months observing couples' interactions. Mr Masters looks at you the way my brother looks at his wife Eliza—as if there is no other person in the world but her. You can feel the thrum of erotic tension in the air."

She could not argue with the last point. When alone with Devon, it was like the stars had collided, throwing her off kilter.

"It is different in my case," she said, moving to pour a glass of port to calm her nerves. "You've seen my husband. He has such a powerful presence, one cannot help but lust after him."

Lillian nodded when Mina offered to pour her a glass,

too. "Then I know the perfect way to pass the time. You will tell me all your secrets, and I shall take notes."

"Notes! I am not discussing my relationship with Devon."

"But I would like to know how things progress in a marriage. How does one move from indifference to lust? When does it become love? And do you think men use desire to control us, to make us think we're the weaker sex?"

"We're not the weaker sex, Lillian. Devon often seeks my opinion before making a decision." Was that why she loved him? Sometimes he looked at her like she was the air he needed to breathe. "Society deems us weak, but not all men treat us so."

"Such men are a rare breed." Lillian accepted the proffered glass of port and sat on the green velvet sofa. "Perhaps men without titles are different. They have fewer expectations."

She was referring to a certain duke she admired.

"Speaking of men obsessed, the Duke of Dounreay rarely takes his eyes off you." Mina sat beside her friend. "He's young and handsome and strikes me as a man who would permit his wife some liberties."

Lillian scoffed. "The handsome ones are highly dangerous. A lady might make a fool of herself over a man like Dounreay. Besides, he won't marry an Englishwoman, nor will he tolerate his wife journeying to Egypt to investigate tombs. And before you ask, yes, he has said as much."

"Is that why you avoid him?"

"I avoid him because his physique would put a Greek god to shame. He makes me all giddy and tongue-tied, and I'll likely ruin myself and be forced to live a life of servitude."

"The mystic said you'd marry a man in a kilt," Mina teased.

"She said I'd marry a man who bears his knees in public."

Lillian took a gulp of port and gave a weary sigh. "But it won't be the Duke of Dounreay."

In the silent pause that followed, Mina could feel her friend's frustration, the conflict between duty and desire. As the sister of Lord Roxburgh, she was expected to marry well, not seek selfish pursuits.

"You're in love with Mr Masters," Lillian said, excited. "I've been studying the signs as part of my research."

Mina laughed. "What signs?"

Lillian began counting on her fingers. "Your face flushed when he whispered in your ear. Regardless of who is talking, you stare at him like you're in a trance. You touch him at every opportunity."

"Is that not lust?"

It was more than that. It was a heady mix of intense attraction and profound tenderness. And it was growing deeper by the day.

"From my observations, those consumed with lust move more frantically. It's less sensual and more urgent."

"Your observations?" Mina felt a slight rush of panic. At balls and soirees, Lillian had taken to disappearing to the ladies' retiring room for long periods. "Please tell me you're not spying on amorous couples."

Lillian shrugged. "Someone has to help innocent women understand their emotions. Do you know how many have been fooled into thinking they've made a love match? Do you know how many young women are ruined because they cannot distinguish between lust and love?"

"Too many," Mina confessed.

She may be in danger of the latter, too. Hence why she had kept her feelings to herself. And poor Miss Howard had been duped by the banyan-wielding Mr Goldman.

"Lillian, please promise me you'll be careful." Heavens

knows what she might witness in a dark corridor at a ball. "Some gentlemen may not take kindly to you interfering in their personal affairs." Amongst the *ton*, there was always treachery afoot.

"If I can save one woman the heartache, is it not worth it, Mina?"

Her thoughts flicked briefly to Arabella. Mina would do anything to help Devon's sister find peace. And she knew better than most how it hurt to be the subject of cruel gossip.

"We have at least two hours to spare," she said, desperate to fill the time. "If explaining my feelings might help prevent someone suffering, then ask me anything, and I shall try to be accommodating. Though I will not speak of our private inter-actions."

Lillian's countenance brightened. "I have a notebook and pencil in my reticule and a long list of questions." She placed her glass on the side table and fumbled in her silk purse. "I've heard lust and love explained as an addiction and …."

Lillian continued mumbling facts, but Mina's thoughts turned to Devon. There were some things a lady needed to know. Namely, craving physical release with a man one desired was like the worst kind of hunger.

Craving love hurt.

Fortune's Den was unlike other gaming establishments. Men came to partake in the serious sport of gambling. Sigmund threw them out if they were too drunk, rowdy, or disturbed other patrons. Aaron Chance dragged them into a nearby alley and let them feel the power of his fists. He made sure they knew not to cause trouble again.

Amid the hush, one could feel the tension with the drop of every card. The best gamblers took time to study their opponents. Men were made and broken at Fortune's Den, and still, they came in droves.

Devon prowled the candlelit room, studying the elated faces of the few who'd won enough money to placate their wives. He watched the losers stumble from their chairs and down liquor to drown their sorrows.

For the first time in years, he felt a flicker of discontent, a pang of distaste for the vice that had made him a wealthy man.

"Will you sit down for the next game?" Bradbury said, itching to play. His skill was average at best. Loose women were his vice, hence why he knew every one of Madame LaRue's Cyprians by name.

"I should have time for one before Wenham arrives"

As Devon stalked about the place, trying to keep his temper, a plan formed in his mind. When it came to the high-stakes game, he would beat the other seven men who had paid to play. Then let them recoup their losses if they agreed to leave him alone with Wenham.

"Why the need for this charade?" Bradbury whispered, a little vexed. "You're not usually so lenient with men who cross you. Let us find Wenham and beat a confession out of him before the real game begins. We'll have better odds of winning if he doesn't play."

Rather than cower in corners as he'd done at school, Bradbury liked to punch first and ask questions later. He enjoyed a fight more than the next man.

"I'd love nothing more than to silence the fool for good. But I need information. I need facts. I'll not risk Sir Oswald charging me with a crime." He would not leave Mina alone in the house while he was locked in a damn prison cell.

186

"You're certain she didn't lie about the attack?"

Unsure if he had heard correctly, Devon said, "If you're referring to Mina, I pray it was a slip of the tongue. She is not a bawdy house wench who invents fantasies for a living. Cursed saints! You've seen the marks on her neck."

Bradbury raised his hands in mock surrender. "I merely meant some women invent stories to get male attention. Some have been known to inflict injuries upon themselves. Under the circumstances, she's probably desperate to keep you at home."

Devon turned on Bradbury, his anger barely contained. "Don't dare insinuate my wife hurt herself," he said, his voice a low growl. "And what circumstances are you referring to?"

Bradbury was quick to diffuse their argument. "I'm sorry. I mean, she might have heard about Belinda and sought a means to keep you from straying."

God's teeth!

He had invented the name when Bradbury persisted in asking questions. He hated that anyone thought him capable of betraying his wife. Yes, they'd not married for love, but he'd made vows, all the same. Despite the odds, he had developed a deep connection to the woman who bore his name.

"There is no Belinda," he whispered.

Bradbury blinked in shock. "What? You gave your mistress of three years her congé to please the Stanford chit?"

Stanford chit!

What the hell was Bradbury's problem?

As he could not betray Arabella, he said, "I don't give a damn about her but I do care about my wife. Say one more word and Belinda won't be the only person receiving their congé."

Bradbury's arrogant snort grated. "We've been friends for

187

seventeen years. Surely you know I have your best interests at heart. The woman has you under a spell. How do you know she isn't intent on ruining your life because she blames you for her brother's death?"

Devon noticed Aaron Chance leaning against the door jamb, watching them, and so took a calming breath. "I suggest we sit down to play the next game before we're thrown out for brawling with each other."

Bradbury frowned.

But then Wenham strode into the card room with Lord Peterson, a fool who had invested in so many lame schemes he'd been close to bankruptcy three times or more.

The fop must have read something sinister in Devon's expression because as soon as their gazes locked, Wenham backed slowly out of the room and bolted.

Devon marched through the card room and broke into a sprint as soon as he burst out onto Aldgate Street.

Bradbury was hot on his heels. "The bastard turned left," Bradbury cried, pointing to a figure dodging people on the pavement.

They gave chase.

Devon came to an abrupt halt on the corner of Houndsditch. He stared down the dark street, listening for the clip of booted footsteps. He heard the grim moans of hungry children huddled in doorways. The wails of babes and their mothers' desperate efforts to quieten them.

"Let's try the churchyard." Bradbury was already crossing the street, heading towards the looming shadow of St Ann's. "Only guilty men run. Wenham clearly has something to hide."

Unless Wenham feared he'd get a beating.

"When we find him, we need to question him," Devon

reiterated. "Once we gain a confession, I mean to take him to the Great Marlborough Street police office."

The rickety wooden gate to the churchyard was open. They crept quietly along the grass verge, not the gravel path, peering around crooked headstones as they passed.

Black clouds filled the night sky. It was so dark one could barely see more than a foot or two in front. Devon pointed for Bradbury to inspect the east corner while he followed the wrought-iron fence to the west.

The eerie whisper of the wind breezing through the trees raised the hairs on Devon's nape. Then he saw a black mound huddled behind a tombstone. He reached out and grabbed Wenham by the arm.

"Don't think you can hide from me," Devon snarled.

But then Bradbury's loud curse rent the air.

A muffled argument ensued.

Devon looked down to find he'd dragged a vagabond from his makeshift bed, but the man was too drunk to notice.

Fearing what Bradbury might do to Wenham, Devon raced across the graveyard, almost tripping on broken stones.

"We know it was you!" Bradbury punched Wenham on the nose, the crack preceding the sudden spurt of blood. "Else, why run?"

Wenham took a hard thump to the stomach, and his legs buckled.

"Let him speak," Devon demanded.

"Why don't we just kill the bastard?" Bradbury yanked Wenham up by the scruff of his coat and shook him. "If a man hurt my wife, I'd bury him six feet under."

Wenham struggled to catch his breath but cried, "Wait! If this is about the apology you want posted in *The Times*, I mean to do it tomorrow."

"It's about the attack on his wife," Bradbury growled.

"Attack? I explained that when you found us."

He was referring to the incident at Captain Howard's ball.

Devon stepped into the fray. He gripped Bradbury's arm, a silent instruction for him to release the gent. "Stanford knew the deed to the land you planned to mine was fake. When you found out he'd broken into your house and stolen it, you killed him."

Wenham shook his head vehemently. "What? He only stole the deed to punish me for not marrying his sister."

The thought of Mina marrying this fool turned Devon's stomach.

"So you killed him," Bradbury snapped.

"No! He had my damn deed. I needed it back."

"Perhaps your temper got the better of you," Devon said. One might mean to bargain or barter, only to stab a man in a sudden fit of rage. "Stanford hired a former runner from Bow Street to investigate your claim. He went to Staffordshire and spoke to the landowner."

Wenham's eyes widened in horror.

"I have your deed," Devon said, though went on to lie. "I have proof it's a forgery. The landowner has passed the matter to the local magistrate, and a warrant has been issued for your arrest. I'm to take you to Great Marlborough Street for questioning."

"No!" Wenham dropped to his knees. "It's all lies."

"Then you won't mind answering Sir Oswald's questions."

Bradbury yanked the fellow to his feet. "Admit you met with Stanford on Waterloo Bridge," he cried, his nostrils flaring. He gripped Wenham by the throat and squeezed his jugular. "Admit you hurled him into the river when he refused to give you the deed."

Devon let Bradbury apply a reasonable amount of pressure. "Answer him!"

"No! I—I arranged to meet him on the bridge," Wenham croaked as Bradbury choked him, "but only because he wished to negotiate a price for the deed." Panicked, he hit Bradbury's hand. "I—I swear."

Mother of all saints!

Bradbury was right.

Wenham was guilty.

Devon instructed Bradbury to release the villain before he crushed his windpipe. "Let him breathe. We need to hear his recount of the event." He faced the pathetic creature. "So you stabbed Stanford when he refused to hand over the document, then threw him into the Thames."

"No! He tried to blackmail me." Wenham gasped for breath. He rubbed his throat as if it pained him. "He wanted money in exchange for the deed, else he threatened to tell everyone I don't own the land."

"Liar!" Bradbury cried.

"It's the truth. Stanford gave me a day to think on the matter."

"Yet he's not here to verify your claim," Devon said.

"Why would I kill him when I need the deed back?"

"Because you expected to break into his house and find it there." Devon was tired of listening to the fop's excuses. But he didn't trust Sir Oswald to investigate the matter properly. "I'm taking you to Peel." He grabbed Wenham by the scruff of his coat. "You can explain it all to him."

"Wait! Mrs Fitzroy saw me."

The comment stole the wind from Devon's sails. "What?"

"I saw Mrs Fitzroy heading along Wellington Street. She wore a blue cloak like she'd been to the opera, but it was late."

"How late?" Devon said.

"Three o'clock. Stanford wanted to meet after the game at Boodle's. Maybe she followed him. I saw her outside the club earlier that evening."

Bradbury gave a mocking snort. "You better hope she supports your claim. Though if she murdered Stanford, I doubt she'll confirm she was there."

"I'll make a statement," Wenham blurted.

Devon stared down his nose. "Damn right you will."

Chapter Sixteen

Devon was quiet, subdued, lost in his thoughts.

Mina studied her husband as he sat in the dark confines of their carriage, his face and expression hidden in the shadows.

After escorting Mr Wenham to the Queen Street police office, he had returned to Fortune's Den and hardly spoken since. Mr Chance sensed a problem and reassured them he knew the magistrate well and they could trust Sir James to uncover the truth.

"Is everything all right?" she said when the silence became unbearable. The pressure to solve the case had taken its toll.

"Yes." His heavy tone confirmed a problem.

"You were quite abrupt with Mr Bradbury when we parted ways. And you barely said two words to Lillian when we took her home."

"I have a lot on my mind."

A lady did not question her husband. She did not make demands upon him, but theirs was not a marriage by usual standards, and he always sought her counsel.

"Don't shut me out, Devon. Something is troubling you. I can sense when you're worried." He had acted in much the same way before leaving for Aylesbury. What was he hiding?

Did he have another secret?

"It's been a long night. And you're tired."

She sat forward. "I'm never too tired to share your burden."

After a brief pause he exhaled deeply, his demeanour relaxing. "I've known Bradbury for seventeen years, but I've never known him to be so irrational, so volatile. He would have murdered Wenham had I given my permission."

In truth, she disliked Mr Bradbury. Tonight, she had caught him looking at her as if she were dirt on his shoe. During dinner, he had been amusing and quite affable. The man had stared at her with his angelic blue eyes, though she feared they masked a terrible darkness.

"He's quite protective of you."

"I'm one of the few people he respects."

Yet she could not see what Devon gained from their friendship. "He seemed convinced Mr Wenham murdered my brother. Based on nothing but supposition, he condemned what might be an innocent man."

Being insightful, he caught the distrust in her tone. "What are you saying? He wanted us to think Wenham was guilty?"

She thought for a moment. "The question we must ask ourselves is why Mr Bradbury was prepared to throttle a man before hearing a confession." The hairs on her nape prickled to attention as she considered all possibilities. "Logic says there are only two, perhaps three reasons."

It did not take Devon long to come to the same conclusion. Indeed, he quickly proved their thoughts were aligned.

"Bradbury may have prior knowledge of Wenham's

guilt," he said, though did not sound convinced, "and for some reason unbeknown cannot reveal how or why."

"Perhaps he was there that night."

"Then why not say so? And what would he be doing near Waterloo Bridge at three o'clock in the morning?"

She shrugged. Who knew what the man did during the witching hour? "Perhaps it's something scandalous and he doesn't want you to think ill of him, which brings me to the second reason. Mr Bradbury thinks so highly of you, he would hurt anyone you despised."

Devon gave an incredulous snort. "I'm quite capable of fighting my own battles, and Bradbury knows it. Yes, he looks upon me as a brother, but he wouldn't risk his neck on a hunch."

"Then logic suggests something quite terrifying." Nerves fluttered in her chest, but she had sworn never to lie to him. "What if Mr Bradbury murdered my brother?"

She should dismiss the notion, yet a pang in her gut said there was some truth to the claim. Devon disagreed, of course.

"Bradbury didn't kill your brother. He had no motive. No reason to commit such a heinous crime. And I doubt he would hide the truth from me. He's a braggart."

"Well, he must be involved in some capacity. Else why would he be desperate to hurt Mr Wenham?"

Tension crackled in the air. With it came the realisation that Mr Bradbury kept his own secrets.

"I study men closely," Devon said, his tone more subdued. "I can read what they're thinking by their expressions, by their actions and the way they move their bodies. I would know if Bradbury meant to deceive me."

Would he?

Sometimes people missed the obvious.

"There is a difference." She knew so from her experiences with Thomas and his endless lies. "When you trust someone, when you care about them and think those feelings are reciprocated, you're blind to the fact they might deceive you."

She had trusted Thomas' word in the beginning, but like a dying rose come winter, her faith had withered and blown away with the wind.

A chilly silence descended.

Seconds passed, the clip of hooves on the road like the ticking of a clock. Then Devon rapped on the roof and instructed Simpkin to take a detour and stop outside Mrs Fitzroy's abode in Golden Square.

"I need to question the widow tonight." His tone rang with steely determination. "I'll be damned if I'll wait until morning. I need to know if she killed your brother, else I shall go out of my mind wondering if Bradbury has played me for a fool."

"You're not a fool, Devon." Keen to calm his volatile temper, she reached across and gripped his hand. "You're the most intelligent man I know. None of this is your fault."

And yet he had not noticed the tender way she looked at him now. He had not considered she might be in lust and in love with him. Which only went to prove her point about Mr Bradbury.

"You're biased," he said, his tone lighter.

"Because I'm your wife?"

"Because we've been intimate."

She laughed. "You think my need for you clouds my judgement?"

"No, but you might see the man who pleasures you in a more flattering light. You do like me pleasuring you, Mina?"

"You know I do."

Even in the gloom, she could see the haze of desire in his eyes as he looked at her lips. She knew he sought a distraction from unwanted thoughts. He confirmed her theory when he pulled her across the carriage and into his lap.

He settled his hands on her waist. His mouth found her jaw, then her lips, and they fell into a passionate kiss that left her pushing her hands into his hair and writhing like a wanton.

I love you!

It was too soon to tell him.

But she could hint at the possibility.

"I love the way you kiss me," she breathed when he moved to suck her earlobe. "I love everything you do to me, Devon. I could spend my life in your arms and die happy."

I love you so much it hurts!

"Straddle me," he growled.

She quickly unbuttoned her pelisse, hiked her skirts to her thighs and came to sit astride him—a mound of material swamping them both.

He gripped her hips, rocking her back and forth, simulating the act they were both desperate to perform. "I need to be inside you. I can't wait until we get home. I need to own you, Mina. I need to possess you, to drive into you over and over, to think about nothing but you hugging my cock."

"Do it then." She could barely catch her breath. "Own me."

Their gazes locked in the darkness.

It was a moment of pure magic.

He unbuttoned his trousers, and though she could not see his throbbing erection, she felt it slide into her seconds later.

"God, love, you were made for me." Holding her, he pushed deeper into her body. "I love how good you feel."

She could stay like this forever. "Don't worry about my

pleasure." Hearing his lustful groans was enough. "Take what you need."

While she sensed his desperation, while he'd made it clear in words, he confirmed he was determined to lose control.

"I'll make it up to you later. Make you come so hard, love."

And then he was thrusting into her, the rocking of the carriage helping him to drive in and out with frantic momentum.

Enchanted by the power in every plunge, she watched his face. Lillian might say this was a lewd act, but Devon Masters was making love to her. This was an act of intimacy, of dependency, of trust.

He told her what he needed.

He whispered words he meant.

He watched her, those dark eyes devouring hers as if she were his life force. He wasn't owning her.

He was proving she owned him. And the rush of hope filling her heart was as satisfying as the deepest climax.

The church bells struck the midnight hour. Devon knocked on Mrs Fitzroy's door for the fifth time. The four-storey townhouse was in darkness, though he persisted in trying to rouse someone from their bed.

Mina climbed down from the carriage and glanced up at the facade. "Devon, she is probably at a party or entertaining Captain Howard."

Since learning Mrs Fitzroy was near Waterloo Bridge on

the night Thomas died, Mina couldn't help but wonder if the widow had acted at the captain's behest.

Had the military man used tactics to persuade his lover to commit murder? Was she wracked with remorse? So much so, she had come to the churchyard to see Thomas' grave?

Devon stepped away from the door. "I'm not leaving until I've spoken to her. We will wait in the carriage until dawn if necessary."

His suspicions about Mr Bradbury were eating away at him like a slow-acting poison.

"Very well, but should we not be a little more inconspicuous?" A person could remain at home for days, especially if it meant avoiding the hangman's noose. "Should we not wait on the opposite side of the square or hide in the gardens?"

"Yes, you're right. But it's too cold to wait outdoors." He stepped away, cupped her elbow and drew her back to their carriage.

They were about to climb inside when the creak of rusty iron hinges stole their attention. They turned to find a maid closing the gate to the servants' quarters. She wore a heavy travelling cloak, the raised hood obscuring her face. She carried a basket on her arm, though Mina knew of no markets open at this hour.

"How fortuitous," Mina whispered.

"Indeed." Devon cleared his throat. "Excuse me. Might you tell me if your mistress is home? We need to speak to Mrs Fitzroy as a matter of urgency."

The shy maid kept her hood raised and barely met their gaze. "She ain't home, sir. She went to Brighton yesterday and won't be back for a week."

"Damnation," Devon muttered under his breath.

Mina could feel his frustration. For the next seven days, his distrust for Mr Bradbury would fester like an open wound.

"Might we ask you one question?" Mina said, keen to discover if Mrs Fitzroy was away from home on the night of Thomas' murder.

"I can't stop now." The maid hurried along the street, clinging to her basket as if it contained the Crown Jewels.

Mina studied the servant. Why would the maid leave at this hour? It was most odd. Then she noticed the woman wore a sparkling ring on her finger and knew the cloaked figure wasn't a maid at all.

"Wait!" Mina picked up her skirts and charged after the woman. "Mrs Fitzroy! We just want to ask you a few questions."

A carriage turned into the square, and the woman waved frantically at the coachman. "Cribbins! Stop! For heaven's sake, stop!"

Devon broke into a sprint. He grabbed the woman by the arm before the coachman could tug the reins.

"Let me go! Release me at once!" Amid her cries and protests, her hood fell back, revealing the widow's famed auburn curls.

"Mrs Fitzroy, we mean you no harm," Mina said. The woman acted like they meant to accuse her of witchcraft, bind her legs and throw her head first into the Thames. "We want to ask you a few questions about the night Thomas was killed. A witness places you at the scene. Running only makes you look guilty."

Mrs Fitzroy's face crumpled in fear. "What? You think I had something to do with your brother's death?"

"We know Thomas acted as a model for your painting lessons at Mr Goldman's studio," Devon said, releasing her before she hit him with the basket. "We know you're Captain Howard's mistress, and you're blackmailing Miss Howard."

Panicked, Mrs Fitzroy glanced up and down the street.

"None of that matters now. Please, you must let me leave before it's too late. I pitied Thomas. I didn't kill him. But someone means to kill me."

"Were you on the bridge that night?" Devon pressed.

Tears filled the widow's eyes. "Please, Mr Masters, I must leave before the devil returns to murder me in my bed."

Mina touched the woman's arm. "Who means you harm?"

She shook her head. "It doesn't matter."

"We're not leaving until you tell us what you know," Devon said.

He needed answers, and they were close to discovering the truth. Mina could feel it in her bones.

"A witness places you at the scene," Mina said, making one last attempt to force a confession. "Miss Howard has agreed to make a statement to say you're blackmailing her. Sir Oswald will issue a warrant for your arrest. They're looking for someone to blame, so I doubt you'll get a fair trial. You'll hang if you don't trust us with the truth."

Mrs Fitzroy swallowed hard and her shoulders slumped. "I'm not blackmailing Miss Howard."

Cribbins brought the carriage to a crashing halt a few feet away. "Everythin' all right, ma'am? Do you want me to climb down and thump the blighter?"

Devon sneered at the scrawny fellow seated atop the box. "You're welcome to try, though you must consider how you'll drive this vehicle when I've broken all your fingers."

Cribbins made to climb down, but Mrs Fitzroy raised a staying hand before facing Devon. "I'll speak to you, but only in my carriage. You have five minutes, Mr Masters, no more."

They settled inside the vehicle and Devon closed the door.

"Begin by explaining why you're blackmailing the sister

of your lover," Devon said, wasting no time. "Are you in cahoots with Goldman? Was extorting money from the Howards always your plan?"

"In cahoots?" Mrs Fitzroy screwed up her nose in disdain. "Goldman is the worst kind of predator. He lies and cheats and knows how to turn young girls' heads. I was attempting to save Sir Thomas and Miss Howard from that manipulating serpent of Satan."

"By threatening to tell Captain Howard?" Mina asked.

"By scaring her enough that she might consider her reputation and cease visiting that den of iniquity."

"And yet you tricked my brother. He agreed to sit for no one but Miss Howard. He was obsessed with her and would not have embarrassed himself for any other woman."

The widow sat forward. "I thought he had agreed to sit for me. I soon realised Goldman had the poor fellow smoking opium to lull him into submission. I have been back to the studio once since. To collect my materials."

Goldman knew she could provide Captain Howard with an alibi for the night of the murder. An alibi that contradicted Mr Wenham's statement. Mrs Fitzroy could not entertain her lover in bed and be on Waterloo Bridge.

Mina told her as much. "Mr Wenham saw you dressed in a blue cloak and heading towards the bridge at a ridiculous hour. So which is it? Were you in bed or on the bridge?"

"Both. But it's a complicated story."

"We're not leaving until you tell us."

After a tense pause, the widow said, "After attending Goldman's opium parties, Sir Thomas had grown anxious and was suffering from paranoia. I heard about the duel and knew you would kill him, Mr Masters. So, I waited outside Boodle's, hoping to speak to him and prevent a tragedy."

That supported Mr Wenham's claim that he had seen her outside the gentlemen's club.

"Mr Wenham followed Sir Thomas out, and an argument ensued. I heard them agree to meet on the bridge. But Captain Howard saw me waiting and presumed I'd come seeking a liaison." A blush touched her cheeks. "We were not unfamiliar with each other, you see."

"And so you left with Captain Howard?" Mina confirmed.

"Yes. I saw Sir Thomas speaking to Mr Bradbury and assumed he was seeking an apology. I hoped it would be the end of the matter."

"Bradbury?" The muscles in Devon's jaw tensed.

Mr Bradbury said he had not seen Thomas.

He'd said he had waited at the Albany for an hour.

He had lied, and the thought filled Mina with dread.

"Yes," Mrs Fitzroy said. "They spoke briefly and parted ways. Captain Howard climbed into my carriage and we returned to Golden Square."

"But you said you were on the bridge."

The widow shifted uncomfortably. "Clarence was drunk and fell asleep as soon as his head hit the pillow. I couldn't shake the thought that something terrible might happen, so Cribbins took me as far as Wellington Street and waited while I walked the short distance to the bridge. I hoped to persuade Sir Thomas to offer Mr Masters an apology."

"Did you see Wenham?" Devon snapped.

"Yes, we passed each other on Wellington Street but never spoke."

"And what of my brother?" Mina coughed against a sudden rush of emotion. "Did you see him?"

"No. I presumed he had walked the other way. I returned home and found Clarence still asleep in bed."

A heavy silence ensued.

Had Mr Wenham murdered Thomas?

Was Mrs Fitzroy lying?

Had she encountered Thomas on the bridge?

"None of this explains why you're leaving town in fear of your life," Mina said, though she wondered if Mr Wenham had made threats.

The widow peered out into the dark street. "Because someone broke into my house in the dead of night, believing your brother had given me a document for safekeeping. He appeared in my chamber and frightened me to death. Thankfully, he left, but not before ransacking drawers and upturning the furniture."

Devon was quick to reply. "You speak of Mr Wenham. He came looking for a land deed. When he saw you in Wellington Street at three in the morning, he must have presumed you'd met Thomas Stanford."

Mrs Fitzroy nodded. "He said he would kill me if he discovered I'd lied. I've never seen him so angry, so deranged."

"Rest assured, the gentleman is currently being questioned at the Queen Street police office," Mina said, somewhat relieved Mr Wenham wasn't roaming the streets, a lunatic free to cause mayhem. "He knows we have the deed, so you have nothing to fear."

Mrs Fitzroy collapsed back in the seat and sighed with relief. "Thank heavens. I've hardly slept the last few nights and planned to visit my sister in Worcester for a few weeks."

The atmosphere turned tense.

Devon sat forward. "Madam, I must advise you to leave town until we find the person who murdered Thomas Stanford. It's not safe for you here, not when you were seen in the vicinity of Waterloo Bridge."

The lady clutched her throat. "Is Mr Wenham not the killer?"

"No. In front of witnesses, he placed you at the scene of the crime. He may say as much in his statement." Devon's tone was grave. "If the magistrate doesn't come knocking, the real killer may think you saw him on the bridge. He may seek to silence you for good."

The widow whimpered. "Then I must ask you to leave my carriage, Mr Masters, so I might be on my way."

"Not until you confirm or deny you were the person who sent the letter to Sir Oswald blaming me for the crime," Devon said.

Mrs Fitzroy had the decency to look embarrassed. "When I saw Mr Bradbury talking to Sir Thomas and discovered the poor fellow was dead hours later, I assumed you were to blame. But then you married Miss Stanford, and that fiend Wenham broke into my home. I accept I made a mistake."

"A mistake that may have cost my husband his life," Mina cried.

Devon was the obvious choice of villain.

But this case proved the devil wore a less obvious disguise.

"Did you visit the churchyard on the day of my brother's funeral?" Mina added, as who else could it be?

"I went to pay my respects and to atone. I might have prevented a murder had I intervened. I blame Goldman, of course. He used Sir Thomas and manipulated events to suit his purpose."

"Don't worry about Goldman," Devon said, his tone dangerously dark. "I shall ensure he receives his come-uppance."

The lady nodded profusely. "I've told you all I know. Please, I must ask you to leave."

Devon moved to the edge of the seat and opened the carriage door. "From Worcester, you will write to Sir Oswald and tell him you'd made a mistake. And you will make a statement detailing Wenham's threatening manner."

"Yes, yes," the widow said, ushering them to alight.

Indeed, as soon as their feet touched the pavement, the coachman flicked the reins, and the vehicle charged away into the night.

Chapter Seventeen

Office of the Order
Hart Street, Covent Garden

Devon had not slept a wink last night.

He could not make love to his wife because the thoughts crippling his mind would undoubtedly affect his performance. This morning, he had sat at the breakfast table, staring at the eggs on his plate as the devil's darkness consumed him.

Bradbury would feel more than the sharp edge of his tongue.

And yet that was not what disturbed him.

If Bradbury had lied about seeing Sir Thomas on the night of the murder, what else had he lied about? Mina said her attacker was taller than Wenham, broader than Lord Kinver. Bradbury fitted the profile and knew Devon went to Aylesbury every Thursday.

He blinked and shook his head to dismiss the grim thought.

"Well? Are you going to knock on the door?" Mina said.

They were standing on the steps of Lucius Daventry's

Hart Street office, where troubled people called to hire an enquiry agent.

"Yes." For fear of scaring her, he had not explained his fears fully. "We need help, and there is only one man I trust implicitly."

Dismissing all doubts—for he was about to name Bradbury as a suspect in the case—he seized the brass knocker and hammered twice.

A stout woman answered, her warm smile banishing the coldness chasing his bones. "Can I help you, sir?"

"I'm Devon Masters. I have a noon appointment with Lucius Daventry." He gestured to Mina, his friend, his lover, the constant object of his affection. "And this is my wife Mina."

As he introduced her, something stirred in his chest, maybe pride at marrying such an exceptional woman, maybe something else.

They were welcomed inside and shown into an elegant drawing room, not an office or study. After directing them to one of two sofas positioned around a low table, the house-keeper—as she proudly informed them—went to fetch tea.

"How long have you known Mr Daventry?" Mina said, scanning the painting of the goddess Themis on the wall before taking a seat.

"Daventry makes himself known to all the *dangerous* men of the *ton*. We met at White's a few years ago, spent the evening drinking brandy and putting the world to rights."

"Does he know about Arabella?"

"Love, no one knows about Arabella but you."

Did she not understand what that meant? That their connection was so profound, he had told her his greatest secret?

Perhaps she did because she smiled like he had given her

a precious gift. "Did you not think to hire him to find out who'd hurt her?"

"What was the point when Kinver admitted responsibility?" He had no reason to suspect another man was involved. "But I cannot tell Daventry about Arabella without speaking to her first."

"I understand," she said, proving she was his greatest ally.

Daventry strode into the room moments later, power radiating from his calm persona. He was the overseer, a man who advised his agents but rarely became embroiled in cases.

Devon inclined his head. "Thank you for agreeing to meet us at such short notice." Devon had delivered a note to the office after leaving Mrs Fitzroy last night and had received a reply a little over an hour ago.

"You're capable of dealing with most problems yourself. I know you wouldn't ask unless it was important." Daventry greeted Mina with a respectful bow. "You look radiant, Mrs Masters. Married life suits you."

A pink blush touched her cheeks, and Devon knew erotic visions of their lovemaking filled her head.

"Thank you, sir. Fate opened a door, and I took a chance and stepped through." She looked at him, not Daventry, and he felt a wild rush of energy coursing in his veins. "Thank heavens I did. My life has changed for the better."

"Most people fail to appreciate Masters' good qualities."

"Do not count me amongst them, sir." Her gaze pinned Devon to the spot, stroking him like a sensual caress. "I appreciate him more with each passing day."

Devon inhaled deeply. The addiction that had him thrusting into her body like a rampant buck, the addiction that made her the constant focus of his attention, was not addiction at all.

It was love.

Holy Mother Mary!

He had fallen in love with his wife!

"But we've not had the easiest of starts," she said, her sad tone compelling him to put things right, to make her happy.

"Hence why we're here."

Daventry motioned to the sofa. He waited for Devon to sit and then dropped into the seat opposite. The housekeeper returned with the tea tray and poured three cups before leaving them and closing the door.

"I assume it has something to do with Thomas Stanford's murder." Daventry reached for the leather notebook and pencil on the table. "Doubtless, the leads brought you to a dead end."

Devon gave him a brief overview of events. He revealed what they knew about Goldman and Miss Howard. Mina mentioned her brother's obsession and her dealings with Wenham.

Daventry scribbled a few notes and looked up. "So you took Wenham to the magistrate in Queen Street?"

"Yes, Sir Oswald is incompetent, and I feared Bradbury might kill him if we didn't place him in custody."

"*Incompetent* is too mild a word for Sir Oswald." Daventry paused. "I have friends who would kill men to protect me. Maybe Bradbury is the possessive sort. Maybe he feels the need to make himself useful to you."

Devon shifted in the seat, distrust of his friend's motives surfacing. "Bradbury lied to me. He met with Stanford outside Boodle's on the night of the murder."

Daventry narrowed his gaze. "Maybe Mrs Fitzroy lied. You said she admitted to being in the vicinity of the bridge. She is connected to all suspects, and you caught her fleeing town after dark."

Mina swallowed a sip of tea and returned the china cup

and saucer to the table. "She seemed genuinely terrified. I felt the same way when the intruder tried to strangle me."

"Intruder?" Daventry straightened. "Someone attacked you?"

"Yes, he broke into the house last Thursday while Devon was away and tried to strangle me with a length of rope." She touched her neck, though the marks were hidden beneath a high-collared pelisse. "Thank heavens for Miss Marmalade. Her quick response saved my life."

"Miss Marmalade?" Daventry sounded intrigued.

"An insolent parrot," Devon said, though he ignored the bird's insults now. "Mina brought the cage to our bedchamber." And thank the Lord she had. "It was so dark, the blackguard thought he had been disturbed by a maid and ran."

Like Devon, Daventry found nothing amusing about the incident. "Did you see his face? Did the devil say anything? Was it Wenham come in search of the deed?"

"He wore a mask and merely called me vile names."

Daventry looked at Devon and frowned. "Do you think it might be Goldman?"

Devon shook his head, his heart a heavy weight hanging in his chest. "We're here because I suspect it might be Bradbury."

Mina gasped. "Mr Bradbury!"

Having seen betrayal played out in so many ways, Daventry was not shocked. "What evidence do you have?"

"None. Just a feeling deep in my gut."

In St Ann's churchyard, Bradbury had shown a cruel side of his character, a side he usually kept hidden. And Devon hated the way he spoke about Mina. The night at Fortune's Den had been an epiphany of sorts, and now he couldn't shake the sense that Bradbury was the root of all his troubles.

Tears filled Mina's eyes, and Devon drew her close. "But why would your friend want to hurt me? It makes no sense."

"Jealousy. Vengeance," Daventry said before explaining his point. "Masters had to marry you. And now Bradbury may feel like he has lost his friend. Perhaps he killed your brother because he persisted in making Devon's life miserable. Bradbury may believe you're doing the same."

Dumbstruck, Mina sat in silence.

"I need to know if my fears are founded," he said. "But before we continue, I must correct your misconception. I married Mina because I felt connected to her in a way I cannot explain."

Daventry smiled. "I understand perfectly. Such feelings are too powerful to ignore." He thought for a moment. "Tell me about your relationship with Bradbury. I believe you said you met at Harrow."

Bradbury had been the older pupils' whipping boy, a small and weak child with a scrawny physique. Devon was more of a rebel with a conscience and had grown tired of hearing the boy's whimpers at night.

"I befriended him when no one else would."

"And you've been close ever since?"

"Yes. We meet most days."

"You've barely seen him since we married," Mina said.

"Things are different now. Focusing on the case has left little time for anything else." He found it hard to believe Bradbury was jealous. "A man doesn't strangle a woman because his friend missed a few card games."

"That depends on the man and what demons plague him," Daventry said in the wise way many people respected. "Most murderers are possessed by an inner rage that is far from logical."

A heavy silence descended.

Devon had always known Bradbury was a little unhinged. One did not suffer trauma at school and not nurse some ill will. Was his devil-may-care attitude a means to hide a black heart? Was he rotten to the core?

"I study people closely," he said, trying to understand how he had missed the signs, how he had made such a terrible mistake. "While I know he's capable of killing a man—"

"Or a woman," Mina added.

He nodded in acknowledgement, the thought chilling him to the bone. "I'm his closest friend, yet his potential actions have brought me nothing but pain."

"Sometimes people want others to hurt as much as they do," Daventry said. "It gives them a sense of belonging. Some feel immensely powerful when they're the one offering support."

The comment hit a nerve.

Bradbury had been his constant companion during those months after Arabella's supposed death. He'd been strong and dependable. Had mentioned it was his way of repaying Devon's kindness in school. Looking back, his manner had bordered on possessive.

"What is it?" Daventry said. There was no man more astute. "You've turned a deathly shade of pale. What have you remembered?"

"Just that Bradbury was a pillar of support when I lost Arabella."

The latter part wasn't a lie. Arabella might be alive, but the light inside her had died that day.

"Remind me what happened to her?" Daventry said.

Devon narrowed his gaze. They had spoken about the incident on at least two occasions. Daventry made it his business to know everything that happened in the *ton*. His mind was as sharp as Captain Howard's rapier, which meant he sensed cracks in the story.

"It's as I've told you before," he said, keeping his nerve despite his heart hammering against his ribcage. "She ran from the garden after an interlude and was hit by a carriage charging into the mews."

The man rubbed his jaw as he contemplated the information.

Perhaps Daventry heard deceit in his tone. Perhaps Mina clasping Devon's hand had added to his suspicions.

"And yet your sister did not die at the hospital," came the comment Devon feared most. "And she's not buried in London."

"Since when did you decide to investigate me?" He hoped his mocking snort hid the inner rush of panic.

"I make it my business to investigate every possible murder amongst the aristocrats and gentry. It's why I initially asked you to drink with me at White's."

"Murder? You feared I'd killed my own sister?"

Daventry nodded. "Or your father had hurt her unintentionally. And your parents' trip to Boston proved timely. But then you explained your situation, and we became friends, and I thought you had a personal reason for keeping her condition a secret."

"Her condition?" he repeated, sounding like the parrot.

"If she's not dead, she's injured and recuperating somewhere. You keep it a secret because you fear the person who attacked her might seek to silence her for good." Daventry paused for breath. "You're not sure it was Lord Kinver, which explains why he's still alive."

Relief replaced panic.

It was like Daventry had lifted a ton weight off his shoulders, and he could finally breathe easily again. Keeping the secret had taken its toll, had made him less trusting. Now, the two people he respected most knew the truth.

Devon released the sigh he'd been holding for years. "All you say is true. Though it is Arabella's desire to remain hidden from society, not mine. She cannot remember what happened that night, and the thought of not knowing who attacked her only enhances her fears."

"The truth is the only thing that can set her free."

"We spoke to Lord Kinver," Mina said, squeezing his hand gently. "He believes someone else accosted Arabella that night. He has a list and has spent the last three years trying to find the culprit."

Daventry hummed. "Not quite the actions of a guilty man."

"No. Devon promised to consider other possibilities once we've caught my brother's murderer." There was a hint of pride in her voice, which doubtless stemmed from his willingness to concede.

Daventry glanced at his notes. "So, you want an agent to investigate the possibility Bradbury murdered Stanford and attacked your wife?"

Devon dragged his hand down his face. "I need to know if I can trust him. And though we've had some success uncovering information, I need the matter dealt with quickly." He glanced at the woman beside him, his heart softening. "I need to know Mina is safe."

"And you need to know if Bradbury attacked your sister."

Devon's breath caught in his throat. "What?"

"Bradbury was there that night. Maybe he saw her with Kinver and meant to berate her as you would have done. Or maybe he had a more sinister motive in mind."

Nausea roiled in his gut.

It couldn't be Bradbury.

Bradbury was capable of throwing Stanford into the Thames, but he would not hurt Arabella. He had no reason to despise her; he knew she loved Lord Kinver.

Mina sighed. "There is something unsavoury about him, Devon."

"He can be intimidating," he admitted.

"He has an inherent dislike for most people," she added. "He told Lillian he found her modern views distasteful. He said she was no different from a Covent Garden strumpet."

Bradbury's lofty opinions often got the better of him.

"Had you told me, I would have addressed the matter."

Had Bradbury been spying on Arabella that night and witnessed her kiss Lord Kinver? Had he made derogatory comments, enough to make her fear for her safety?

Sensing Devon's growing unease, Daventry said, "I have an idea. We'll approach this from a different angle. We'll tackle the mystery of your sister's attack first. You'll tell Bradbury she's alive."

"What the blazes!" Devon reeled like he'd been slapped. "No!"

"Do you want justice for her or not?"

"You know damn well I do."

"If Bradbury is innocent, he will merely think you trust him with your secret. You might say Mrs Masters had a positive influence on your decision."

"And if he is guilty?" Mina said a little apprehensively.

"Then my agents will be there to take him into custody. But we must be certain he is the culprit before we act." He arched a brow. "You understand what I am suggesting?"

"Yes, you want to use Arabella to lure him into a trap," he snapped. He wanted to risk the life of a woman who had already suffered beyond measure. "She's not strong enough to withstand another trauma."

Mina gripped his arm. "Devon, she will gain confidence knowing she helped catch the man who hurt her. We will prepare her. And we should tell Lord Kinver she's alive. He may still be our culprit. For Arabella's sake, we must know for sure."

"It's time she came home," Daventry said respectfully.

Devon closed his eyes against the image of his sister's scarred face.

He had sworn to protect her. Now, like a lamb to the slaughter, he would offer her as bait to trap the devil who'd betrayed them.

He made a quick mental calculation, weighing his options.

They were limited.

So, with a heavy heart, he said, "Very well."

The instincts that made men fear him said Bradbury was guilty.

Chapter Eighteen

Just like Mina had known knocking on Devon's door was the only way to solve her problems, she knew it was right that Arabella should be involved in catching her attacker.

She just prayed the woman had her brother's fortitude.

That said, Devon sat quietly in the carriage as they journeyed to Aylesbury, watching raindrops run down the windowpane, sighing like he was off to war and leaving everything he loved behind.

"None of this is your fault, Devon."

He looked at her. The pain in his eyes hurt her heart. "If Bradbury admits to attacking Arabella, I mean to kill him, Mina."

The cold finality of his words unnerved her.

"And you would hang, leaving your wife and sister without protection. What happens when a new devil tries to take advantage?"

To a penniless lord, a rich widow was a prime target.

"I've failed you both. I've let that scoundrel put his hands on you. You're stronger without me. You came to a rogue's home at midnight and got what you wanted." His gaze slipped over her body, his lips parting as if recalling their first scintillating kiss. "Surely you've realised I'm but a slave to your wants and desires."

That night, her life depended upon reasoning with him.

But she was no longer a woman satisfied with a warm place to sleep and a hearty meal. He had given her passion and excitement, a life that could be glorious if they could find a way through their current predicament.

"What is this really about, Devon?" Marriage was about honesty and compromise. Knowing when to offer support and when to ask for help in return. "I understand you're worried about Arabella, but—"

"I'm worried about you, Mina."

"Me?"

With some frustration, he dragged his hand through his sable locks. "I don't want to leave you at the convent. I can't be without you, not even for one night, and it's killing me. I feel so damn weak and vulnerable."

She sat quietly and listened.

"I'm Devon Masters. I don't tolerate betrayal." His voice brimmed with raw emotion. "Hell, men cross the street if I make eye contact. I should kill Bradbury. Yet here I am, caring about nothing but losing myself in your body, wanting you so desperately I can hardly breathe."

Her heart soared.

She struggled to calm her racing pulse whenever they were together. She could curl into his naked body and spend a lifetime in his bed.

"What do you think it means?" She would not put words into his mouth for fear of drawing the wrong conclusion.

"I know what it means." His dark gaze caressed her slowly. "I'm in love with you, Mina."

Her heart missed a beat. "It might be lust."

Lord help her! He was in love with her!

"It's not lust, though I need to bury myself inside your body with shocking frequency. I can't leave you alone tonight."

Happiness bubbled to her throat. "I'll be with Arabella."

"No, Daventry wants you to wear a nun's habit and prowl the corridors, waiting for the villain to strike."

She had to commend Mr Daventry. He did not stop to consider she might be scared, but assumed she could assist his agents in trapping the blackguard.

"I've almost lost you once, Mina. I can't risk losing you again."

She crossed the carriage and fell into his lap. "You won't lose me, Devon. I'm in love with you and plan to seduce you into bed with shocking frequency. I'd kill Mr Bradbury myself before I'd let him ruin what we have."

His mouth curled into a sinful grin. "You love me?"

"How could I not?" She pushed an errant lock of hair from his brow. "You're handsome and kind and always considerate. You saved me."

He slid his hand under her skirts and stroked her thigh. "You forgot the part where I'm wicked and ravish you senseless most days."

Her smile became a sweet moan as he edged higher, his thumb massaging her sex. "Yes, you're very wicked, Mr Masters."

"But you like me making mischief." He pushed two fingers inside her.

"I love it. I love you."

His mouth closed over hers, his tongue sweeping through her lips, seeking its mate. The deep exploration had them clawing at each other's clothes, making love until they were but a mile from Aylesbury.

"Devon, don't tug the bell pull, not yet." Mina stood at the gate, staring through the wrought iron bars. Night was upon them, and the convent gardens were dark, eerie. "My skirts are creased, and my hair is a dreadful mess. The nuns will take one look at me and know we've sinned."

He laughed as he brushed a stray lock of hair behind her ear and kissed her forehead. "We're married. It's not a sin for a man to make love to his wife."

"No, but it makes us seem desperate."

"We are desperate. Desperately in love," he said, his voice soft, his smile tender, his lips kissable. "Spare a thought for me travelling back to London alone. Forced to spend six hours in a vehicle that carries the sweet scent of our arousal."

Heat filled her chest.

Happiness brought a surge of euphoria.

But a shadow appeared in the garden, reminding her of what they risked by being here, by tempting the devil to reveal himself.

She tapped Devon's arm and gestured to the approaching figure. A woman appeared, a stream of moonlight drawing attention to her compassionate blue eyes and kind countenance.

"Good evening, Reverend Mother," Devon said warmly.

The graceful lady smiled through bars made to separate her from the trials of the external world. "It's unlike you to make a mistake, Mr Masters. Have you lost track of days?"

Devon chuckled. "No, I'm aware it's Monday. But I need your help with a matter of great importance and beg a private audience."

Without her assistance, they would have to move Arabella to another location, one that would carry a greater risk of her being hurt.

That said, while it was likely Mr Bradbury had murdered Thomas, and he was undoubtedly wicked to the core, Mina feared he was not to blame for Arabella's accident. How could anyone so close to Devon hurt him like that?

Still, the plan was in place.

They would know the truth soon.

The Mother Superior looked at Mina, prompting Devon to say, "This is Mina Masters. My wife."

The lady's smile brightened. "Arabella said you were married. You'd best come inside before you catch a chill. I'll make sure Arabella knows you're here. She is used to routine, not sudden surprises."

The serene woman unlocked the gate—that a man of athletic build could easily climb—and bid them entrance.

An instant feeling of peace settled around Mina's shoulders as she stepped into the pretty garden. It was a moment to reflect. The calm before the storm. Having spent years at her brother's mercy, a life of quietude was all she'd craved. Now, as long as Devon stood beside her, she didn't care what problems they faced.

They followed the Mother Superior's slow, graceful steps to an office. The room was spotlessly clean, the polished walnut desk uncluttered.

"Please sit down." She gestured to the chairs facing the desk. "Tell me what brings you all this way on a Monday."

They sat, and Devon reiterated why his sister chose to live peacefully at the convent and not return to London.

"For three years, you have been patient with her," he said, emotion choking his voice. "You have not asked her to leave or pressed her to take her vows."

The Mother Superior watched them over hands clasped in prayer. "We are merely tending one of the Lord's flock, an injured lamb who has lost her way. Besides, one cannot make vows to the Lord when one is in love with a man. Indeed, that is what hinders Arabella's progress."

Devon sighed. "You know I despise Lord Kinver, but I have reason to believe he may not be the person who attacked Arabella in the garden."

After hearing Lord Kinver's desperate pleas and seeing the list, Devon wanted to consider other possibilities. Yet distrust still lingered in his tone.

"We want to take her home." Mina couldn't bear the thought of Arabella sitting alone in her room, so far away from her family. "We want to help her understand what happened that night, so she might make clear decisions about her future."

The Mother Superior nodded. "And I would support such an endeavour, but I fail to see how you might achieve your goal."

Devon gave a brief recount of events.

He spoke of Thomas' murder, the late-night attack last Thursday, the visit to Mr Daventry, and what they hoped to achieve with her help.

"I see." She sat back in the chair.

"The devil is at work," Mina said, using the only means of persuasion at her disposal. "We must stop him before he hurts someone else. We believe the same person hurt Arabella three years ago."

Devon spoke of Mr Bradbury. "He thinks Arabella is dead. I shall explain she is alive and that her memory is returning. Daventry seems convinced Bradbury will come here, and his agents mean to capture the villain. We merely need your assistance."

Seconds passed in silence.

The lady pushed to her feet. "I shall need time to reflect."

Devon stood. "I intend to return to London tonight and set the wheels in motion. I ask that Mina remain here, where I know she is safe."

Mina offered the woman a warm smile. "We understand your dilemma. We act only in Arabella's best interests. Perhaps we might explain the situation to her first."

"Give me an hour to pray, and you shall have your answer." She gripped the cross hanging around her neck. "In the meantime, you may visit Arabella. I'm sure she would like to meet her sister-in-law."

They thanked her and waited in the corridor outside Arabella's room while Sister Agatha explained she had visitors.

It nearly broke Mina's heart when she entered the sparse room and saw the young woman struggling to stand. The scar marring Arabella's delicate face was not as shocking as Devon had described. Perhaps because Arabella had her brother's dark features and handsome looks, and her brown eyes were bright with excitement.

"Oh, I cannot tell you how happy I am to meet you." Arabella reached out to grasp Mina's hand, taking a small step at the same time. "Devon spoke so fondly of you on his last visit."

"He did?" Mina glanced at Devon and he winked.

He wore the same devil-may-care look she'd seen when he'd charged out of the tub like Poseidon, when she'd struggled to tear her gaze away from every carved muscle. Yet beneath his facade, he was angry and scared of what tomorrow would bring.

It was easy to have sympathy for Arabella's plight.

But Devon had made the trip every week for the last three

years, knowing his sister's condition came as a result of a decision he had made.

How she longed to take away his pain.

I love you!

She would spend a lifetime making sure he knew.

"Why have you come on a Monday?" Arabella laughed like it was such a strange thing to do. She turned to Mina. "He visits every Thursday at seven o'clock, not a minute later." Her amusement died. "I pray there is nothing wrong." She frowned. "Tell me there is nothing wrong, Devon."

Mina took Arabella's hand. "Might we sit together on the bed?"

"Yes, of course."

"We have news that might prove disturbing." Devon remained standing while they sat. "But you're a grown woman and deserve to hear the truth."

Arabella shuffled nervously. "Is it about Lord Kinver?"

It was a logical guess. What else might affect a woman who spent her days in quiet solitude many miles from home?

"Is he to marry?" Tears welled in the woman's eyes. "Have you hurt him? Has he confessed to hurting me?"

Mina patted Arabella's hand. "It is none of those things."

A relieved sigh left the woman's lips. "Thank heavens."

Devon explained Lord Kinver's theory that someone else was in the garden that night. "Do you recall seeing anyone hiding in the shrubbery? Can you remember who chased you to the mews?"

Arabella's brow furrowed in concentration. "No."

Mina looked at Devon and shook her head. It was pointless pressing her for information. The mind often invented stories, and they needed facts.

"How do you feel about Mr Bradbury?" Mina said.

Arabella looked at her. "Devon's friend?"

225

"Yes."

She shrugged. "He can be quite intense. He feels strongly about many subjects but is always polite. Why? Has something happened to Mr Bradbury?"

"No." Devon inhaled deeply and paused before adding. "We want you to come home, Arabella. Things have changed."

His sister's gasp conveyed a wealth of panic. "No! I feel safe here. No one bothers me. I can sit peacefully in the grounds. You know how people are in London. I'll not suffer their cruel comments and pitying stares." She stroked the scar on her cheek. "I want to stay here, Devon."

"What if I told you Lord Kinver might be innocent?"

She jerked her head. "Innocent?"

"What if we could catch the person who hurt you that night? Would you come home, Arabella?" He gestured to her legs. "You should be walking the length of the garden. You should be able to stand without aid. Yet I fear your slow recovery stems from fear, not problems with your mobility."

Were Arabella's thoughts hindering her progress?

The prospect of being in a crowded room, not knowing who had attacked her, must be terrifying. For anyone suffering a trauma, survival became the only focus. Where better to hide than a convent? It was a frightened woman's sanctuary.

"Do you know how I met your brother?" Mina said.

She recalled the night with perfect clarity. Could envisage herself standing on the dark street, choosing the path to ruination.

"Devon said you came to plead for your brother's life."

She'd been so desperate, she would have sold her soul to the devil that night. "I stood outside his house in Dover Street, shaking to my bones. I cannot recall ever being so scared." She had considered walking away many times. "But a feeling deep in my gut made me knock on his door." Looking up, she met Devon's gaze and her heart fluttered. "That feeling has never left me. It wasn't courage or determination that made me ask for his help. It was destiny's guiding hand."

His mouth curled into a sensual smile. "And now we're in love."

"The future is bright, Arabella." How could she make her see the importance of taking a chance? "Your future could be bright, too."

Arabella sat in silence.

Devon watched her intently before saying, "Someone attacked Mina at home last Thursday while I was here visiting you. It might be Kinver or Goldman. It might be Bradbury."

"Mr Bradbury? Good heavens!" Arabella sat bolt upright, her gaze scanning the length of Mina's body. "Are you all right, Mina? Were you hurt?"

Arabella needed to hear the truth. Sparing her feelings only hindered her progress. "I would have died had my parrot not saved me, but that is another story." She offered a reassuring smile. "With the help of the most skilled enquiry agent in London, we want to set a trap to catch the person who hurt you."

"A trap? But how?"

Devon explained Mr Daventry's plan. "If the Reverend Mother agrees, I shall leave Mina here with you and return tomorrow to lie in wait."

The woman, who upon their arrival had sat bathed in the glow of happiness, turned ghostly pale. "You mean to lure the devil here? To the convent?"

"Yes," he said, his voice tight.

"Arabella, you must do what you feel is right, not what is easy." Mina had faced a similar dilemma. "You must seek justice. You owe it to other women who may suffer at the villain's hands."

They waited while Arabella processed the information. She sat with her head bowed, muttering to herself. Then the atmosphere changed, and the sudden spark of energy in the air brought renewed hope.

"Very well." Arabella managed to smile. "I will do whatever you ask of me. In return, you will allow me to decide my own fate. If I want to remain at the convent, you must accept my decision."

Devon nodded. "Once you have all the facts and the culprit is in custody, you will be free to choose your own destiny."

A light knock on the door brought the Mother Superior. "Forgive the interruption. May I have a moment in private, Mr Masters?"

"You may speak freely in front of Arabella," Devon said.

The woman gave a graceful nod and entered the room. "I have had time to reflect and must inform you I cannot permit your enquiry agents to run amok in God's house. The sisters are unused to the company of men, and we have already made many allowances in your case."

Drat!

Mr Daventry's other plan involved Arabella returning to London, though Mina doubted she would leave the convent.

"I see," Devon said, clearly annoyed.

Mina stood. "Might there be another solution, Reverend Mother?" She could feel the heat of Devon's penetrating stare. "You serve the Lord in His fight against evil. With my guidance, the sisters could help catch one of Satan's minions."

"We'll find another way," he said, his voice tight with disapproval. "If you think I'd leave you to face the villain alone, you're mistaken."

"Mrs Masters would not be alone," said the Mother Superior. "I accept the terrible deed cannot go unpunished. A compromise is needed. I'm certain the sisters would rally together to help your cause."

Mina closed the gap between them and touched his arm. "Please, Devon. If we lure the scoundrel here, it's safer for all concerned."

He fell silent, his gaze searching her face.

"All will be well," she assured him.

He lowered his voice. "I'll not lose you to that fiend."

"You won't."

He turned abruptly, fighting an inner turmoil.

She wished she could massage his tense shoulders and kiss away his fears. But all she could do was focus on one important fact. "We must do this for Arabella."

London
The next morning

After meeting Daventry at the Order's office in Hart Street, and explaining his agents could not storm the convent's grounds, Devon returned to Dover Street to await Lord Kinver.

He paced the study, listening to the incessant ticking of the mantel clock. Without Mina, the house was too cold and quiet. He had missed holding her warm body in bed last night. He had missed seeing her sweet smile at breakfast this morning.

Love was a blessing and a curse.

Separation proved unbearable.

Yet he had never been happier.

At the sudden sound of the door knocker hitting the plate, Devon checked the time. Impatient to learn why Devon had summoned him, Kinver was ten minutes early. Indeed, he heard the panic in the lord's voice as he greeted Bates.

Devon sat behind his desk and waited for Bates to enter.

"Lord Kinver is here, sir."

"Show him in, Bates."

Kinver burst into the study as the last word left Devon's lips. "Tell me you've identified our mystery monster. Tell me you have good news. Three years and I've discovered nothing, and you find a clue within days."

Devon waved to the chair opposite. "Sit down."

Kinver brushed a lock of brown hair from his brow and flopped down into the seat. He was breathless and looked harried.

"I have news regarding Arabella's grave."

Disappointment flashed in Kinver's eyes. If he'd faked it, then he was more skilled than any actor working on the Covent Garden stage.

"Oh! I thought you'd discovered who spied on us in the garden that night. I presumed you'd bribed the men in your debt."

"I punished you for the crime. No man in his right mind would confess to hurting my sister for fear I'd shoot him dead."

Kinver looked deflated but gathered himself. "Yes, of course. Forgive me. I should be grateful for simply knowing where Arabella is buried."

A stab of guilt hit him in the chest. If this were a card game, he would stake everything on Kinver's innocence.

"Brace yourself for shocking news." Devon should have offered the lord brandy to lessen the blow. "Arabella did not die in the accident."

Kinver stared at him, his eyes wide.

"Did you hear me?"

For long, drawn-out seconds, the lord said nothing. "What do you mean? She died later, at the hospital?"

"No. Arabella is alive."

Kinver jumped from the chair. "Alive!"

"Arabella was injured quite badly. She cannot walk and has a dreadful scar on her face." Devon's heart felt as heavy as a block of lead. "She wished to hide away from society."

"She's alive?" He dropped into the seat. Shock gave way to a smile. "Where is she? Why has she not contacted me? I must speak to her."

"Arabella cannot remember what happened that night." This was where he had to tread carefully and follow Daventry's plan. "She is frightened and doesn't know who hurt her. But her memory is slowly returning. I'm sure it won't be long until she recalls the event in great detail."

"Surely she knows I would never hurt her."

"When one has no memory, the mind conjures many terrifying scenarios. But she is living at a convent in Aylesbury. The Sisters of St Margaret take exceptional care of her. She means to remain there for the foreseeable future."

Kinver was on his feet now, barely able to keep still. "I must write to her. Ask to visit. When her memory returns, she will know I did nothing but search for her that night."

An unexpected feeling filled Devon's chest.

He pitied the man he had despised all these years.

"I will speak to her on your behalf. But you must swear to

231

keep her secret. Fail to do so, and I shall ensure you never see her again."

The lord didn't know what to do with himself.

His actions during the next twelve hours would determine whether he deserved Arabella's love.

Devon pulled out his pocket watch and checked the time. Bradbury would arrive within the hour, and he needed to get rid of Lord Kinver.

"I have a pressing appointment." Devon stood. "I shall be in touch in due course. But I ask that you respect Arabella's wishes until she can make informed decisions."

Still dazed, the lord ambled to the door. Before leaving, he gripped the jamb and said, "When she remembers I'm innocent, you will tell her I still love her?"

Devon bowed respectfully. "Of course."

Bradbury arrived forty minutes later. He sauntered into the study and helped himself to brandy. "Any news on Wenham? Has the rogue confessed to killing Stanford? There's no mention of it in the broadsheets."

Devon watched him—this serpent of Eden—and fought to maintain his steely composure. "He maintains he bought the land off an agent who has since disappeared. They'll charge him with fraud, but whether they charge him with murder remains to be seen."

"He admits to being on the bridge and has a motive. That should be enough." Bradbury glanced at the door. "Is Mina out?"

"She's gone to stay with Miss Ware."

Bradbury frowned. "Trouble in paradise?"

"Something like that." Devon noted the flicker of satisfaction in his friend's eyes. "I thought about what you said at Fortune's Den. Maybe I've been too trusting. She is, after all, my enemy's sister. Last night, she demanded I stop gambling. You can imagine what I said."

He would give his soul to save his marriage.

Bradbury assumed all men were like him, shallow, unforgiving. Indeed, the fact he found Devon's marriage troubles amusing fired his blood.

"Excellent." Bradbury grinned. "Does that mean you'll attend the game at the Blue Sapphire tonight?"

"I can't. I'm to dine with Sir Frederick Morton."

"The fellow who deals with the lunes in Bedlam?"

"Yes."

Bradbury swallowed his brandy. "What the hell for?"

"Arabella is alive."

Bradbury almost choked. He coughed and spluttered. "What the blazes! Have you been drinking?" He called over his shoulder. "Bates, fetch a doctor."

With his temper hanging by a flimsy thread, Devon took a calming breath and relayed the same story he had told Kinver.

"Sir Frederick knows of methods to recover trapped memories. We hope Arabella will soon recall it was Kinver who hurt her that night. Then I'll shoot the bastard."

And there it was.

The faint flicker of panic in the rogue's eyes.

He masked it quickly.

"Well, I'll be damned. Why the devil didn't you say so before?"

"I made a promise to Arabella. Due to the extent of her injuries, she wanted to hide from polite society." *Injuries you inflicted*, he added silently. "But when her memory is restored, and I've dealt with Kinver, I mean to persuade her to return to town."

"And she's a cripple, you say?"

Always so crass. "She is learning to walk, but it's a slow

233

process. That's why I called you here. Arabella agreed I could contact Sir Frederick, and with you being my closest friend, I didn't want the doctor gossiping and you finding out from someone else."

"No, quite right." He snorted. "So the Belinda thing was just a cover story for your visits to the convent?"

"Yes, but you understand why I couldn't reveal the truth?"

Bradbury nodded. He continued asking questions and cursing Lord Kinver to the devil. Then, as expected, he excused himself on the pretence of a previous engagement.

Devon stood at the window and watched Bradbury bark orders at his coachman and climb into his carriage.

The wheels were soon in motion.

His thoughts turned to the plan and how a group of ageing nuns would bring a devil like Bradbury to his knees.

Chapter Nineteen

"We pray the Lord will watch over us," Sister Agatha uttered as Mina and Arabella formed a circle with the nuns of St Margaret's convent and pressed their hands together. "We place our faith and trust in Him, for He will protect and deliver us from the clutches of evil."

A whimper left Arabella's lips.

Mina opened her eyes and glanced at the poor woman. She looked pale, sickly, and her body trembled as she tried to support her weight on the wooden crutches.

If Devon were here, he would gather his sister into his arms and carry her back to bed. He would know what to say to soothe her and settle her fears. He radiated strength and confidence even when he was broken inside.

Mina's heart ached at the thought of how much she missed him. One night spent apart felt like a lifetime, and she'd been counting the hours since dawn.

Love brought extreme pleasure and intense pain.

Doubtless, because her feelings were so raw and new.

She closed her eyes briefly and silently begged the Lord to deliver them safely from their dealings with a devil.

Sister Agatha, a middle-aged woman whose healthy glow lit up a room, brought the prayers to an end and instructed Sister Mary to escort Arabella back to her chamber.

Mina made to follow, but Sister Agatha wanted a private word.

"Let us walk outside for a while." Sister Agatha led the way and brought them out into the herb garden. She glanced up at the inky sky. "I've always known this day would come." Her voice was as soft and as gentle as the night breeze. "I've always known Arabella would leave us."

The words carried a sense of wisdom, not regret.

"Devon said he met you at St Thomas' hospital. That you appeared like an angel in a moment of darkness. Your presence gave him strength."

Sister Agatha smiled. "Arabella wasn't the only person injured in the accident." She gestured for them to walk along the cobbled path. "Her brother's wounds were as clear as this cloudless sky."

Mina swallowed against an image of Devon pacing frantically while the physician tended to his sister's injuries. "Guilt leaves an invisible scar, though it can be just as painful."

"It has barely healed the past three years."

Silence descended.

Stillness had a way of bringing one's deepest fears to the surface. "If Lord Kinver is not the man who mauled Arabella, Devon will blame himself for keeping them apart."

"And if he is the monster you seek, Mr Masters will blame himself for taking his sister to the ball that night." Sister Agatha looked up at the scattering of stars. "He must acknowledge his feelings and understand why he made certain choices. Then he must ask for forgiveness."

"Arabella would forgive Devon anything."

Sister Agatha stopped walking. "It is not his sister's

forgiveness he needs. Mr Masters must accept he is fallible. Then he must forgive himself." She cupped Mina's cheek. "Have faith. Be his angel in the darkness, and all will be well."

They looped the garden in companionable silence.

A moment to reflect on the sister's wise words.

Sister Agatha led them back through the cloisters, bringing them to a halt outside Arabella's door. "We should begin our preparations, ensure we're ready to welcome the intruder."

A shiver of trepidation ran down Mina's spine. "We must attempt to gain a confession before cornering him. We will give Arabella a code word which she must say when she needs us to capture the devil."

"You're certain he will come?"

Mr Daventry seemed convinced. He knew the criminal mind better than any man. "He won't risk the chance of Arabella revealing his identity. There is too much at stake."

Devon would hunt the fiend and shoot him dead.

Of course, she did not say that to a woman who valued the Lord's commandments.

The sudden sound of sobbing reached Mina's ears.

Sister Agatha heard it, too, and nodded to the door. "It is as I feared. Arabella has spent so much time in seclusion she is unequipped to deal with the slightest upset."

Having spent many hours talking to Arabella last night, Mina knew her worries amounted to more than that.

"She is terrified Lord Kinver will come and prove he's the one who hurt her so despicably." For three years, she'd hoped there had been a dreadful mistake. "Arabella cannot believe the man she meant to marry could be so wicked."

Sister Agatha gestured for them to enter Arabella's room. "Then we must pray the other fellow is responsible."

They found Arabella curled up on the bed, weeping into her lace handkerchief. Her shoulders shook as she tried to suppress the sound.

Mina sat on the bed and stroked her sister-in-law's arm. "Don't cry. Please don't cry. All will be well. You'll see."

Arabella gripped Mina's hand. "I'm sorry, but I cannot go ahead with the plan." Another sob escaped, and she heaved to catch her breath.

A flurry of panic filled Mina's chest. "He will be here soon. All you need do is lie in bed and get him to admit to hurting you."

"I'm afraid I'll burst into tears and ruin everything."

"You won't," Mina reassured her.

Still, she understood completely. Arabella might see the villain creeping up to the bed and remember what he did to her that night. And Sister Agatha was right. Hiding at the convent had left Arabella unprepared to face her past.

Arabella sat up. "You could pretend to be me, Mina."

Mina glanced heavenward. "You're so slight. My hips are too wide. And I'm much larger in other areas."

"It will be dark, and you'll be beneath the blankets."

A vision of her own attacker burst into her mind. The skin on her neck was still red and sore, proof of how close she had come to dying.

"We sound nothing alike."

"You can make your voice sound sleepy." Arabella squeezed Mina's hand. "You're much braver than I am. That's why Devon loves you."

"But do you not want to catch the devil who hurt you?"

Arabella sagged. "Yes, but it has all happened so quickly. I'm not ready to face him. Imagine being in a dark room, not knowing who will jump out from the shadows."

Imagine being strangled in your bed by a man in a hood.

Still, they had come this far. With luck, they would solve this mystery and discover if the same devil had killed Thomas.

"Very well," Mina said with some reluctance. She dismissed all reservations. "I shall act in your stead. But time is of the essence. We must hurry."

Sister Agatha took Arabella to hide in the mother superior's office. She returned minutes later with Sister Mary in tow. They helped Mina into bed and drew the coverlet up around her shoulders. Then they took to their hiding places. One moved behind the curtain. The other squeezed into the gap between the armoire and the wall.

"Remember, we must hear a confession," she said.

They would not have the blackguard denying culpability once the magistrate arrived. And questioning the word of a nun was sacrilege.

A heavy silence fell over the room.

Mina's heartbeat hammered in her ears.

Her body trembled, and not from the cold.

What if the devil tied a rope around her neck and pulled tightly? What if the nuns were too weak to loosen his grip?

A light knock on the door sent her nerves skittering.

Sister Frances peered around the door. In a hushed but panicked voice, she said, "Mr D'Angelo came to the back gate. He said to tell you Lord Kinver's carriage stopped on the road and parked three hundred yards away."

"Lord Kinver!" Mina's heart sank.

"The gentleman climbed down and marched towards the convent."

"He is sure it is Lord Kinver?" Mr Daventry's agents were highly skilled and would not make a mistake.

"Yes, his coach bears his coat of arms." Sister Frances glanced behind her before quickly adding, "Be prepared. He should be here any moment." She closed the door and hurried away, her steps echoing along the corridor.

Mina shuffled down beneath the coverlet and tried to calm her ragged breathing. She would rather wrestle with Lord Kinver than Mr Bradbury, but couldn't bear the thought of breaking the news to Arabella.

She would not recover and would likely stay at the convent and take her vows. In one way, Devon would be relieved to know his friend was innocent. But watching Arabella spiral into a depression would kill him.

She released a sigh, then tried to focus on the task ahead.

Devon had told the suspects that Arabella's room faced the fountain in the garth. It wouldn't take Lord Kinver long to find her—but what did he plan to do?

Minutes ticked by.

The sisters never moved, fidgeted or complained.

Mina struggled against an inner restlessness.

But then the door creaked open, and instinct forced her to focus. The air shifted as if a malevolent force had breached this place of sanctity. The door clicked closed, and the heavy presence pressed forward.

The devil had arrived at St Margaret's.

Chapter Twenty

"You're certain it's Lord Kinver's carriage?" Devon stared at Dante D'Angelo, one of Daventry's best enquiry agents, shock shaking him to his core. "His coat of arms bears two stags and a castle tower."

Devon had made a point of learning everything about Lord Kinver, though the devil had fooled him into believing he cared about Arabella.

Cursed saints!

He would have staked his house on Bradbury being guilty.

So much for being the best gambler in London!

"I don't make a habit of giving false information," D'Angelo said as they stood hidden in the wooded area near the gate to St Margaret's.

"Did you see Kinver?" Daventry said impatiently.

"It was dark and impossible to identify him without making myself known. He climbed down and marched towards the convent."

Daventry frowned. "Did he speak to his coachman?"

"No."

Devon's mind was a whirl of confusion. What the hell was Kinver thinking? "Maybe he is desperate to see Arabella?"

Men in love were often irrational.

"Then why not park outside the convent and ring the damn bell?" Daventry muttered a curse. He liked to control every situation and did not take kindly to being left outside the convent walls.

Nausea roiled in Devon's stomach.

The beast had torn Arabella's gown off her shoulder. Left ugly purple bruises where he'd grabbed her tightly and shaken her like a doll.

What sort of man did that to a woman?

Yes, the need to thrust deep into Mina's body had Devon's blood pumping hot and wild in his veins. But he had no desire to hurt her. Her pleasure was his only consideration.

Mina!

He'd missed her last night.

He'd missed the warmth of her body next to his.

He'd missed watching her sleep.

"Question his coachman." Daventry's firm order to his agent dragged Devon from his musings. "Threaten him until he reveals Kinver's plans. Scale the convent wall if necessary."

D'Angelo broke into a sprint and disappeared into the darkness.

Daventry's unease sent Devon's pulse skittering.

"You think Kinver means to hurt her?" His thoughts turned to his sister, waiting nervously in bed. She still loved the lord, and that made her vulnerable.

"Instinct says Kinver loves her and is desperate for a reunion. But I cannot shake the sense we've missed something."

Devon felt the same growing discomfort. "I'll not leave them alone like sitting ducks. I have a blade in my boot. I'll scale the wall and watch from the shadows."

It would mean breaking his oath to the Reverend Mother. A man was only as good as his word, but he could not risk losing Arabella.

And what if Kinver hurt Mina in the process?

Daventry thought for a moment before cupping his hands to his mouth and making a birdcall. "Wait for Sloane and then enter the convent. He'll follow behind and keep to the shadows. The Reverend Mother will understand your need to break a vow."

Sloane appeared from the gloom, his long hair tied in a queue. The style was popular fifty years ago, but Sloane liked to embrace his pirate heritage.

Daventry beckoned his agent forward. "Enter the convent with Masters. Keep out of sight. Intervene only if you deem it necessary, and don't let the sisters see you."

Sloane nodded. "We'll climb the east wall."

They were about to move away when D'Angelo burst into view, pointing to a place in the distance. He was breathless by the time he reached them.

"Kinver is … Kinver is in the carriage." D'Angelo pressed his hand to his chest and heaved a breath like his lungs burned. "Hurry. Someone needs to enter the convent."

"But you said you saw Kinver alight."

"I said I saw someone alight, but it wasn't Kinver. I found the lord beaten, bound and gagged in his carriage. Kinver was held at knifepoint and forced to instruct his coachman to wait before Bradbury shoved a rag down his throat."

"Bradbury!" Devon felt the blood drain from his face.

"The coachman had no idea Bradbury had beaten his master."

Devon's legs moved before his brain engaged, and he was at the wall in seconds. Sloane followed and helped him over before climbing the wall himself.

"Call if you need me," Sloane said, staying out of sight.

Devon took a second to focus his vision. He was so angry, so damn scared, he could hardly see straight.

Then he heard Bradbury's booming voice breaching the silence.

"Move out of my way, or I'll kill her."

Devon ran, vaulting the low topiary hedge. He came to a crashing halt at Arabella's door to find Sister Mary and Sister Agatha with their backs pressed to the wall, the bedsheets strewn over the floor, the side table upturned.

What the hell had happened in here?

Bradbury had Arabella in a choke hold, the sharp tip of a blade pressed to her throat.

Devon blinked rapidly.

It wasn't Arabella. It was Mina.

Mina, my love!

She gripped Bradbury's muscular arm as she fought for breath. "Devon!" Fear swam in her wide eyes. Tears ran down her cheeks.

Don't cry, love. I mean to put this bastard in a grave.

Bradbury paled. His gaze flicked left and right.

"Get your hands off my wife!" Devon cried, the devil's wrath burning in his chest. "If you want to live, you'll release her. Now!"

Bradbury gathered himself and stood like a monument to conceit. "If I slit her throat, I'd be doing you a favour. She's a whore who lured you into a trap, and you're too damn blind to see it."

Devon fought the urge to charge forward and knock the fiend's head off his shoulders.

Keep calm!
Talk him down!
Gain a confession!

"And yet you came here for Arabella."

"You fooled me into thinking she was alive," Bradbury spat.

"She is alive and has named you as the man who attacked her in the garden." Devon gestured to the room, though the visible signs of a struggle filled him with rage. "This is all a trap to catch a liar, a traitor, a deceiver. You've been plotting behind my back, Bradbury."

How the hell had he missed it?

"I'm your closest ally," Bradbury cried.

"Ally!" Devon snorted. "You have a knife pressed to my wife's throat. My sister is scarred and crippled because of you. You've brought Lord Kinver here because you plan to kill Arabella and blame him, make it look like he took his own life. Please tell me how you're serving my best interests."

"I love Arabella," he said, yet his eyes were cold and hard like a mortuary slab, his voice full of hatred.

"I love my wife deeply." So deeply it consumed him. "Ask her if I would ever hurt her. Ask her if I have ever marked her skin in a fit of temper." He'd not bruised her, not even during their vigorous lovemaking.

"I didn't mean to hurt Arabella, but she wouldn't listen to reason. Sometimes, a man must take the moral high ground. Sometimes he must do what's necessary to make a woman listen."

Devon shrugged. "So, you saw her kissing Lord Kinver."

"He had his damn hands all over her."

"They're in love."

"No, they're not! He was making a fool of her, making a fool of you. Someone had to intervene."

God's teeth! Bradbury was the devil incarnate.

"Just like you intervened in my argument with Thomas Stanford." He pictured Bradbury strolling onto Bromley Common without a care in the world. "You killed him and threw his body into the Thames."

"Because you were too damn weak to deal with him."

Mina's eyes widened, and more tears fell.

Devon wanted to take her in his arms, comfort her, kiss her, and he would when he'd dealt with this miscreant.

"Did you stop to think why Stanford behaved as he did?" Goldman was to blame, and he would damn well pay. "He'd smoked so much opium it affected his mind. The man couldn't rouse a logical thought." Why else would he have posed naked in the artist's studio?

Had they met on the field, Stanford would have shot Devon.

Devon would have fired back.

And Mina would despise him now.

"More reason to bring the matter to a swift conclusion." Bradbury firmed his grip as Mina struggled. He pressed the point of the blade so close to her neck it pierced the skin, drew blood. "You should thank me. I saved your damn life."

Devon gritted his teeth as he watched the crimson drop trickle down the column of her throat. "Let my wife go. We'll go somewhere and talk about this." He was so damn scared of losing her his temper got the better of him. "Let her go!"

"It's too late." Bradbury's frustration surfaced. "You've made that impossible now. The only hope I have of surviving this ordeal is to take her with me." He pressed his lips to Mina's hair and kissed her.

"Don't touch her!"

"We'll board a ship to the Indies, love," he said in Mina's ear. "I can afford to keep you, and I'll soon rid you of these modern habits. Masters will move on quite quickly. He's not short of female admirers."

Move on quickly?

He would rather die than live without her.

Did Bradbury know nothing about love?

Devon mentally shook himself. He had to treat this like he did a card game before his emotions made him weak. He needed to assess his odds, ensure every move brought him a step closer to the end goal.

"Go with him, love." He stared at her intently, hoping she knew to have faith, to trust him. He would track her to the ends of the earth if necessary. "Don't be scared."

She pursed her lips, trying not to weep. He could read the terror in her eyes, but she was clever enough to know he had a plan. "Move aside and let us pass. I'll go with him freely. There's no need for anyone to intervene."

Bradbury grinned. "Courageous little thing, aren't you?"

"It's one of the reasons I love her," Devon said.

The rogue's eyes brightened. "You always win, Masters. It's only fair another man gets a chance to sample her delights."

Curse this ingrate to Hades!

He was going to murder Bradbury with his bare hands.

"Before you go, let me ask you one thing." Devon stepped aside. "I thought we were as close as brothers. How long have you been hiding your disdain?"

"Since you stopped listening to reason." Bradbury gripped Mina around the waist and pulled her tight to his chest. He swiped the blade close to her neck—a sinister warning. "Since I realised I'd have to spend my life living in your shadow."

"I've never expected anything but friendship."

Bradbury scoffed. "Have you thought I might want men to cross the street when I approach? I want them to look at me and piss their pantaloons. I want to win and wallow in the adoration. I want to see fear in their eyes when I take their bounty."

"And yet it brings little to no reward."

Falling in love with Mina had helped Devon learn what truly mattered. Money could not buy happiness. It could not rid Arabella of her scars. It could not bring Thomas Stanford back.

Bradbury continued complaining.

Those who expected life to be fair would always be unhappy.

Devon backed out into the covered walkway and stepped aside. He might have goaded the rogue, asked him how he planned to get to Dover with someone chasing his heels.

But Bradbury had nothing to lose.

Out of spite, he might take Mina's life.

"Move into the garden and open the front gate," Bradbury commanded, dragging Mina with him. "Do it now!"

"I scaled the wall. I don't have the key."

Bradbury glared at Sister Mary. "Fetch the damn key."

She inclined her head and hurried away along the corridor.

Sister Agatha remained inside the room. She caught Devon's eye and revealed the object she had hidden behind her back—a hooked window pole, solid enough to hurt a man if it landed with some force.

Unaware Sister Agatha crept slowly behind, Bradbury followed Devon through the herb garden until they came to a halt at the wrought-iron gate.

The Reverend Mother appeared with her chatelaine of

keys, unfazed by the imminent threat. "Mr Bradbury, might I suggest you take a moment to reflect? You'll need the Lord on your side if this plan is to work."

And this rogue had sided with Satan.

Devon gestured to the knife pressed to Mina's throat. "I'm afraid he refuses to listen to reason. We should let them leave."

Daventry and D'Angelo were waiting outside. Bradbury would not get far when pitted against London's most skilled enquiry agents.

"Just open the damn gate!" Bradbury yelled.

The Reverend Mother took her time finding the right key. That's when Evan Sloane slipped into view, the blade in his hand glinting in the moonlight.

But it was Arabella's voice that caused Bradbury to glance right. She came hobbling towards him on her crutches, calling his name.

"Mr Bradbury! Wait!"

"Arabella!" The fool looked genuinely shocked. He'd thought Devon had invented the tale, a ruse to catch a killer. "You're alive."

"I have been recuperating at the convent, sir." She shot Devon a look filled with disdain. "I couldn't bear to live with my brother, not after he let Lord Kinver assault me in such a wicked fashion."

"Neither man deserves you. That's what I was trying to tell you in Lord Kinver's garden, my dear."

Arabella came one step closer. "Might I leave with you, sir? I cannot stay here and do not want to return home. My memory has no hope of returning, and I know how people judge."

Bradbury grinned at Devon. "I'd rather take your sister than your wife. Arabella is much more amenable." He turned, relaxing his hold on Mina. "Come here, Arabella, and we shall make the trade."

She shuffled closer, but her crutch slipped from underneath her, and she tumbled to the ground.

Bradbury released Mina and lunged forward to catch Arabella. That's when Sister Agatha charged into the fray and hit Bradbury on the back with the heavy pole.

Bradbury's knees buckled, and he howled like a beast.

The Reverend Mother kicked him in the ballocks before looking heavenward and begging the Lord's forgiveness.

Like a bloodhound let off its leash, Devon attacked Bradbury. He yanked him to his feet and punched him so hard in the face he thought he'd broken his knuckles.

Chaos erupted.

Fists flew.

Devon had nothing but murder on his mind.

The Reverend Mother opened the gate and Daventry appeared.

Before Devon could object, the agents took over, dragging Bradbury outside the convent walls, restraining him and binding his hands.

"We'll take him to the local magistrate," Daventry said, punching Bradbury himself for good measure. He shook his wrist to ease the ache. "We'll remain with Bradbury until he's charged and detained, but you must give a statement."

Angry and shaken, Devon nodded.

"Have the sisters make written statements." Daventry gestured to Lord Kinver, who hobbled closer, clutching his ribs and nursing a blackened eye. "I'll need a detailed account from Kinver, too, but I imagine he wishes to be reunited with Arabella."

"I'll deal with everything here." Devon took one last look at Bradbury, the Judas who had fooled him for the last seventeen years, before turning his back on him forever and escorting Lord Kinver into the convent.

"Bella!" Lord Kinver cried as he locked gazes with Arabella. Tears trickled down the lord's cheeks as he closed the gap between them.

"Henry!" Arabella tried hiding her face from him. "Don't look at me. I have terrible scars."

He captured her chin between shaky fingers and lifted her face to his. "I don't care about your scars. God, how I've missed you, Bella. This is like a dream come true."

Arabella started crying. "I can hardly walk, Henry."

He smiled. "Then I have an excuse to carry you everywhere. I love you, Bella. I don't care about the insignificant things."

Arabella fell into his arms, and they held each other close.

Tears dripped from Devon's eyes. Guilt choked him.

He scanned the group of nuns, searching for Mina.

Sensing his silent call, she quickly finished her conversation with the Reverend Mother, ran towards him and threw herself into his open arms.

"It's not your fault," she whispered against his ear. "Don't blame yourself, Devon. It's all been a terrible misunderstanding."

He pulled away and looked at her, dashed tears from her cheeks with his thumbs. "If only Arabella hadn't lost her memory, then we—"

"Don't torture yourself." She planted a chaste kiss on his lips. "It has all worked out for the best in the end."

"Has it?" He was struggling to see how.

"Devon, look at them."

He glanced at Arabella huddled against Lord Kinver's chest, his heart bursting with happiness for the darling girl who had suffered so greatly.

"To be undeterred by her injuries, he must love her deeply," Mina said. "They will cherish every second they have together. They'll be happier than ever." She pushed a lock of hair from his brow. "You know she fell on purpose. She wanted to help save me."

He sighed to release the tension in his chest. "I've always feared she resented me on some level, but I knew she was acting when she agreed to leave with Bradbury."

"Arabella loves you. I love you, Devon. Desperately so."

"I love you." He tangled his fingers in her silky brown locks, his only preference now. "Now it's all over I need to focus on the serious business of making love to my wife."

Mina kissed him, her tongue slipping into his mouth, mating with his, heating his blood.

He held her tightly, relishing the feel of her body against his, his heart aching at the realisation that he might have lost her tonight.

Damn Justin Bradbury.

The most painful betrayal didn't come from one's enemies.

It came from those one trusted most.

Chapter Twenty One

The Strand, London
One month later

Carriages lined the road outside Somerset House on the Strand, home of the Royal Academy. Mr Goldman had been invited to unveil his most recent painting, that of the stallion Emilius, a bay horse owned by the Earl of Chesterton and the winner of many prestigious races.

Mina hugged Devon's arm as they navigated the busy street, nerves churning in her stomach. "Do you think this plan will work?"

Devon cast her a sidelong glance and smiled. "Mrs Fitzroy has fulfilled her part of the bargain. By now, every gossip in London knows of Mr Goldman's lecherous ways."

"And she promised not to mention Miss Howard?"

He patted her hand. "She pities Miss Howard, and agreed not to name any of the students Goldman has seduced. I've arranged for the clerk to place copies of today's *Scandal Sheet* inside the programme. Hopefully, the audience will read it before Goldman takes to the stage."

Mina had glimpsed a copy this morning. Mr Goldman's name was spread across the top of the page in bold letters. The article mentioned a prominent artist's love of satanic rituals and stealing maidens' virtues.

They made their way into the building and found Mr Daventry and his wife Sybil waiting inside the opulent entrance hall. They exchanged greetings, though had dined with the couple only last night.

"The clerk swapped the paintings this morning," Daventry whispered, "and will blame the delivery firm for the mistake."

A frisson of excitement raced to Mina's toes. "Many prominent members of the *ton* will be in the audience to witness the spectacle."

The arrogant Mr Goldman would get his just deserts.

Devon grinned. "Let's hear Goldman explain why he's showing a painting of himself with a sword for a phallus."

Using all the techniques she had learnt at the studio, Mrs Fitzroy had spent three weeks perfecting the portrait of her art master, a depiction of Mr Goldman as a slayer of virgins.

"In exposing Mr Goldman, we will embarrass the earl," Mina said, slightly worried. After all their troubles with Mr Bradbury, she sought a peaceful life, not to be hounded by a man with a vendetta. "Do we want to make an enemy of a man like that?"

Mr Daventry lowered his voice. "No one will know we're involved. Besides, Chesterton can weather the storm. Once he denounces Goldman, he'll be seen as the victim."

An attendant dressed in blue livery arrived to summon the gathering crowd into the Great Room. Everyone joined the queue and found a seat amid the rows of benches in the auditorium. With much excitement and enthusiasm, people pointed to the makeshift stage and the square canvas balanced on the easel.

A swathe of red velvet hid the painting from view, but everyone chatted about the earl's magnificent beast, winner of the Derby.

Devon found them a seat with an excellent view of the stage, then checked the programme and noted the *Scandal Sheet* slipped inside.

It did not take long for the atmosphere in the room to change.

Enthusiasm died like a withering flame.

Stunned gasps rippled through the auditorium as people sat down to read about Emilius' racing history, only to learn of Mr Goldman's lewd pursuits.

Devon reached for her hand and gripped it tightly. "Relax. Enjoy the show. This man was instrumental in causing your brother's downfall. And he's about to receive his come-uppance."

Her mind drifted to the events of the past year. She had been unable to explain Thomas' manic episodes and strange obsessions. One could not reason with him. If she had known about his activities at Mr Goldman's studio, she might have found a way to save him.

But then she wouldn't have married Devon.

And she would rather die than be without him.

She squeezed his hand and met his gaze. They were so in tune with one another they could speak silently. Like her errant thoughts, she knew his mind conjured images of what they might do when alone in their chamber tonight.

Indeed, his lips curled into a sinful smile. He leant forward, his mouth daringly close, and whispered, "I mean to own you tonight. You'll be clawing my shoulders and begging for release."

She arched a brow. "Not when you discover what I have planned. Make no mistake, you'll be on your knees, Mr Masters."

Desire burned in his dark eyes. "You presume you will beat me at chess, love. That you will win the wager. That it will be your turn to decide what we do."

To even the odds, they had chosen a different game than cards, and she had won her first bout last night.

"It won't matter if I win or lose," she said coyly.

"And why is that?" he drawled.

She moistened her lips, made sure he knew she meant to take him in her mouth. "You'll have to wait to find out."

He gave an intrigued hum, but the auditorium door swung open, and the president of the Royal Society entered the room.

Sir Martin gave Mr Goldman a glowing introduction, regaling his early studies at the academy, mentioning his most famous works to date. He introduced the earl, seated in the front row, who received a tepid greeting from the audience.

The earl frowned, clearly confused by the crowd's lack of support. Perhaps because the clerk had avoided leaving copies of the *Scandal Sheet* in the front row.

"Allow me to present the artist," Sir Martin said, his ruddy cheeks reddening further upon hearing the disgruntled whispers and grumbles of unease. "The extremely talented Mr Jasper Goldman."

Mr Goldman swept into the room with his usual flamboyant air and bowed to the audience. Along with the earl, Sir Martin started clapping most heartily, though few in the audience followed suit.

The sound died, leaving a heavy silence.

Mr Goldman's arrogant grin faltered.

Stuttering, he began his speech, gesturing to the earl when

he spoke of how they met while watching Emilius race at Newmarket and Cheltenham.

"There was such power in those muscular legs." Mr Goldman laughed. No one else did. "I speak of Emilius, not his lordship. The stallion dominated every race, and one could almost hear the young fillies whimpering."

A couple in the audience stood. They pushed past those seated on the benches and made a quick exit. Two other ladies did the same.

Unsure what had caused the crowd's hostile mood, the earl called for Mr Goldman to reveal the painting. "Do it now!"

With a dramatic yank of the velvet cover, Mr Goldman called, "Ladies and Gentlemen, I present Emilius. The people's stallion."

The stunned silence lasted for two seconds.

Shrieks and gasps rent the air as all eyes fell upon Mrs Fitzroy's grotesque painting of Mr Goldman. The man stood naked, his phallus a giant sword dripping with virgin blood. Scattered around his feet was a mound of helpless victims.

The earl shot up, outraged.

Mr Goldman stared at his own image, dumbstruck.

A lady swooned.

A riot erupted.

Gentlemen shook their fists, threatening to teach the profligate a lesson. As people clambered out of the auditorium, a matron took to the stage and whacked Mr Goldman with her reticule.

Sir Martin grabbed the length of red velvet and attempted to cover the vile image, but men gathered on the stage, desperate to destroy the disgusting portrait.

"I don't think I've ever seen anything so entertaining,"

Devon said, laughing from his seat. "The panic in Goldman's eyes is priceless."

"He does look quite terrified," Sybil Daventry said, amused.

"He'll be forced to close his studio and leave town." Daventry stood and suggested they depart before a host of baton-wielding constables arrived.

"The earl might throttle him before he escapes the auditorium." Mina watched the lord grab Mr Goldman by his cravat and shake him violently. "Still, let's hope the man learns a valuable lesson."

"Shall we take coffee at Simpsons?" Daventry suggested.

Devon nodded. "We have two hours to spare before we take Arabella out for her daily walk."

Since leaving the convent, Arabella had made excellent progress, which had much to do with her upcoming wedding to Lord Kinver. She wanted to walk down the aisle without the aid of crutches.

"Excellent." Daventry ushered them out into the entrance hall and then onto the Strand. "Well, that's all loose ends tied up, and the case solved. Wenham will serve three years for fraud, and Bradbury will hang next week. What do you intend to do with yourselves now?"

She met Devon's gaze. While he seemed himself to those who didn't know him better, he still struggled with the depth of Mr Bradbury's betrayal. "We have Arabella's wedding to arrange and must focus our efforts on ensuring she has the support she needs."

Devon smiled. "I've never seen my sister so happy."

Daventry agreed. "She's suffered enough, and Kinver seems keen to prove he'll make a good husband."

With it being a dry day, they opted to walk to the coffeehouse.

"May I ask you a question, Mrs Masters?" Daventry said, mischief twinkling in his dark eyes. "It relates to your recent visit to the Bartholomew Fair."

A blush rose to her cheeks. "Of course."

Did he mean to ask about the fortune teller?

"Mrs St Clair told me about the mystic's predictions. She was to marry a man who fell in a cowpat, and the prophecy came true. It made me wonder what the visionary told you."

I'd see my husband's buttocks before I'd see his face.

An image of Devon's pert behind flashed into her mind. She had never seen anything as spectacular as his toned physique. Indeed, the thought left her flushed in a rather intimate place.

She glanced at her husband, recalling how he had cursed Miss Marmalade this morning. "She said I would marry a man who loved parrots."

Lord and Lady Kinver's wedding ball
New Cavendish Street, London
Another month later

Lillian was not in the ladies' retiring room, despite insisting she needed to tidy her hair. She was not hiding outside in the garden, but Mina had stumbled upon Lord Kinver and Arabella dancing beneath the moonlight and could not control the sudden flood of tears.

Lord Kinver cradled his wife close to his body. Arabella placed her small slippered feet on his, and the lord waltzed with her while supporting her weight.

Other than the look of devotion in Devon's eyes whenever they made love, it was the most beautiful thing Mina had ever seen.

Not wanting to disturb them, she slipped away quietly and returned to the ballroom. She dried her eyes and went to find Devon, who was busy watching play in the card room.

He had not gambled since they had married.

Well, he made illicit wagers with her before they played their nightly chess game, but he lost as many times as he won —often deliberately because he liked it when she took command.

He spotted her within seconds of her entering the room. Their eyes met, and he moved through the crowd as if pulled by the earth's magnetic force.

Mina's soul sighed.

Her heart was so full of love it was set to burst.

Devon reached her, his arm snaking around her waist as he drew her out into the hall. "Did you find Lillian?"

"No. I imagine she's hiding somewhere, spying on amorous couples and making notes for her book." By now, Lillian should have enough information to fill an entire library.

"I thought you warned her against sneaking off along dark corridors. Lord knows who she might encounter."

"I did, but she has an adventurous spirit and is as stubborn as a mule." Mina glanced back along the quiet hallway. "She might be watching us now through her newly acquired telescope. It collapses and fits into her reticule."

Devon grinned. "Then let's give her something to write about." He drew her back into the alcove. "Let's show her how passionate lovers kiss when no one is looking."

He took her mouth in a slow, drugging kiss that turned her

insides molten. His tongue slipped over hers as he deepened the kiss, causing the telltale tightening low in her belly.

"I need to get you home," he breathed against her lips. "I need you naked and beneath me, panting my name."

His words made her as giddy as his kisses. "But I must locate Lillian before she finds herself in a heap of trouble."

"She's perfectly safe."

"How do you know?"

"Dounreay is missing too."

"What? Why didn't you say so before?"

He stroked her cheek with the backs of his fingers. "Lord MacTavish and his daughter came looking for them. He found me in the card room and asked if I'd seen Dounreay."

Mina frowned. "Well, they can't be together. After hearing the fortune teller's prediction, Lillian avoids the duke like the plague."

"And yet Dounreay can't take his eyes off her whenever they're together in the same room. He's probably gone to look for her." Devon captured her hand. He slid her glove slowly down and pressed a lingering kiss to the inside of her wrist. "Come, let us wander the corridors until we find her."

"You don't mind sneaking about upstairs?"

Doubtless, he would rather watch the card game than traipse about after her wayward friend. Lillian needed to stop her foolish antics before she ruined her reputation for good.

"I'd do anything for you, love." He reached into his waistcoat pocket and showed her the tiny pearl. "I could buy you expensive trinkets, but I know you value my time more than precious gems."

Oh, this man was beautiful inside and out.

"You give me everything I need, Devon."

His gaze clung to hers, the way she clung to his sweat-soaked body as they made love. "I do have a gift for you," he said smoothly.

Her breath caught in her throat.

She had a gift for him, too, but planned to wait until Arabella and Lord Kinver left for their honeymoon tomorrow before revealing her surprise.

"What is it?" she said, her mind conjuring all the ways she might thank him for his thoughtfulness. "Do tell me."

"It's actually a gift for both of us," he said, sounding almost apologetic. "I've arranged a week away at a cottage on the grounds of Lord Deville's estate in Whitstable. It's quiet, and we won't be disturbed. We can spend our days walking along the beach. Our nights sprawled naked by a roaring fire."

Heat flooded her body. "It sounds divine."

It was the middle of winter, but they would keep each other warm. Indeed, the need to feel physically close to him was a craving she couldn't sate.

"I'll make you a necklace out of seashells," he said, remembering what she had said that night at Woodcroft Jewellers. "It will be a symbol of hope, of my esteem, of my undying love."

"Oh, Devon!" She checked they were alone in the corridor before devouring his mouth, the feel of his tongue making her giddy. "I have a gift for you, too. An exceptional gift."

He quirked a brow. "You do?"

"It's actually a gift for both of us."

"Is it a week in Brighton?"

"No." It was something infinitely more precious.

Clearly intrigued, he narrowed his gaze. "I don't imagine it's expensive," he mused, "and it must convey some level of sentiment."

"It is priceless. Rare. One of a kind."

He studied her silently.

"I'm glad you've no interest in playing cards," she said, laughing. "Based on your current observational skills, you'd likely lose every penny. How can you have lived with me for almost three months and not have noticed the obvious?"

His smile proved blinding. "You mean the fact we've made love every day without fail? Have you not noticed I'm more careful of late, that I spend a little longer raining kisses over your abdomen as I'm edging my way south?"

"If you know, why didn't you say something?"

"Because I wanted to hear the words from your lips."

She reached for his hands and held them tightly. "I'm most certainly with child. I've felt nauseous every morning for the last two weeks." She paused, unsure how he felt. "Are you pleased?"

"Pleased? I'm ecstatic."

"I wasn't sure if—"

"I love you, Mina. You're my life, my love, my everything. I'd pay a king's ransom to have a family and share my life with you."

Oh, she would never grow tired of hearing his romantic confessions. "And I love you, more than I could ever express in words."

"You can show me in kind later," he teased, winking.

She smiled as she remembered looking through his portfolio of vowels, him daring to offer a scandalous proposal. "You paid twenty thousand pounds for a kiss, and now you expect one for free."

"I paid twenty thousand pounds for two kisses and to put my wicked hands on your body."

She touched his chest, aware of the hard muscles flexing

beneath her fingers. "If only I'd known you weren't so wicked."

"Not wicked? You will change your assessment when you've heard how I mean to worship your body tonight." His mouth curled into a devilish smile, his dark eyes burning with desire. He brushed his mouth over her ear and spoke of his erotic musings.

Mina's pulse rose more than a notch. Heat flooded her body. Had she been holding a thermometer, mercury would have burst out through the glass tube.

"You're right," she said, swallowing hard. "You're not wicked, Mr Masters. You're downright devilish."

Thank you!

I hope you enjoyed reading *Not so Wicked.*

Is Miss Ware busy taking notes on the *ton*'s amorous antics?
Will she find herself in a dark corner with a handsome duke
who leaves her breathless? Will she stumble upon something
more sinister instead?

Find out in …

Never a Duchess
Scandal Sheet Survivors - Book 3

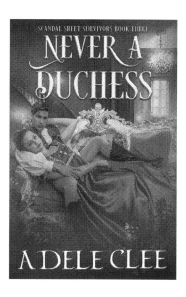

More titles by Adele Clee

Scandalous Sons

And the Widow Wore Scarlet

The Mark of a Rogue

When Scandal Came to Town

The Mystery of Mr Daventry

Gentlemen of the Order

Dauntless

Raven

Valiant

Dark Angel

Ladies of the Order

The Devereaux Affair

More than a Masquerade

Mine at Midnight

Your Scarred Heart

No Life for a Lady

Scandal Sheet Survivors

More than Tempted

Not so Wicked

Never a Duchess

Made in United States
Orlando, FL
01 June 2023

33709305R00162